Before I Let You In

JENNY BLACKHURST

EMILY BESTLER BOOKS
—
ATRIA

New York London Toronto Sydney New Delhi

An Imprint of Simon & Schuster, Inc.
1230 Avenue of the Americas
New York, NY 10020

First Emily Bestler Books/Atria Paperback edition April 2018

EMILY BESTLER BOOKS/ATRIA PAPERBACK and colophon are trademarks of Simon & Schuster, Inc.

For information about special discounts for bulk purchases, please contact Simon & Schuster Special Sales at 1-866-506-1949 or business@simonandschuster.com.

The Simon & Schuster Speakers Bureau can bring authors to your live event. For more information or to book an event, contact the Simon & Schuster Speakers Bureau at 1-866-248-3049 or visit our website at www.simonspeakers.com.

Interior design by Laura Levatino

Manufactured in the United States of America

10 9 8 7 6 5 4 3 2 1

Library of Congress Cataloging-in-Publication Data
Names: Blackhurst, Jenny, author.
Title: Before I let you in : a novel / Jenny Blackhurst.
Description: First Emily Bestler Books/Atria Paperback edition. | New York : Emily Bestler Books/Atria, 2018.
Identifiers: LCCN 2017039030 (print) | LCCN 2017045080 (ebook) | ISBN 9781501168857 (Ebook) | ISBN 9781501168840 (paperback)
Subjects: LCSH: Psychological fiction. | BISAC: FICTION / Thrillers. | FICTION / Psychological. | FICTION / General.
Classification: LCC PR6102.L3349 (ebook) | LCC PR6102.L3349 B44 2018 (print) | DDC 823/.92—dc23
LC record available at https://lccn.loc.gov/2017039030

ISBN 978-1-5011-6884-0
ISBN 978-1-5011-6885-7 (ebook)

*To Ash, and to Connor, who never gives up
and always finds a way. Love you, chicken nugget.*

Before
I Let
You In

PART 1

– 1 –

NOW

Where would you like to start?

Hmm.

Is something funny?

That's what I always used to say to my patients. It gives them a sense of control over the session. Except we both know I'm not in control here, don't we?

Is it important for you to believe that?

I know what you're trying to do. You're trying to put me at ease so I open up and confess my darkest fears and then you can tell them I'm crazy. I feel crazy. You can write that down.

Why don't you start at the beginning, Karen? When you first met Jessica Hamilton.

That's not the beginning. It's where all *this* started, I suppose, but it's not really the beginning. It started way before all that, before I met Bea and Eleanor, Michael. It started with what happened when I was four years old.

Would you like to talk about that? What happened to you when you were a child?

No. I don't want to talk about that, and they don't want to hear about it. They want to know about how she died.

Go on.

You can't fix me.

Pardon?

Those were some of the first words Jessica Hamilton ever said to me, the words I still hear on a loop in my mind. I remember thinking she was wrong, I fixed people all the time; it was my job. What I didn't realize then was that she never wanted to be fixed in the first place; that was never her intention. I didn't know it yet, but she was there to fix *me*.

- 2 -

KAREN

A standard session at the Cecil Baxter Institute was three thousand seconds long. Some patients spent the entire time in silence, a fact that often confused some of the junior psychiatrists—why spend £150 to sit mute for fifty minutes? Not Dr. Karen Browning, though; she understood. She understood it in the same way she understood professional men who visited prostitutes. It wasn't about the money or the silence. It was about the control.

The soft click of heels on wooden flooring alerted Karen to the presence of her secretary, Molly, just outside her office door. *Our* secretary, she reminded herself—Molly worked for all four junior psychiatrists on the second floor; only the directors on the top floor had personal assistants. There was a light tap on the door. Karen ran some gloss over her lips, slipped the tube back into the top drawer, and waited for Molly to come in. All the offices were set like a stage, and Karen was particularly proud of hers, a symbol of everything she had achieved.

And don't they say pride comes before a fall?

She'd gotten to work early that morning to read over her case notes for this session, making sure she knew as much about Jessica Hamilton as possible before she even walked through the door. Miss Hamilton was her only new client that week—all the others were ongoing cases—and she had little information about her, which irritated her beyond words. Whoever had done the initial referral notes had been nowhere near as thorough as she herself would have been. The scrawling signature on them could have been any of the others, and she made a mental note to bring it up as non-accusatorily as possible at the next team briefing.

Age: 23
Medical history: no diagnosed history of depression or generalized anxiety disorder. Family background unknown. No medication at present. Self-referral.
Reason for visit: tension headaches and irrational cognitive activity.

As she always did from the initial notes, Karen couldn't help putting together a picture of the woman about to walk through the door. Probably well-off, judging from the amount of money she was paying for fifty minutes of Karen's time. Karen did a certain amount of pro bono work, but Jessica Hamilton was self-referred and self-funded. She imagined that her friends called her Jess and her family called her Jessica.

There was a second knock, which was unusual for Molly. If Karen's "In Session" sign wasn't on the door, she usually entered straightaway. Karen got up, smoothing down her suit jacket, and opened the door to find not the smiling face of her assistant on the other side but a slight, timid-looking girl with a pale face, blossoms of red spreading out over her cheeks.

Karen hoped her own face hadn't revealed her surprise, doubted it had. Eight years of psychiatry had taught her reactions to hover below the surface, never breaking through to the onlooker. The ultimate poker player.

The young, attractive, rich-girl image the name Jessica Hamilton had conjured up couldn't have been further from the reality standing opposite her now. Karen put out a hand for her to shake, registering quickly the bitten nails and the grip as weak as the smile she herself offered.

"Jessica?" She cast her eyes around the reception area, but Molly was nowhere to be seen. "My apologies. Our receptionist would usually be here to greet you. Come in." She ushered the woman inside, mentally cursing Molly and her out-of-character unprofessionalism.

"Please, take a scat."

Either Jessica Hamilton didn't hear her or she ignored Karen's request. Instead she walked slowly away from the sofa and around to the bookcases on the far wall of the office. She seemed to be drinking in every detail of the mahogany shelves, the leather-bound books chosen for their aesthetics rather than their subject matter. For the first time in a long time, Karen felt as though her space was being scrutinized and found wanting.

"Would you like to sit down so we can start?"

She thought for a second that Jessica was going to ignore her again, but after a moment she took a seat opposite and sat silently, waiting for Karen to lead the session.

Jessica wasn't unattractive; certainly if her face weren't so ruddied from the cold outside—or perhaps from nerves—she could pass for pretty. Her hair fell in natural waves down to her shoulders and was a blonde so dark, it looked devoid of color entirely. Her whole look was designed to elicit the least amount of interest, it seemed.

"My name is Dr. Karen Browning. I don't know if you've seen other psychiatrists, but here we like our clients to be comfortable. So I'd like you to call me Karen; though if you don't want to, that's fine. Similarly I'd like to call you Jessica, but if you'd prefer Miss, Mrs., or Ms. Hamilton, I'm fine with that too."

She threw Jessica a wide smile, hoping to put her at ease. She sympathized with all of her patients; this had to be a daunting experience for them the first time around, sharing their fears and perceived shortcomings with someone who had no reason to care other than the money they were paying them. That was one of the reasons she tried to look as approachable as possible: no designer labels on her suits like some of the other psychiatrists, no severe bun on the top of her head, and no diamonds the size of the Blarney Stone—not that the last one was her choice.

Jessica nodded at the standard spiel as though she'd heard something profound but gave no indication of what she'd like to be called.

"Can I get you something to drink?"

She shook her head almost imperceptibly. Karen poured herself a glass of water from the cooler in the corner and sat on the chair facing her. It was purposely an inch lower than the sofa, giving her patients the sense of control many didn't feel in the outside world.

"Okay. I notice that the reason for your visit is tension headaches. Would you like to tell me about them?"

Jessica's eyes locked on to Karen's, something she wasn't used to, at least in initial sessions. She'd kept her office sparsely decorated so that people didn't have anything to focus on or be distracted by—the sofa, her desk, and two small bookcases; the one photograph, no trinkets, and a large painting of a jetty over a mass of relaxing turquoise water—yet they still found somewhere to look other than at her. Not Jessica Hamilton, though.

"You can't fix me."

There was a vicious challenging tone to her voice that was so at odds with her demeanor that it hit Karen harder than the actual words she'd used. But she had been shocked in her job thousands of times, and she'd gotten hellishly good at concealing her reactions; her face remained an impassive mask without a flinch.

"Is that what you think is going to happen here, Jessica? That I'm going to try and fix you?"

"Isn't that what you do, Dr. Browning? Fix the poor little mental cases, make their lives as perfect as yours?"

She didn't break eye contact. Her eyes were blue but too dark to be striking, with flecks of brown that dulled the effect further. Unremarkable—like the rest of her appearance.

"No, Jessica, that's not what we do. I'm just here to listen to what you have to say and try and help you come to terms with what's going on."

"Listen and help, doesn't sound very proactive to me. Why is it that people pay you so much money just to act as a brick wall? What's so special about you?"

It wasn't unusual for patients to be angry or confrontational, Karen told herself, trying not to let the anger that resonated from this girl rattle her on a personal level. Sometimes people were furious at life itself when they walked into their session; sometimes the vitriol was directed at their psychiatrist. Jessica Hamilton was no different from anyone else. And yet that was how she seemed: different.

"It's often easier to share our problems with someone who has no personal investment in our lives; it makes people feel less judged and gives them a safe place to air their issues. I'm not here to judge you, Jessica, nor am I here to try and improve you. We don't see people as being broken, and it's not our job to fix them. If you're happy to talk to me, I'd like to try and understand what's going on in your life. Is there somewhere you'd be comfortable starting?"

She saw Jessica processing her words and almost felt her disappointment that Karen wasn't going to rise to her attack. She couldn't help but wonder what the girl thought therapy was going to achieve, or why she'd come in the first place if she felt so strongly about the profession.

"I'm having sex with a married man."

If her first words were meant to challenge, now she meant to shock. Karen was already writing up her notes in her mind. *Patient is looking to shock as a way of eliciting judgment. Possibly looking to diminish feelings of guilt.* She'd have to look a lot further than she had so far; Karen had heard far worse admissions inside these walls.

"Is that all it is, just sex? Other people might have chosen the words 'sleeping with' or 'having an affair.'"

Jessica's face was blank, unreadable. "I'm not in love with him. There's no point. I'm not some stupid girl who thinks he's going to leave his wife to be with me."

Patient is using denial as a defense mechanism against admitting her feelings. Signs of a different problem?

"Would you like to start at the beginning and talk about how the two of you met?"

It was a difficult profession, being a psychiatrist, but Karen had never considered a different one, and in all the years she'd been practicing she had never regretted her choice. It had come naturally to her to treat the client like a wounded bird: no sudden movements, keep a neutral voice, listen, lead but don't dictate. With some people it felt like one wrong word and they would try to escape, seeing you as a captor rather than a savior. At first you could be the enemy—especially if therapy wasn't their choice.

Jessica ignored the question and, placing her elbows on her thighs, leaned in to decrease the distance between them.

"What makes a person good or evil, do you think?" she asked, her voice so low that Karen had to inch forward on her seat to hear her. "Their thoughts? Or is it when you actually do the things you're thinking of? A lack of morals? Empathy?"

"Are you concerned about thoughts you've been having?"

Jessica smirked slightly, her unremarkable face becoming unattractive with the expression. "Not exactly. You haven't answered me."

"It's a complicated question, Jessica, and not one I'm sure I'm qualified to answer. But if you're worried about your thoughts, I'd say that the fact that you are here trying to get help with them shows that they are a product of your situation rather than an inherent cognitive dysfunction."

"Do you always sound like a textbook?"

"I'm sorry—"

"And do you always apologize so much?"

"I—"

"Okay, what does Freud say about hurting people by accident?"

A tiny thread of tension twisted a knot inside Karen's chest. It wasn't often she lost control of a session, but it definitely felt as though this one was becoming counterproductive. "Have you hurt someone by accident?"

"Who says I was talking about me?"

The dread inside her caused her hand to tremble almost imperceptibly, and she wondered if Jessica had noticed her discomfort. She couldn't have known the reaction she'd get from that question, and yet the ghost of a smile that settled fleetingly on her lips before her face reverted to impassive suggested she had.

"An accident is just that, Jessica. Accidental. It's often the way we deal with the fallout of our actions that defines our character."

"My father always had this funny way of looking at accidents. Not the tripping-over type, but the really bad things that we allow to happen in life because we've taken our eye off the ball. He'd say that nothing in this life was accidental, that accidents don't just happen. He said they were the way our subconscious was allowing us to act out our true feelings under the guise of being unintentional. Do you think that makes sense, Dr. Browning?"

The tension tethered them together like a rope, her innocent question thick with unspoken meaning.

"I think you'd like my father."

Karen's thoughts scrambled to join themselves into coherent sentences. Buzz words from her training—"father," "subconscious"—triggered automatic questions, and yet she struggled to voice them. Before she could say anything, Jessica started to speak again.

"It was at a charity gala." Her eyes were fixed on a loose piece of skin at the edge of her thumbnail, the jagged skin suggesting an anxiety disorder perhaps. Her nails were short and uneven—bitten down rather than filed—and free of nail polish.

It took Karen a second to realize that Jessica was answering her original question, the mask she'd arrived with having slid back down into place. She allowed herself a second to gather her work persona, slotted her professionalism back into place, and continued the session as though the last few minutes had never happened.

"Are you involved in the charity world?"

"Not really. Someone I know had a spare ticket. He was at the bar and he looked just as bored as me. He made some joke about paying me to stay there with him, and I said I wasn't a prostitute. He got really flustered and started saying he hadn't meant that; he was worried that he'd insulted me. That's when I noticed how good-looking he was."

She looked up from her hands and smiled, not the smirk that had played across her lips a minute earlier, but a real smile at the memory. It didn't transform her face the way some people's smiles did. If anything, it made her plainness stand out more, the fact that even a smile couldn't light her up. It made a difference, physical appearance, as to how people treated you, and Karen could well imagine this girl being swept away by the attention of an attractive man. "He was cute, though, not all cocky and self-assured like some good-looking men."

"Is that your experience of men?"

She didn't miss a beat with her story, as though Karen hadn't even spoken. She described in great detail the evening she'd met her married lover, the jokes he'd told, the way his hand had rested so close to her knee that every time she laughed it brushed the satin of her dress. But as her story went on, her body language changed again and she reverted to a hard-shouldered stance, bracing herself against the part that was causing the negative feelings.

Classic indicators of cognitive dissonance.

"So what happened when the gala ended?"

Jessica crossed her arms. *The patient is uncomfortable with the memory.* "We went back to his hotel room and we fucked."

"And how did you feel about that?" Karen knew it was a cliché, and a bloody awful one at that. She nearly cringed every time she had to say it. It had become a running joke with her friends; for the first twelve months after Karen had told her she wanted to be a psychiatrist, her best friend Bea would ask her at least once every time they spoke: *And how did that make you feel?* But sometimes—okay, a lot of the time—it was exactly the question that needed to be asked. Because that was what she was there for: to get to the root of how the client felt about what they were telling her. A lot of the time they were so lost in their own story that they didn't even notice the corniness, almost like they were expecting it anyway.

Jessica raised her eyebrows, as though she couldn't believe Karen had pulled the feelings card so soon.

"I didn't come, if that's what you mean. It was fine, over a bit quickly and hardly romantic love-at-first-fuck, but it was okay."

The patient uses humor and shocking language to divert from the question of feelings. Karen couldn't stand bad language; it made her feel uncomfortable and insecure. She supposed it stemmed from her days at school, reminding her of the goody-goody she'd been, afraid to use bad words while the cool kids peppered their conversation with gutter talk. Or maybe from before that. Long before.

"The second time was better. And before long there was a third, and a fourth. Now we meet up all the time during the week. He isn't office-based; he practically lives at my place."

"Aren't you afraid his wife might find out?"

Jessica scowled. "For a while I thought she might. I kept waiting for a phone call or for her to turn up, to say 'I know what you're doing. I know what you've done.' But she's so wrapped up in the children, she wouldn't realize what was going on if we shagged in her car while she was driving it. She doesn't even care what he does."

"Is that what he says?"

"He doesn't have to actually say it; it's obvious from the other things he says. She doesn't have time for him."

"And you do."

Jessica shot her a glare. "What difference does that make? I don't want him to leave her or anything. I just don't understand how she can not know what's going on with her own husband." Her eyes were back on her fingernails, and her voice lowered. "I think about it a lot."

So there they were. It hadn't taken as long as Karen had expected for them to get to the next layer of the problem. This was the reason Jessica was there, and if she pushed too hard now, it would ruin the entire session's work. She tried to reassure herself that Jessica was just a girl who had got herself into a situation that was causing her an internal struggle. All the defiance from the beginning of the session, the feeling that Jessica was there to challenge her—it was her own hang-ups manifesting themselves in her client's innocent questions about life. She was nearly convinced of it.

"About his wife . . ." She kept her words low and quiet, leaned toward Jessica slightly. Jessica responded with a nod, still not looking at her but not scowling anymore.

"How she could let herself be treated like that? I mean, does she know and not care? Or is she just so stupid that she can't see what he's doing? He bought another phone, you know. So he can contact me without her knowing. She does all the finances, but he's got his own account that she doesn't know about. What kind of husband feels like they have to do that? Because his wife is such a controlling bitch, that's the only way he can get his own money."

To spend on sleeping with other women.

"I've done these things, just little things. I messed with a few things on her calendar, made sure she missed a few appointments. It made me feel good, in control."

"You've been in this woman's home?"

"Yes."

The unease that had been mounting now threatened to suffocate her completely.

"Jessica, I'm afraid I have to ask you this. It's part of my responsibility as a professional, and I wouldn't be doing my job if I didn't. Do you understand that?"

Jessica nodded.

"Do you feel like your behavior is in danger of escalating? That your thoughts towards this woman may lead to actions beyond your control?"

"No." She shook her head slowly. "None of those things. She disgusts me and I hate her, but I'm not evil."

- 3 -

BEA

Hi, everyone, my name is Eleanor, and my Fuck This Shit Friday is . . ." Eleanor paused for maximum dramatic effect, something she had been good at since they were children. "I had to change at least sixteen nappies today, and I managed to drop one of them on my feet. Literally shit."

Neither Bea nor Karen could stop the burst of laughter that resonated around the small café. Bea saw a couple of people look up from their newspapers as though the three of them were raucous teenagers in a library. She resisted the urge to stick her tongue out. As Karen continued to remind her on a weekly basis, they were grown-ups now, although whenever they were together, the last fifteen years seemed to melt away, and they were back under Eleanor's bunk bed with a bottle of Mad Dog 20/20.

Eleanor screwed up her face and took a swig of her drink.

"You can laugh, you bastards. You're not the ones cleaning shit off your new flat-heeled, so-sensible-I-could-kill-myself shoes. Right. I nominate Karen."

Karen picked up her mug and raised it to the group, but Bea saw her hesitate. It was only a fraction of a second; most people wouldn't have noticed, but most people hadn't known their friends since reception year at school. "Pleasure to be here with you all on this lovely Friday afternoon. Thanks for the nomination, Eleanor. My FTS is that I've been so busy at work that last week I missed a dentist's appointment and a talk by a leading psychiatrist that I'd been looking forward to for months. Clean forgot to write them on the calendar."

Bea and Eleanor groaned theatrically, and Eleanor threw her head onto her arm on the table. "For God's sake, Karen Browning, you could at least make something up if your life is so bloody *Little House on the Prairie*," she mumbled through her sleeve. She looked up. "I've missed so many midwife visits lately that I'm certain they have social services on speed dial. Bea, your turn. And this had better be worse than poo on your feet. I don't think I could handle winning this game a third week in a row."

Bea topped up her glass of juice from the jug standing on the chintzy red-and-white tablecloth and braced herself.

"Hi, everyone, my name is Bea."

"Hi, Bea," the other two chorused. Bea raised the glass and nodded in the direction of Eleanor, who was waiting eagerly.

"I'd like to thank Eleanor for my nomination. My Fuck This Shit Friday is that I forgot to—" She stopped short, remembering that the thing she'd forgotten to do couldn't be mentioned in front of Karen. Thinking on her feet, she recalled her morning at work. "I forgot to book one of our major clients at work into our senior management seminar and received a royal rollicking from my prick of a boss, who called me incompetent in front of the entire office."

"What a wanker," Eleanor murmured, reaching over to rub Bea's shoulder, the thumb of her other hand swiping through the text message she'd just received. "Oh, for God's sake, Noah's still asleep. He'll never sleep tonight if Mum lets him nap all day."

Bea felt a momentary flicker of annoyance, but at the last second Eleanor redeemed herself and dropped the mobile into the yawning mouth of her overstuffed handbag.

"He's not worth worrying about."

As Eleanor took Bea's juice-free hand, Bea couldn't help noticing faint Biro marks on the back, the ghost of a reminder or a phone number that a ninety-second shower hadn't quite erased.

Her phone buzzed again from under the table, and to her credit she barely threw a glance at it.

"That's what Fran said." Bea grinned. "Just a touch more colorfully."

Karen raised her eyebrows. "Isn't it a bit late for big sister to be flying to the rescue?"

"Oh, leave off her, Karen," Bea said good-naturedly. "Fran's always had my back; you've just never given her a look-in. It's nice to finally feel like I can talk to my sister. There's no bond like a sisterly one, you know." She flung a hand to her mouth, remembering what had happened to the sister Karen had had once upon a time. "Oh shit, sorry, hun."

Karen smiled, but her mouth was a tight line that made it look like more of a grimace. "It's okay, you don't have to apologize for loving your sister. And I'm glad you're getting on better with Fran, honestly."

She smiled properly this time and lifted her mug. "Okay, Eleanor wins today. To your shitty life."

Bea followed suit, raising her mug above the table and clinking it with Karen's. Eleanor lifted her own mug and sighed.

"To my shitty life."

"So gym mum says to working mum, 'Oh, no, I'm just surprised *you* had the time to . . .'" She stopped and looked from Bea to Karen and back again. "Oh God, I'm boring, aren't I?" She hid her face in her hands. "You can leave if you want to. I'll look away and you can just sneak out."

Bea laughed. "No, seriously, I really wanted to know what gym mummy said to that other one . . . vegan mummy?"

Eleanor groaned. "All right, all right. But you should know that those sixteen minutes of adult interaction during the school pickup are all I get most days. I'm not sitting in an office gossiping about who stole whose turkey sandwich or fixing people's heads. Feuding mums are all I have."

"Have you thought about when you'll go back to work?" Bea saw the crestfallen look on her friend's face and immediately regretted asking the question.

"Adam thinks I should take some time out. Just until Noah goes to school. What with childcare costs being so high, he thinks I may as well spend the time with the boys while they're young. And it's not as if we can't afford to live on his wage."

"And what do you think?" Karen probed gently. Eleanor let out another sigh.

"I think I don't want to be a middle-class asshole moaning about having the chance to actually bring up my own children when there are a ton of women who don't have any choice but to go back to work who would kill to be in my position."

"Okaaaay," Bea replied, digging her fork into the carrot cake left over on Karen's plate. "But what do you think when your friends don't care that you're a middle-class asshole?"

"I think I'll go crazy if I don't do something that makes me feel like me again. I'm too selfish to devote my every waking moment to being someone's mummy or someone's wife."

"You could set up your own business," Karen suggested. "Then you get to be mummy and super-businesswoman. Noah could go to nursery a couple of mornings a week—he'd benefit from the interaction with other babies, and you could network. I have some contacts I could put you in touch with; I know a lot of mums who have done the same thing."

Eleanor looked as though she was rolling the idea over in her mind, poking at it to find the holes.

"I don't know," she said, but underneath the words Bea could see there was a spark of interest that she hadn't seen in Eleanor since she'd taken maternity leave from her advertising job. "I mean, at Fresh I had a pretty stable client base. This would mean starting from scratch. It would be a lot of work . . . I'll think about it. Beats going back to my old job and having to pump my boobs in the disabled loos."

"I thought you'd practically stopped breastfeeding?"

"I practically have, but the bastards—sorry, Karen—won't stop filling up. I wake up in a puddle of milk every morning."

Bea screwed up her face. "Ew."

"Oh, Bea, one day . . . when you have kids . . ."

Bea pretended to shudder. "Jesus, I can't have kids. For one thing, I have a cream sofa."

Eleanor laughed. "You will. You know you will. I knew this woman who—"

"Seriously, Eleanor," Bea cut in. "If you tell me one more time about Moira at work who had her first child at forty-two, I'm going to throw up."

A hurt look briefly crossed Eleanor's face, then she broke into a grin. "Well, she did! So it's never too late."

"Absolutely. In fact I think I'll start right away. The very next bloke I sleep with, I'll give him a questionnaire about his family history first. You know, those ones you get at the doctor's. 'Excuse me, sir, before you take off those boxers, would you mind telling me if anyone in your family has a history of heart disease? No? Fantastic! Now, when you're ready, if you could just stick your willy in this tube for me.' " She mimed twirling a test tube between her fingers.

"Vulgar, Bea." Karen shook her head. "Speaking of which, how are things on the romance front?"

"Bill!" Bea shouted, turning in faux desperation to the waitress. "Can we get the bill, *please*?"

As the only singleton of the three of them, Bea was obliged to keep the others stocked up with graphic tales of her love life, her friends greedily feasting on her every word, reliving their dating days through her. What they didn't know, would never know, was that it was all bravado, lies, and posturing for their sake, so that they didn't worry about her. Bea hadn't been with anyone in years, and her few token dates had been to keep Karen off her back. They had never been given a real chance.

As they were waiting for the bemused waitress to bring the bill over, Karen turned to her.

"Look, I know this guy from the work crowd. He's single . . ."

Bea groaned theatrically. "Please, Karen, no more blind dates! I love you, but the blokes you've found for me in the past are . . . Well, let's just say I've not managed to find my Prince Charming amongst them."

Karen smiled. "I know, Tim was a bit of a wet blanket, and Sean . . ."

"Was an utter cockblanket," Bea finished for her. "Seriously, Karen, how these men made it as psychiatrists when they have so many Freudian issues themselves, I do not know."

"David's not like that," Karen protested. "He's not even a psychiatrist. He works in IT."

"Oh, for fuck's sake—like that's better!"

Eleanor laughed. "Don't be so fussy, Bea. At least if he's rubbish in bed, you might get your twenty-year-old laptop upgraded."

"Bitch." Bea grinned at Karen. "Fine, give him my number. He'd better not be another Sean, though."

"I promise. But it's no wonder you can't find a decent man, with language like yours. You could at least try and sound like a lady."

"False advertising." Bea pointed at Eleanor. "Isn't that illegal, Els?"

The waitress arrived with the bill, and Karen handed over her card, as always. Bea shot a frustrated look at Eleanor, who shook her head almost imperceptibly. They had both tried to pay countless times, but in the end it was easier just to let her get the tab.

"I've got to shoot off back to work," Karen said. "I have a

patient this afternoon and I need to leave straight after the session. Michael's away this weekend; I want to say good-bye before he goes."

"Somewhere nice?"

Karen pulled a face. "Doncaster, I think. Love you both."

She took her card back from the waitress, and the others both hugged her good-bye.

"I'd better go too." Eleanor pretended to glance at her watch, but Bea knew she was desperate to get back to her son. "Good luck with work, call me if you need to talk it through."

Bea grimaced. "Thanks, hun, I will. Love to Tweedledum and Tweedledee."

Eleanor grinned. "I'll tell Toby and Noah their old fogy auntie Bea said hi. They won't have any idea who Tweedledum and Tweedledee are."

"What are they teaching kids in schools these days? Wink."

"You know one of these days you'll actually *learn* to wink. And learn to be funny."

"All right, cow. Still okay to pop those passport forms over after the gym later?"

"Not bedtime, Bea; you always turn up at bedtime and Tobes goes wild."

"Not bedtime, I promise."

- 4 -

KAREN

The tension around the table was palpable, but not because they were worried about what they were about to be told—bad news was never delivered in a team environment; that wasn't the way things were done round here. Instead it was communicated behind closed doors, as quietly as possible: no fuss, no muss. No, the rest of the junior psychiatrists, six in all including Karen, were all looking anxious for the same reason her own leg was jiggling impatiently, and she'd glanced at the door constantly since they'd been gathered in the large conference room.

It was Friday, and everyone had been hoping to slope off early to start their weekend. Michael was leaving tonight and she'd been desperate to get back and see him before he set off. She always treated weekends as though he might never come back; in fact every time she said good-bye to anyone she loved she treated it as though it would be the last time. If she didn't see him, she'd spend the weekend obsessing about him being in some kind of accident and worrying that the last words she'd ever said to him were "Oh, can you stick the garbage out before nine?"

After what felt like an eternity, the door to the conference room opened, and two of the senior partners, Robert and Jonathan, walked in, both completely oblivious to the fact that it was the end of the week and their staff looked like a group of sulky teens in detention.

"Thanks for coming, everyone." Jonathan looked round the

table and his gaze fell on Karen, already in her coat. "Are we keeping you, Karen?"

Embarrassment at being singled out warmed her cheeks, but she wasn't about to be shamed. She'd always got the impression Jonathan didn't particularly like her; he was a misogynistic bastard and his deprecating comments were always aimed at her or at the only other female junior.

"Nothing that can't wait until after we're done," she replied, meeting his eyes. She suspected that Jonathan had always secretly hoped she'd get pregnant, a baby instantly flipping the switch in her brain from career woman to mum. As it stood, she was a hundred times more committed than her male counterparts, and there was no way any of them could dispute that, or question her drive. What poor Jonathan didn't know was that Karen wouldn't ever have children. She'd been so tempted on occasion to tell him, to destroy his dream of her slipping off into a station wagon and an apron, but to tell him would mean having to tell him why, and she couldn't do that.

Robert, sensing the tension between them, cleared his throat. "Right, then, we won't keep you long. The reason we've got you all here is because, as you know, Ken Williams is retiring this summer."

"As you know" was an understatement; the knowledge of Ken's retirement had sat in each and every one of their offices since he'd announced his plans two months earlier. It had watched them during their sessions and whispered to them as they filed their paperwork. Notes had become more comprehensive, referrals had flowed like champagne in the Playboy Mansion. Ken's departure would leave a hole in the second-floor infrastructure that each one of them was desperate to plug.

Karen already knew who it was going to be, and it really was a case of plugging the hole full of dung. And from the expression on his face at the table, it looked as though he knew it too. Travis Yapp was the embodiment of every cuss word Bea had ever uttered.

What was the word for someone who wore too much gel for a man of his age and still referred to his car as a female? She made a mental note to ask Bea later.

Karen knew that Robert didn't like Travis, but she also knew that Travis had impressed the right people, said and done everything that was expected of him. Karen didn't like the implication that she hadn't. She knew she wasn't always as diplomatic as she could be; she wasn't the yes man she was expected to be, but she'd always hoped that when it came to the crunch, Robert would stick his neck out for her. It wasn't enough, he'd told her, and then added, as if sealing her fate as a junior psychiatrist for the rest of her life, "You wouldn't be happy on the second floor anyway: too much politics, not enough hands-on work. You'd suffocate." Travis, he'd said, was exactly the kind of political schmuck they wanted on the top floor. "What does that make you?" she'd wanted to ask, but he was still her boss, and anyhow, she hadn't wanted him to know how much it pained her not to get the job.

Jonathan was now doing the talking—some long drawn-out speech about the years of experience Ken would be taking with him and how much he'd learned from his colleague. Karen must have been frowning in anticipation of Travis's coronation, because Robert was looking at her now, mouthing, "You okay?"

She flicked her eyes down to her lap, ignoring his concern—childish, she knew, but this whole charade was causing anxiety and irritation to flare up inside her. She might have to sit there and congratulate Yapp, smile and say he was the best man for the job, but she didn't have to make Robert feel better about what a coward he'd been. She hadn't really believed in the whole glass-ceiling thing when she was at medical school, but the doubt she'd held so strongly about its existence was beginning to wane.

". . . and that's why we're very excited to invite Karen to join us as a member of the senior consulting team. What do you say, Karen?"

Karen shook her head slightly, convinced she'd misheard. "Sorry, what?"

Robert laughed, saving her embarrassment, as the rest of the team gauged one another's reactions. Clearly they'd all been expecting this to be Travis's coronation too.

"Well, shock and disbelief is as good a reaction as any, I suppose." Robert grinned. "I'm sure you'll all join me in congratulating Karen—assuming of course that she wants the position?"

Karen composed herself, smiled, and nodded graciously. "Of course. I'm thrilled and honored. Thank you both for the opportunity. I hope I live up to your expectations."

Her colleagues all recovered as quickly as she did, none more so than Travis Yapp, who plastered a white-toothed poster-boy grin on his face and held up an invisible glass in toast. "Congratulations, Karen—it must be great to see all your hard work paying off."

———————

"'Congratulations, Karen—it must be great to see all your hard work paying off,'" Karen mimicked in a childish voice. "What a . . . a . . ." She searched for a suitable word and remembered Bea's creative command of the English language from just a couple of hours before. "What a cockblanket."

Robert let out a laugh so spontaneous and genuine that Karen couldn't help smiling through her fury.

"I don't know what you're laughing at," she chided, her anger dissipating. "You realize he was insinuating that I've been sleeping with you to get a promotion?"

"It's standard Misogyny 101—if a man gets a promotion, it's because he worked for it; if a woman gets one, it's because she slept with someone for it. They teach it on the first day of the 'Aren't You Glad You Have a Penis' course."

"Hmm, quite the feminist, aren't we?" Karen checked her watch.

"I really have to get home. I just wanted to catch you to say thank you for the opportunity. I won't let you down."

"I know you won't." Robert smiled. "Welcome to the career of your dreams, Dr. Browning."

Karen descended the steps of the Cecil Baxter building, her mind reeling. Partner. Everything she'd worked for, everything she wanted was within her grasp now. She might not have the family she'd hoped for as a child but at least she had her career—finally she felt her choices were going to be vindicated.

As she made her way to her car she looked both ways down the street before she crossed, but what she saw made her stop sharply at the side of the road. To her right, no more than three hundred yards was a silver Fiat parked up as though its occupant was waiting for someone. And sitting behind the wheel, waiting, watching her walk from the building despite it being hours since their session that morning, was her newest patient, Jessica Hamilton.

– 5 –

KAREN

Yes!" She had been fumbling for her keys for a few minutes, and as her fingers closed around them and she pulled them out of her bag, a crumpled piece of white paper followed them and landed on the doorstep. Grabbing it off the ground, she let herself in and threw her bag into the foyer.

"Hello? Michael?" She resisted the urge to shout, "Honey, I'm home!" and anyway, it would have fallen on deaf ears—Michael wasn't here. Although the house was hers (well, the bank's), he had his own key and treated the place as his own when he was there during the week. They weren't like any of the other couples Karen knew, constantly checking in with each other, and although she found it hard at times, it worked for them. Mostly. She hated having to keep the nature of their relationship a secret, but telling those around her where Michael really went on his weekends "at work" simply wasn't an option.

She wandered through to the living room, smoothing out the piece of paper as she walked. A cheerful-looking yellow logo was emblazoned across the top; her old school and the one Toby attended now. The words "Keeping in Touch" were written under the logo in large print. It was some kind of newsletter detailing the children's achievements of the term so far. Karen shoved it on to the TV cabinet without reading the rest.

She was used to the still silence that came with too much time home alone, but today it unsettled her, and she switched the TV on to fill the void where a bustling after-school routine might have been. It flickered into life and she left it on the channel it was already tuned to, ignoring the predictable fodder of the retired and unemployed that came on and heading upstairs to fix her makeup before Michael arrived. She wanted his mental picture of her to be a good one, to last him the few days he'd be away. In the couple of years they'd been together, they had made sure never to let themselves go, become comfortable in the way they might have done had things been different. Their time together was always cherished, knowing that he might have to leave at any minute if a family emergency arose.

As she refreshed her lipstick and mascara and applied more blush to her cheekbones, she thought of poor exhausted Eleanor and the way she never had a second to spend on herself anymore, and of Bea and the fact that all she had was time. And her job, which didn't exactly seem to be going swimmingly at the moment. She should offer to do more for both of them, she decided: take the boys off Eleanor's hands for the day so she could get some well-deserved rest, spend some more time with Bea and try to find her someone who made her happy. Not that that had exactly gone well last time she'd tried—a fact Bea didn't hesitate to remind her of. In retrospect it had probably been a silly idea to set her friend up with someone she worked with, though Bea could have shown a bit more gratitude and at least waited until Sean had left before calling him a total wanker under her breath.

The fact was, Karen only ever wanted the best for her friends.

When her face began to feel heavy from the makeup she would remove in a few hours' time, she flicked the screen of her phone, dreading a message telling her that Michael had had to leave while she was still at work. There was nothing, just a couple of emails that could wait until later, and a text from Bea.

E looking harassed. Do all mums look like that? Thank God we r happily sprogless!!! Xx

Karen smiled at Bea's way of telling her she was worried about Eleanor while trying not to look interfering. She fired off two text messages, one replying to Bea—*Sure she's fine but texting her now. Maybe we should offer to take boys this wkend?*—and one to Eleanor: *Love our lunches. Miss u as always. Anything I can do to help with the little men? Xx*

Bea replied almost instantly.

Sounds good. Let me know when. Xx

Karen was just about to tap out another message, her thumb hovering above the screen, when she heard Michael's key in the door.

- 6 -

ELEANOR

As Eleanor left the café, she felt the calm and freedom seep away from her like a physical drain on her body. She had to go and pick Noah up from her mum's, then it would be back to school for Toby, followed by tea and bath time. When Adam arrived home, he was usually too knackered to put the boys to bed, so she'd end up doing that too. It would be eight thirty before she could sit down, and then she'd be listening for the monitor all evening, eventually crawling into bed for her three hours' sleep before Noah woke again.

As she drove, she thought of Bea and Karen and what they would be doing with their evenings. With Michael away, Karen would probably work, typing up notes, making referrals and sorting invoices, all done from the comfort of her own sofa with a glass of wine in her hand and a trashy movie on TV. Bea would spend her evening at the gym, popping over to Eleanor's long enough to disturb the kids—no matter what she promised—then getting changed to head out with the girls from work, no doubt. She'd drink and laugh until late and then climb into bed safe in the knowledge that tomorrow was Saturday and she could sleep in before lunch out with Karen or one of her other friends.

Eleanor's evening looked a bit different. If Noah went down okay, she had calls to make about the surprise party she and Bea were arranging for Karen's birthday in six weeks, and she wanted to make a list of decorations they would need for the VIP booth in the restaurant she'd booked—she still hadn't decided if they should have a theme. She and Bea had spent a whole afternoon window-shopping for ideas when they'd first started planning it months ago, and all they'd managed to decide was *no pink*. Then tomorrow Toby had football at 10 a.m., so she and Noah would go to that with him while Adam worked, then they'd all have lunch together before a birthday party with the other mums from the school, followed by takeout and a film in the evening. Such a glamorous life.

She often tried to remind herself that this was what she'd wanted—that this stage of the boys' lives wouldn't last forever and she'd miss it when they were teenagers and she could do what she liked. By then, though, she was pretty sure she'd be too knackered from the last ten years to get her glad rags on and go to a nightclub. Did nightclubs even let you in over forty? Maybe there was a special room for people who'd spent their thirties covered in baby sick. And by the time Noah was old enough, Toby would be eighteen, and the thought of bumping into him at a bar sent her into a cold sweat.

Her phone rang, Adam's name flashing on the caller ID.

"Hey, love." She put him on hands-free and shouted into the receiver.

"Hey, how are you?"

"Good, thanks, what's up?" It wasn't that Adam never called her in the day anymore; it was just that there was always a reason, which usually involved adding to her to-do list. Can you just pick me up . . . ? Can you just post that . . . ? "Just" had become a dirty word in their household.

"Okay. Work's hectic, though. Just calling to say I'll be a bit late. Overran today, and I've got to fit another call in before I can break for tonight."

Her heart sank a little at the words. She envied Adam his ability to let his life "run over a bit," safe in the knowledge that she'd be there to sort everything out. The tea, the house, the kids. Was this how she'd imagined her life when she'd met him? Was domestic drudgery to be her only reward for taking on him and his eighteen-month-old son?

That wasn't how she really felt, of course. Toby was every bit her son. She'd raised him for seven years, he called her Mum, and he was none the wiser that it wasn't true. She knew the girls thought she and Adam should tell him about his real mother, but the truth was that she couldn't bear the thought of their perfect family becoming a little less perfect. Having him shout, "You're not my real mum" during an argument, or going off to look for the egg donor who dared to call herself his natural mother. There was nothing natural about choosing drink and drugs over your kids. That woman hadn't earned the right to be the shadow that hung over their lives. And yet she was, because deep down Eleanor knew she was being an awful person for keeping Toby from knowing where he came from. She knew it was selfish and mean, and she justified it by telling herself—and anyone who would listen—that it was for his own good. What kid wanted to know his mother had abandoned him before he could even tell her how much he loved her and needed her? Toby didn't need that; they didn't need to be a problem family.

"Okay, baby, I'll take care of things." Eleanor tried not to sigh but didn't quite manage it. If he noticed, though, he didn't say anything.

"Thanks, love." There was relief in his voice; there wouldn't be a fight right now. And even if she was furious later, he could give her a hug and a kiss and say he was sorry, and it would all be done with. She couldn't bear to drag out fights and Adam knew it. "You're a star." That was her, Eleanor the star, Eleanor the supermum. Eleanor the selfish, lying actress.

"Hello, baba!" As she walked into her mum's house, Noah started to kick his legs in delight. "How's he been?"

"Absolute gold."

She scooped the little boy up and realized how much her arms had missed his weight.

Just as her mum got up to put the kettle on, Eleanor's mobile rang.

Private number. "Did someone forget to claim their Payment Protection Insurance back?" she murmured to Noah, and canceled the call. Seconds later, it rang again.

"Hello?"

"Mrs. Whitney? It's Georgia Fenton, from Toby's school."

Her stomach lurched. *Oh God, what's happened?*

"What's wrong? Is Toby okay?"

"Yes, Toby's fine, don't worry." The school secretary's voice was calm as always. She could be ringing to say that Toby's leg had fallen off and she'd deliver the news in a panic-free tone. "It's just that it's the last day of term and all the children leave early today, but no one's here to collect Toby. We sent out a newsletter weeks ago."

Shit. How had she missed that? She always checked Toby's bag in the evenings, after he'd gone to bed. Maybe not every night, but definitely in the last two weeks.

"Oh God, I'm so sorry, I had no idea. I'll be straight there for him."

"Great, thanks. It's not a problem for someone to wait with him; it's just that we have our end-of-term meeting in ten minutes . . ." *And you, useless mother, are an inconvenience.*

"I'm so sorry. I'll be there as quickly as I can."

It took her ten minutes just to collect Noah's things together and bundle him into the car. By the time she arrived at the school, out of breath and disheveled, it had been half an hour since the call. Toby was sitting in the office looking thoroughly fed up.

"I'm so sorry," she repeated, aiming her apology at both the secretary and her son. "Are you okay, dude?"

He glared at her. "Everyone left ages ago."

"I'm sorry, mate, really I am. I didn't know." She looked up at Mrs. Fenton, who tried not to look as annoyed as Toby. "I'm sorry about your meeting."

"It's fine, Mrs. Whitney, really. I bet you've got a lot on your plate at the moment." She shot a pointed look at the car seat, where Noah was cooing happily at the sight of his brother.

"Yes, well, it won't happen again. I'm not usually disorganized; I mean, I have a whole routine . . ." It sounded pathetic even to her. Georgia Fenton might not believe her, but it was true. She ran the house with precision and had promised herself that a new baby wouldn't change that. She was not the type of person to let things fall apart.

"Even the best-laid plans of mice and men . . ." Mrs. Fenton ushered them towards the door.

"That was so embarrassing!" Toby hadn't stopped glaring since she'd picked him up, and after a silent car journey home he made his announcement the minute she opened the front door. "I bet you wouldn't have forgotten that thing!" He shot a killer look at the car seat, where Noah was now sleeping soundly.

"Tobes, come on, I didn't forget . . ." But it was no good. He'd already run upstairs and slammed his bedroom door behind him.

- 7 -

NOW

What happened to the newsletter?

Which newsletter? The one from Toby's school? I threw it away.

You put it in the garbage? At home or at work?

At home, I think. Why is this relevant? It was just a newsletter. Come and visit our school, bake sale, et cetera. I barely read it.

Did you know it was from Toby's school?

Of course I did. He goes to our old school.

How did you think the newsletter got into your bag?

I thought Eleanor had dropped it there at lunch.

Was it at the top of your bag?

No, it wasn't.

What do you think now about how the letter got in there?

I know what you want me to say. That *she* put it in there. That she'd been planning this long before we even knew she existed. You're right, it must have been her . . .

Aren't you going to say anything?

Obsession. It starts slowly, like a train pulling out of a station. You can still see the houses and trees around you, you can still make out the details of people in their windows or dark green tractors in their light green fields; then it starts to gain momentum, and the houses are still there, but the people aren't visible in the windows anymore. Colors start to blur, dark green bleeds into light, and you realize that if you don't find a way to get off now, you are going to spin off the track altogether.

That's how it was with me, at least. I've been watching them for years now—ever since they were little girls—and I never saw the train speeding up, never noticed the colors around me beginning to merge until it was too late. The way they bounced off one another even as five-years-olds—I wanted it, I craved it. I prayed that one day they would need me the way they needed each other.

As they grew older, they grew closer—not like other girls I studied, so easily torn apart by boys or differing interests. They were like sisters—closer even, because they had chosen each other.

If you asked me to pin down the moment it all changed, I would tell you it was impossible. A series of unfortunate events that jolted our lives off their tracks. Sliding-door moments, they call them. If I had chosen to prepare my letters before entering the post office that day; if I had remembered to pick up the packet of envelopes from my kitchen drawer rather than having to steal a dozen loose ones from the stationery cupboard at work; if a family of rats hadn't chosen that week to chew through the wiring at the local post office, forcing me into the town, things would have turned out differently for three women.

I had been rushing, the task I had set myself that day firm and unerring in my mind. I'd already been put so far behind by my uncharacteristic disorganization, I didn't have time to mess around. I was determined not to be sidetracked by the books that lined the shelves of WHSmith, or by the stationery strategically placed at the entrance of the post office contained within the bookstore. So determined was I to beat the lunchtime rush that I almost didn't see them, probably wouldn't have if Bea hadn't chosen that moment to let out a shrieking laugh, a laugh I would have picked out at a Justin Bieber concert, and in that instant I almost felt the flapping of the butterfly wings that would cause a tsunami in our lives.

I froze, my breath catching in my throat.

They walked past the entrance to the post office, just the two of them that day, Eleanor heavily pregnant and insisting they use the lift, her hand resting on her stomach to emphasize her encumbered state, Bea humoring her, although I was certain she would be groaning inwardly at her friend's theatrics.

I turned away from them too quickly, almost stumbling into the woman next to me in the line. I muttered an apology, or perhaps the words had formed in my mind but got lost before they had crossed my lips. Ignoring the rush of blood to my face and shoving my mail back into my bag, I bolted towards the stairs, not knowing what I planned to do when I reached the top and saw them leave the lift.

In truth, I did nothing, just watched from behind a gondola of brightly colored cards emblazoned with birthday greetings as they linked arms like carefree fifteen-year-old girls, rather than the thirtysomething women they were, and left the store, the air inside seeming more alive for having had them in it.

By the time I reached the fresh air of the high street, the roar of blood in my ears had slowed to a steady pulsing, the flames that had blazed under my collar had been extinguished, and my legs no longer shook. I flattened my back against the cool stone wall and let all my senses return to their resting state, allowed my eyes to close for a second as my composure returned.

It might seem irrational—allowing that small act of seeing them in a place that I hadn't expected them to be to shake me to the extent it did. In some ways it was akin to seeing your teachers in their normal clothes and realizing that they continue to exist when you are not looking at them, that their lives carry on even without you holding up the microscope to it. I hadn't been prepared. I hadn't even known Bea had the day off work—and I thought I was at a point where I knew everything about them. Obviously I hadn't been paying close enough attention. I'd let the ball drop and now here we were.

My sliding door, my choice. Would I return home now, letters shoved hastily into my handbag, and let my normal life whitewash over the last ten minutes, ugly graffiti on a wall quickly replaced by a pastel hue? If I had, who knows how differently things would have turned out? That slow IV full of obsession that dripped into my veins over the weeks that followed—would it still have consumed me as completely as if it were heroin?

I wandered around the town without purpose or explanation after that, terrified at the thought that I might see them again and terrified that I wouldn't. When I did—of course in a town this small it was inevitable—I was relieved that my reaction was less physical than the first time. See? I wasn't in the grip of my obsession; I was still in control.

This time I drank in the details of the women who strolled with a casual air of contentment through the shopping center as though I were seeing them for the first time, not the millionth. Bea wore designer heels and clutched her handbag like it was an Oscar, walking slightly ahead of Eleanor as though guarding her groaning baby bump with her very life. Eleanor herself kept one hand on her stomach, stylish even in maternity wear.

And now my reaction was decidedly more measured. Sure, my heart was beating a bit faster, and I noticed how warm it was in the shopping center, but it wasn't like I threw up or passed out or anything dramatic like that. And when I saw them go into the café for lunch—well, I was going to just grab a sandwich from Wilko's with what little time I had left, but the café across the street from them looked nice, and I deserved something good to eat. There was nothing more to it than that. Drip, drip.

What harm could come from just watching them? I'd made an art form of it over the years.

I thought about them on the way home, of course, but that was because I'd just seen them—it's not like they were always at the forefront of my mind. I had my own life. It's hard to believe now, but my existence hadn't always revolved so fully around where they were or what they were doing.

Bea had ordered a glass of wine with her lunch, laughing at the disapproving looks from her abstinent friend. Obviously I couldn't hear what they were saying, but when they laughed I imagined that they were commenting on how Karen—always the sensible one—wouldn't have approved of wine on a workday. Maybe Bea wouldn't return to work at all—why else would she be drinking midweek? I imagined that their voices weren't loud but still managed to practically block out everyone else in the café, and noticed how they didn't even look up to see if anyone was staring with disapproval when they laughed, or when Bea knocked the basket of complimentary crisps flying off the table.

I was still thinking about Eleanor's raucous laughter when my phone rang. It was work asking me to pick up the midweek snacks, and my attention was ripped away from the women as quickly as if I'd never seen them.

- 9 -

ELEANOR

The cupboards heaving with freshly bought produce sure to spoil before it made its way into one of the culinary delights she vowed to make "one of these days," and all visible surfaces wiped over with a baby wipe, Eleanor sighed and flicked on the kettle. She crossed two of the jobs off the everlasting list stuck to the pinboard in the kitchen, and was just adding three more when her mobile started playing "All about That Bass" from the other room.

"Hey, you." She answered Bea's call with her phone under her chin. "Good save the other day. I'm guessing you forgot to book the restaurant?"

Bea sighed. "Yup. And it's taken on the day we wanted it—we'll have to re-send all the bloody invites and I know you worked really hard on them. Sorry, Els. Do we change the date or the venue?"

"Neither." Eleanor grinned, and then realized Bea couldn't see her smugness. "I booked it months ago when we first talked about this birthday thing. Before the baby brain took over."

Eleanor pushed Iron Man to one side with her foot to gather up that morning's discarded pajamas. She picked through the pile of clothes, silently judging which ones were good for another wear before they were added to her ever-increasing washing pile. Pants, wash. Socks, wash. Pajama top, no visible stains . . . She held it against her face and inhaled. Wash.

"You knew I'd forget?"

Washing under one arm, Eleanor picked up a pile of Adam's papers from the dining room table. She cast an eye over them, then, deciding she had no idea what they were or where to put them, put them back down again. How the hell was she supposed to keep this place tidy when the mess was so important to everyone else? Maybe she should try getting her husband a reward chart. It had worked when Toby was acting like a four-year-old. Then again, Toby had actually been four.

"I . . . Well, I suspected."

"You could have just told me and saved me the trouble of forgetting to do it myself," Bea grumbled.

"Where's the fun in that? Do we have many RSVPs?"

"I'll have to check my spreadsheet," Bea replied.

"You mean the napkins you've been writing the plans on?" Eleanor felt her friend cringe.

"You saw that then?"

"Seriously, Bea, you spend all day organizing other people's lives and yet one party and you're a bundle of napkins and Post-its. I sent the invites out last Monday; we should have some replies by now."

Eleanor glanced at the clock guiltily. If she didn't start Noah's story time soon, they'd get behind on lunch and the whole of the rest of the day would be out of whack. But this was important to her friend, and her own life was so dull these days that she had to find her drama from somewhere.

"I'll get you a list, okay?" Before Eleanor could answer, Bea asked, "So what have you been up to today?"

She said it like an afterthought, a token question because she knew the answer would be short and sweet.

"Oh, same old," Eleanor replied, hating herself for not even being bothered to make something up. "This morning we went food shopping and this afternoon we get to have story time and make cupcakes."

"Sounds like fun. Save me a cake?"

"If you fancy risking a bout of food poisoning, there'll be one here with your name on it."

Bea laughed. "Did you think any more about what we talked about at lunch the other day?"

"Not really." In truth she'd thought of little else; the idea of getting her teeth into something again had set off a spark inside her that she hadn't felt since before Noah was born. Excitement at doing something that was just for her. But she'd mentioned it to Adam and he'd been his usual uninspiring self. "Don't you have enough to think about with this place and the kids?" he'd asked, casting a disparaging eye at the plates still stacked in the sink from their dinner. And that had been that.

"You should, you know. It'd do you good to do something that wasn't for everyone else for a change."

"I will," she promised. "I will definitely think about it."

She hung up, taking a look around at all the things she needed to get done before Toby came home from his nan's and she lost any chance. Plus there was story time and tummy time and every other kind of time being a Good Mother required. Just the thought of spending another six hours with no adult to talk to made her want to scream. She took Noah from his bouncer and laid him on his mat, propped up with the special tummy-time contraption that Adam shook his head at, surrounding him with brightly colored and suitably stimulating toys. He kicked his legs happily, and feeling like a complete shit, she flicked on the kettle again, pulled out her laptop, and googled "starting your own business from home" in one window, and "cleaners in the Shrewsbury area" in another.

- 1 0 -

KAREN

Karen stepped up her pace, moving through the crowds with an expert fluidity. So much for the failing high street. She should be in a hurry more often; her bad luck might save some of these shops from bankruptcy.

In a moment of uncharacteristic disorganization Karen had walked out of the house that morning without her lunch, only remembering it was still in the fridge when lunchtime had been marked by the sound of her stomach groaning in protest. Not that she'd minded having to go into town to buy something—it gave her a chance to get out of the office and check out the calf-length leather boots she'd had her eye on for weeks.

Cutting through the shopping center was the obvious choice, and as she passed the Pandora store near the entrance, she glanced at the window instinctively, a gesture that could have been described as either vanity or self-consciousness, to check her hair.

She almost didn't see them. Maybe had the center been less busy, had the throng of shoppers not steered her closer to the doorway than usual, or had the shop itself not been almost empty she might have missed them altogether. As it was, in the exact second that she was passing the doorway, he turned, the movement drawing attention to that trademark teenage haircut that was beginning to look out of place on a man in his thirties. He placed a hand on the arm of the younger girl at his side, and as Karen turned back, the shop almost completely behind her now, she saw her smile, the same smile she'd seen just a few days before when that same girl had sat opposite her and talked about her married lover.

Jessica and Adam. Her patient and her best friend's husband.

The foyer was quiet when she arrived back at work, just the tapping of Molly's fingers on her keyboard. She looked up and smiled when she saw it was Karen.

"Nice lunch?" she asked. Then, registering Karen's expression, "Is everything okay?"

"Fine, thanks, Molly. I had a sandwich." Karen realized too late that that wasn't what the receptionist had asked, and just how distracted she'd managed to make herself sound with the lie. She'd gone straight back to the office after seeing Jessica and Adam together and completely forgotten to eat, questions slamming through her mind like gunfire.

Is Adam her married lover? Did she know we were best friends? Is that why she chose me? What the hell do I do now?

"Can you hold my calls for an hour, please?"

"Sure."

She fumbled to get her key into the office lock, cringing at how all over the place she must look. Once inside, she could feel herself relaxing—no one watching her in here, no one for whom to maintain the professional demeanor.

Sinking down onto the plush beige carpet and leaning her back against the base of the sofa, she closed her eyes and breathed in deeply through her nose to the count of eight. Letting the breath out through her mouth as slowly as she could manage, she felt the panic inside her flow outward, pictured it as a physical entity that she could expel and watch float away. Repeating the exercise twice more, she felt herself relaxing, her thoughts ordering themselves into a list in her mind. She enjoyed lists; they were manageable, organized. They helped her keep control. How anyone got through their lives without a set of bullet-pointed tasks to guide them, she would never understand.

The first item on her list—was it definitely Jessica Hamilton she'd seen in that store? There was no question of whether it was Adam; she'd known him longer than she'd known Michael, had even been with Eleanor when she'd bought him the jacket he'd been wearing that afternoon. The question of Jessica was trickier. She'd met her only once before, and in a different environment. Could she say for certain it was her? She visualized the coat the girl had been wearing, a camel-colored mac with a tie belt at the waist. She didn't remember it from their session—in fact the only colors she could associate with her patient were gray and black. Of course that didn't mean anything; not everyone wore the same coat all the time. Bea had hundreds, it seemed.

She tried to picture Jessica's face but could see only those murky blue eyes, the dark blonde hair. The girl with Adam had been sleek, styled, her face made up. Granted, Karen had seen her for only a second or two, but she'd got the impression of someone infinitely more confident than the girl who had come to her for therapy. And yet her first instinct had been that it was Jessica—why else would her name spring to mind? There must have been something about Adam's companion that had made her instantly recognize her as the girl who had been in her office just a few days ago. But try as she might, she couldn't picture what it was.

Assuming she was wrong and the girl in the shop wasn't her patient, had she also been mistaken about them being together? Adam had certainly laid a hand on the girl's arm, but could there have been an innocent reason? Had he been pushing past her?

No, her first instinct had been right. Whether it was Jessica Hamilton or not, that lying bastard was cheating on her best friend, and now she had to decide what to do about it.

- 11 -

BEA

Mum! It's everywhere!"

Fran threw her son a damp dishcloth.

"Get the worst up, and I'll take care of the rest when you've all gone to bed."

She crossed the kitchen to join her sister at the table, pushing aside a pile of half-term homework to put their coffee down.

"I don't know how you cope," Bea told her with a shake of her head. "Just watching all this is exhausting."

"What, the kids?" Fran grinned. "The secret is to stop caring about the things that aren't really important. Are my surfaces always fingerprint-free? No. Is there an empty milk carton back in the fridge? Probably. Did we have fish finger sandwiches for tea twice this week? Absolutely. But the kids had clean clothes on every day and they were fed and watered. I've learned not to worry too much about the stuff in between. I'll have a perfect home when they've moved out." She snorted. "If they move out."

"I reckon Eleanor could learn something from you." Bea had always envied Fran's simple approach to life. Her sister had never worried about whether her clothes were bang on trend or cared about being at the top of the career ladder. All she ever wanted was to enjoy her family and be happy, and as a result it seemed as though she was. Bea didn't necessarily want her sister's life, but it would be nice to feel as content with the one she had.

Fran snorted. "Don't say that in front of Karen, will you?"

Bea raised her eyebrows. "And what is that supposed to mean?"

"Nothing, just that she's hardly my biggest fan, is she? I mean, she's always seen herself as more of a sister to you than I am."

"That's not true!" Bea's response was a little too fast. "Karen loves you, she's just a bit intense sometimes. It's probably the psychiatrist thing." She wondered if her words sounded as forced to Fran as they did to her. If Fran noticed, she didn't comment.

"Yeah, well, I guess she's got issues of her own."

"What issues?" asked Bea, surprised.

There was a huge crash from the living room, followed by two voices shouting, "Mum!" in unison.

"Oh shit. Look, wait there, I'd better go and see what's going on."

Fran disappeared, leaving Bea staring into her coffee cup and wondering what kind of issues her sister thought Karen was dealing with. After a minute, her sister returned and began rummaging around in the cupboard under the sink.

"Sorry, Bea, they've made a right mess in there, knocked over the bloody side table. I'm going to be scrubbing milk out of the sofa all night or it'll stink like a drain."

"No problem." Bea swilled down the dregs of her drink and put her mug in the sink. "I'll bail out. I'd rather watch my nails dry than watch you clean."

"You're too kind." Fran screwed up her nose.

"What are sisters for?"

- 12 -

KAREN

Michael had arrived home that evening brandishing a bunch of flowers like a fencing sword. They'd chatted about work, and Karen had filled him in on as much as she could about her caseload without breaking her monk-like vow of silence. Three times she'd almost told him about seeing Adam with the mystery woman and three times she'd thought better of it. He'd looked exhausted; his complexion was sallow and he downed the glass of wine she had poured for his meal before she'd even dished up. The last people he'd want to talk about were her friends and their marriage problems.

"Tough weekend?" she asked, snaking her fingers over his shoulders, kneading out the knots in his muscles through his shirt. He nodded but said nothing, just leaned his head back so his forehead nearly touched her chin. She bent forward and kissed it gently.

Michael turned to her and buried his face in her stomach. She kissed the top of his head, then knelt down so they were face-to-face and kissed him harder on the lips. This was how it was between them: they let passion wash away the pain rather than talking through it. She would have laughed had it not been so pitiful—a psychiatrist who couldn't get her own boyfriend to talk about his problems. She recognized the irony, but to push him would be to push him away, and she'd missed him too much to risk an argument tonight.

They took their troubles to the bedroom and cast them away

along with their clothes. The sex was rougher, more urgent than usual. It really must have been a bad weekend.

By the time they got round to eating, the chicken was tough and dry, so Michael called for takeaway and got dressed to go pick it up from their favorite place a few miles out of town.

While he was gone, Karen made herself a coffee and sank herself down on the sofa to read a magazine—one of those real-life "my mother stole my husband" types that she swore she bought only for the quizzes.

The downstairs of Karen's home was modern—sleek lines and chrome kitchen appliances—but it could hardly be called cozy. Everything she owned was a fingerprint hazard, and the custom-made glass patio doors had been a nightmare to find blinds for— even more so considering she never closed them.

The darkness beyond the doors gave the impression that there was nothing there, as though the world began and ended with her house. Silly really, as she was surrounded by other houses; they just weren't packed together like soldiers in a row. When the darkness was this thick, she felt completely cut off from everyone else. It was one of the reasons she'd chosen the house in the first place: you could be surrounded by people and yet still be on your own.

A thump against the back kitchen door pulled Karen's attention from her magazine, but only briefly. That was quick; he'd obviously forgotten something. She wondered why he'd been so uptight when he'd arrived home. Had they fought? Did she know about Karen, or suspect? She assumed he wouldn't be back if his wife knew about her, unless she'd kicked him out.

Lost in thoughts of Michael's marriage ending, it took her a minute to realize he hadn't come in. He couldn't have forgotten his keys; he'd locked the door behind him and she'd heard his car leave. She reached over and cracked the front room curtain open. The car wasn't in the drive.

"Hurry up, Michael, I'm bloody starving," she muttered to herself, picking up her magazine again.

A second noise, like a short blast of hail against the door, pulled Karen to her feet. She dropped her magazine on the sofa, moved towards the kitchen, and peered through the window, but nothing but blackness greeted her. Fumbling with her keys, she pulled open the kitchen door and stared out into the night. There was not a movement or sound anywhere. As she went to close the door again, she glanced down. A jumble of items lay beneath the step: a pair of boots she hadn't worn for years, a sweater, a necklace. Her heart pounded as she picked them up, noticing a card that Michael had sent her for her birthday a year ago, and one of her lipsticks. How had these things got out here? The last time she'd seen any of them they had been in her bedroom, the boots in the closet, the card in a box under her bed.

She scooped up the items and locked the door behind her, throwing one last look into the darkness. The garden was silent; no telltale sniggering or thud of footsteps to indicate that this was the work of bored teenagers.

Shaking slightly, she deposited the items on the sofa and crossed the room to check that Michael really had locked the front door behind him. He had, but she opened it now, staring down the empty street, dimly lit by the eco-friendly lamps the council had replaced the once-harsh streetlights with. Who had thrown those things?

She was about to lock the front door again when she noticed the piece of paper Sellotaped to the stained glass. She pulled it off and slammed the door shut, turning her key in the lock, then switched on the hallway light. Her hands trembled slightly as she unfolded the plain white notepaper and looked down at the words written in neat cursive handwriting.

I know what you're doing. I know what you've done.

"You're sure these things were inside the house? You hadn't thrown them away? It's probably kids going through the garbage to try and scare you."

When Michael had returned, he'd found Karen sitting on the sofa staring at the collection of belongings she'd found at the back door, the letter laid out on the cushions next to her.

"I hadn't thrown any of them away. They were in the house, in my bedroom. Someone's been here, someone's been through my things!"

"We should call the police." Michael picked up the phone. "If you're sure someone's been in here, then it should be reported."

"No," Karen replied quickly. If the police came, they would have too many questions. They would want to know who Michael was; they would blame this on his wife, probably even pay her a visit. Everything would be ruined. Besides, she knew who was responsible for this, and it had nothing to do with her lover and everything to do with her. She could hear those very same words on a loop in her mind—"*I kept waiting for a phone call or for her to turn up, to say I know what you're doing. I know what you've done.*" This was a warning. This was Jessica.

ELEANOR

Wow, this place looks great! I mean, not that it doesn't usually, but . . ." Bea let her sentence trail off, and Eleanor smiled and waved a hand.

"It's okay. I know that the redistribution of toys and general crap hasn't been my strong point lately, but—drumroll, please. . . ." She paused for maximum effect, and Bea drummed her hands on the glass coffee table. "I got a cleaner! Her name is Lesley. And please stop that now, you're getting fingerprints on my nice clean glass."

"Oooh, did you win the lottery?"

"It's not as expensive as you might think," Eleanor replied, handing Bea her green tea and placing Karen's coffee on a coaster. Get her, she was even using coasters again these days! It was amazing how having the house clean encouraged her to keep it that way—suddenly chucking a few things in the washing machine and rinsing off the breakfast dishes didn't seem like climbing a mountain. "And anyway, I switched my energy providers and canceled Netflix and my gym membership—oh, don't look like that, Karen, I wasn't using it anyway—and saved myself nearly sixty quid a month. That pretty much pays for her to do a couple of hours a week. You wouldn't believe what she can get done with no kids to look after. Well, okay, you two probably *would* believe it." Eleanor wondered for a second why she felt like she had to justify how she was spending her own money. "She's a bloody lifesaver."

"So what have you been doing with all your newfound free

time?" Karen asked. Was it Eleanor's imagination, or was her voice a shade cooler than it had been earlier? Surely someone who could do exactly as she pleased the whole time didn't begrudge her a few hours a week?

"I, um . . ." What was wrong with her? She'd been steeped in desperation to tell her friends about her new venture—after all, they were the ones who had encouraged her to take back something for herself. So why did she suddenly feel as though her tongue had been pasted to the bottom of her mouth? "I took your advice," she said, putting extra emphasis on *your,* as if trying to remind them that what she was about to say was their idea. "So while Noah was napping and Lesley was ironing, *I* was putting together a plan. A business plan, I suppose. I'm thinking of going freelance."

In the silence that followed, Eleanor realized why she'd felt so nervous about saying out loud what it was she'd been doing since their last meeting. She'd thought about little else ever since the idea had taken root in her mind and spread like ivy, obscuring every-thing that had seemed so important the previous week, yet she'd not actually told anyone about it. She hadn't even said anything else to Adam after his disparaging remarks about having her hands full already. Maybe her hands wouldn't be so full if he lifted a finger every now and then. *If it were that easy to start your own business,* she could imagine him saying, *everyone would do it. You've done very well at work, but do you really think you have what it takes to get a whole marketing business off the ground? And where are you proposing we find the start-up costs?*

"That's fantastic." At least Bea sounded enthusiastic, even as she reached for her mobile phone, probably to check on more in-teresting people. Karen had stayed oddly silent, and Eleanor won-dered what was wrong with her today.

"What does Adam think about it all?" When her friend finally spoke, her words were tinged with an inexplicable hostility. "His wife the entrepreneur, and this lifesaving cleaner?"

Eleanor's throat constricted, desperate not to allow the words she really wanted to say to spill out unguarded. *What is your problem?*

"Oh, I haven't mentioned it to him yet. I wanted to tell him about it properly when I had it all planned out. You know what he's like, glass half-empty and all that."

"He must love the idea of a cleaner, though?" Karen pushed. "The house looking so immaculate and you getting some rest?"

Eleanor threw Bea a look, one that said "What's wrong with her?" in the hopes of a conspiratorial shrug or grimace to tell her she wasn't imagining Karen's sudden change in attitude. But Bea was tapping at the screen of her mobile, her mouth curled in a half smile at whatever smart-ass status she was posting. Eleanor was instantly annoyed. When did it become socially acceptable to sit in someone's house and hold conversations with people not even in the room? How would they react if she got out a book and started reading it in front of them?

She was being unfair, of course; she was just as bad when it came to her mind being a million miles from her body. It was just that right now she needed Bea to leap to her defense, to tell Karen to stop being so confrontational. Presuming of course she wasn't imagining the sting in the other woman's tone.

"I haven't told him about that either," she replied, trying to keep her voice breezy. "Let him think I've suddenly found the key to domestic goddessness. I'll tell him when I'm ready. Like when I win the small business of the year award or something."

"Is there anything I can help with?"

"It's still just a bullet list at the moment. I spent most of my time researching the technical aspects—tax, website design, market research, and all that boring stuff. I figured I didn't want to get carried away with the fun bits until I was sure I could handle the serious stuff."

"Just make sure you're not taking on too much," Karen warned, sounding much more like herself.

"I'm not taking on anything just yet," Eleanor promised. "It's just nice to be feeling a bit more human again. Thanks to Lesley, I have no FTS at all this week. Bea?"

"No FTS for me this week either. Aren't we all quite the Polly-annas?"

Bea hung back as they were leaving Eleanor's house, letting Karen get almost to the car before she spoke.

"Here." She pulled a padded envelope from her handbag and shoved it into Eleanor's hands. "Table confetti and three hundred silver and lilac balloons. The restaurant said we could string a net from the ceiling and drop a load on her when we shout surprise. I realize three hundred might be a bit excessive, but I wasn't sure how many to get, and seeing as it's pretty much the only responsibility I've been given, I've also taken the liberty of ordering some foil Happy Birthday ones and a giant cock-shaped one for her seat."

Eleanor cringed. "That had better be a joke. And you wonder why you've been given only one responsibility. We'd be having a picnic in the quarry if I'd left it to you. Now, go on, she's looking at you funny."

"Right. What's my next job?"

"I'll keep an eye on the RSVP email account, seeing as I have an actual spreadsheet, not something written on a napkin; you just sort out Karen's mum. You won't forget, will you?"

"Absolutely not," Bea replied confidently. "Karen's mum. Drop me a text to remind me in a week, yeah?"

- 14 -

I'd tried to forget them. It might not seem that way now, but I'd never intended for them to take over my every waking moment. I'd gone years being content to listen in, spend the odd five minutes on Facebook flicking through their photographs and then returning to my normal life. Now I realize it had been like gradually working free a bolt, loosening it and loosening it until finally it gave way, and raw emotion pumped through the hole it had left behind.

Now I thought about them constantly.

It was amazing what people put on social media. I never really understood the need to inform the world what they were having for lunch (complete with pictures) or write cryptic messages to rally "friends" who wouldn't speak to them if they saw them on the street. Although admittedly Facebook—and more so Twitter, which people rarely made private—were useful tools when you wanted to keep an eye on someone, and I was glad that at least Eleanor and Bea weren't security conscious.

Eleanor's Facebook was mostly locked down, save for the odd parenting article she'd shared with the world and her constantly updated profile pictures, but Bea's profile was loaded with information: where she lived, where she worked, what she had for lunch and how many stars she would give the restaurant she ate it in. And not one scrap of it private. Selfie upon selfie, preening, pouting, posing, and laughing. Always laughing.

My eyes settled on Bea's status, still on the screen in front of me: *Lunch plans canceled—what am I going to do without #FTSF? Going to get my shit together and go to the gym #wishmeluck #notcomingoutalive.*

I wasn't a member of a gym. I'd always considered it a waste of money when it was just as easy to not eat like a pig in the first place. And of course I had experience in not eating—not always through choice, but at least it had taught me that some things didn't have to be for pleasure: eating for a start, and when I was older, sex. Some things could be used for control.

When I was younger, my mother had told me—before she practically stopped speaking to me for good—that I should always take good care of my appearance. I'd wanted to laugh at that. Because looking after yourself, with your gym membership and your highlights and your shellac nails, has worked so well for you, right, Mum? Do you think those false nails hide the pain in your eyes? Does your expensive manicure stop your hands shaking when you pour your third glass of red wine? How does your gym pass keep you warm? But I'd taken her advice, and it had stood me in good stead. People responded to you differently when you were well turned out; you were treated with less suspicion. Just because you spent an extra half hour slicking on some makeup on top of the mask you already wore day after day, it was assumed you knew what you were doing. If you were presentable, you must be okay. You could maintain a modicum of control.

And there was that word again, control. I'd lost control once and it had cost me everything. I wouldn't let it happen again. These days everything I did was about the power struggle that existed inside my mind. Me against them. And I knew that I would win. I would have the control I craved; already I could feel them losing it.

- 15 -

BEA

D rink?"

Ian inclined his head towards her and Bea shook hers in return. "Not for me, mate. I could use a night in."

She was going to go home and lose herself in a book—she had a new one that had been recommended by pretty much every blogger whose opinion she respected and trusted, and she'd been waiting for the right moment to get stuck into it. Feeling slightly smug about how much better than her colleagues she was going to feel in the morning, she left the office without so much as a backward glance but still keenly aware of the sidelong looks her friends were giving one another.

Being alone in her flat felt safe and reassuring. She didn't have to put on any airs and graces here by herself. She could just change into her jammies and curl up on the sofa with her book.

Her fleece onesie on and last night's pizza warming in the microwave, she went in search of the parcel from Amazon. She found it balancing precariously on the bathroom shelf, exactly where she'd shoved it hastily the night before. Reopening the package, she pulled the book out by its spine, frowning at the bright blue cover in her hands.

Asking for It. Bea was almost certain this wasn't the book she'd ordered, although the cover and name looked familiar. Probably a one-click impulse buy—ever since joining a glut of Facebook book clubs, she was forever clicking away on Amazon. She turned it over in her hands and paused to read the blurb on the back.

She barely felt the book falling from her hands. Her mind spun in so many different directions that she felt dizzy and nauseous. The pattern on the gray-and-white linoleum rushed up to meet her, and she hardly had time to reach out to grab the bath as she realized the floor wasn't rushing towards her, she was falling towards it.

The room was too hot and the music too loud. A thick plume of smoke sat like fog above the heads of the partygoers, the smell and taste of it making her feel sick to her stomach. Bea clutched her seventh—or was it eighth?—Malibu and Coke so hard, her knuckles were white from the effort it took to stop it spilling over the side of the glass. She had to sit down, but all the grimy student-issue sofas were full of people talking animatedly about subjects they knew nothing about. She couldn't bear the thought of squeezing her way onto a spare arm and having to pretend she wasn't as drunk as she clearly was. Every last space was taken up by people: people in the middle of the floor swaying to the music, couples entwined against the door frames, their faces lost in one another as though their tongues were alien probes searching for the meaning of life. Like tonight their existence depended on one another.

The bottom stair was free, and Bea sank down on the grubby gray tiles and rested her head against the cool wooden banister. She fought to keep her eyes open, to stop herself falling asleep and humiliating herself by dribbling down her chin, but her eyelids were so heavy, she had to blink constantly to stop them closing automatically. If only the room would keep still for a second, if only she could pull herself to her feet and get outside for some fresh air, she was certain she'd feel better, less hemmed in and claustrophobic. But whatever signals her brain was sending to her legs, they seemed determined to ignore them, and she stayed where she was. Her face itched from the weight of the makeup she'd plastered on before heading out to the party with her friends. And where were they anyway? Viv and Ruby? She had a vague memory of Ruby grabbing her arm earlier on, shouting something over the music about did she want to go with them? Was she sure? Would she be okay?

So they'd left then, they must have done. Why had she stayed? Because she'd been having fun, chatting to some guy about using multiple perspectives to break boundaries in art, like one of those students she was now so desperate to avoid. Not for the first time since starting uni, she wished Karen and Eleanor were there with her. They would never have left her behind—Bea could remember nights out at home when Karen had stayed at a club long after it had ceased to be fun for her just to make sure her friends were okay. If we start the night together, we end it together; she could picture her saying it now. But she hadn't started the night with Karen and Eleanor; she'd started it with her new university friends, people whose loyalty was only to themselves. And now she was alone.

"You look like you could do with a kebab and your bed."

For a minute Bea thought it had been herself talking, voicing her inner wishes out loud. But this voice was deeper, male. She forced her eyes open to see Kieran, the guy she'd been talking to when Ruby left, standing in the hallway in front of her. She managed a smile, or at least she thought she had—she no longer felt significantly in control of any part of her body.

"You must be some kind of mind reader," she slurred. Her voice was thick, and speech felt alien to her. "Don't suppose you could add aspirin to that list, could you, Genie of the Lamp?"

"Your wish is my command." Kieran grinned and offered her an arm. "Come on, I promised Rubes I'd get you home safe. I've been looking for you for ages—last time I saw you, you were doing shots of tequila in the kitchen with Freud."

Bea grimaced as a picture of Danny Hooper—known as Freud

owing to his passion for discussing psychology every time he wasn't alone in a room—wielding a bottle of tequila and talking about attribution theory passed briefly through her mind.

"Ergh, no wonder I feel like shit. Karen always stops me mixing my drinks."

"This Karen, she your sister or something?" Kieran asked as Bea took his arm and allowed herself to be lifted to her feet. She wobbled a little, but walking made her feel less like Bambi, with Kieran's steady grip holding her upright.

"Or something," she muttered, not wanting to think what Karen would say if she could see her now. "Look, can we skip the kebab? I just want to crash out, to be honest."

"Yeah, no problem." Kieran bowed slightly. "At your service."

———

Bea woke on the cold bathroom floor with the ghost of a scream still on her lips. She didn't have to wonder what she'd been shouting. She hadn't had one of the nightmares for a long time, but whenever she did, she woke up gasping the same two words over and over again. *Don't go . . . don't go . . . don't go.*

- 16 -

ELEANOR

I thought they'd stopped—the nightmares? I thought you were doing okay with sleep and stuff now?" Eleanor sat down next to her friend and handed her a glass of orange juice and a glue stick. Bea gulped down half the glass in one go, like she'd spent the last week in a desert, and picked up one of the silver foil letters.

"They had. I haven't had one since the day you told me about the accident. That was my first dreamless sleep in years. It's hard to be scared of someone when you know they'll be in a wheelchair the rest of their life. This wasn't like before, though—I literally blacked out. I haven't done that since the very beginning. It was seeing that book, the book I could have practically written myself, sitting on my bathroom shelf."

She started spreading the letters onto the banner they were creating; noticing Eleanor's frown, she picked up the ruler and began measuring the gaps between them. *I'm going to have to redo the whole bloody thing,* Eleanor thought. *That's all I need.*

"I know, that's weird, right?" She slipped down onto the mat next to Noah and flipped him onto his tummy, smiling at his immediate attempt to lift his head, kicking his legs as though he were swimming on dry land. "I mean, how could you order that and not know? You think Amazon sent it to you by mistake?"

"I checked my account. Well, not straightaway; when I woke up, I felt rough as anything, like I could have slept for a week, but I couldn't bear the thought of closing my eyes again, so I just lay on the sofa staring at the ceiling. I must have dropped off again because I woke at about two a.m. and climbed into bed, but at least I didn't dream again. Then at work the next day I checked my Amazon account—I thought if I did it with plenty of people around, there was less chance of me losing it again if I saw the book on there. But there was nothing. Well, nothing but the book I'd originally ordered—the one I thought I was pulling out of the package."

"Didn't you check it when it arrived? How come you didn't realize it was the wrong one then?"

"That's why it was in the bathroom." Bea winced as one of the foil letters stuck to her fingers. "Oh crap—I hope we have spares of these things. I'd taken the parcel up to the loo to open it the night before, ripped it open, then heard *Game of Thrones* starting in the living room and just shoved it on the shelf."

"Must have been a mistake, then; they sent you the wrong one." Noah started to whine, and Eleanor propped him up in his inflatable ring before it could turn into a full-on howl. She was still getting used to a baby's attention span; it seemed like Toby had been so much more content to sit and play, but of course he'd been much older. This was uncharted territory. "You should have called me. Did you tell Fran?"

It was clear from the way Bea hesitated that she still hadn't told her sister about what had happened to her—not this week, but sixteen years ago.

"I thought you were closer to Fran these days?"

Bea nodded. "We are closer, but it happened so long ago, how do you bring that sort of thing up? 'Hey, Fran, guess what . . . ?' " She trailed off, unable to be flippant about what had happened to her a lifetime ago. Which just showed how much it still affected her, Eleanor thought; Bea could be flippant about just about any situation, no matter how bad. Sometimes it made her and Karen cringe, the way she could joke about the most sensitive of subjects—but not this.

It had worried them both at the time that she'd never reported what had happened—she'd just turned up at Eleanor's parents' home one Sunday morning in such a frightening state that Eleanor had been on the phone to Karen within minutes of her arrival. Karen had taken the first train back from Sheffield, where she was at university, and instantly insisted that Bea went to the police, but she'd refused. *Who'd believe me when I can't even remember what happened? It'd be my word against his—and everyone could see what a state I was in. I'd be the drunken slag who cried rape—it'd be me who suffered and he'd be the victim. I won't give him that satisfaction.*

Eleanor hadn't agreed, but at least she'd understood. Karen had pretended to as well, but they all knew that in her black-and-white world, if someone had committed a crime, they should be punished. There was no awful gray area where a girl whose only crime was to have too much to drink got torn apart in the court of human opinion.

As if reading Eleanor's mind, Bea leaned forward and lowered her voice.

"Look, you won't tell Karen about this, will you? I don't really have the energy to be psychoanalyzed today."

Eleanor nodded, knowing exactly what she meant. Karen was amazing, the first person everyone turned to in a crisis. She always knew exactly what to do, but sometimes her concern could be a bit, well, suffocating.

"No problem. I think you should just put it down to the stress at work—your prick of a boss stirring up old wounds or whatever the saying is—and the shock of seeing that book you hadn't ordered. I don't think you need to worry that the nightmares will start again. After all, you slept okay last night, didn't you?"

"Yeah." Bea nodded, reaching over to pick Noah up from the mat. "I don't need to dissect it—all that 'How does that make you feel?' bull. I just want to forget about it."

"Forget about what?" Karen's voice came from the doorway, and both women's heads snapped up in shock. Bea shoved the banner under the sofa just as Karen walked into the room. "Adam let me in—he's just got home. Forget about what?"

Eleanor cast a surreptitious glance at Bea, who looked about three shades paler. *How much had she heard?*

Bea ignored Eleanor's look and laughed. "All right, bat ears! I was just telling Eleanor about the latest in the saga that is the office. Gary is still acting like David Brent, Sandra said we should spike his coffee, but I reckon I should just forget about it. Get on with my work, you know—be all growed up and stuff."

Karen raised her eyebrows, and in that moment Eleanor was certain she had heard everything.

"Sounds like a good plan—have you had a bump to the head?"

Bea stuck her middle finger up in response and stood up to hand Noah over to Karen's open arms, kicking a silver foil letter farther under the settee as she did.

"You're just in time, Grandma—I need a glass of wine."

- 17 -

BEA

She hadn't had the dream for three days—hadn't dreamed at all, in fact. She'd been scared to go to sleep at first; the thought of seeing his face when she closed her eyes had terrified her so much that she'd sat up on the sofa watching *Doctor Who* box sets until her head pounded with exhaustion, and she'd barely made it to bed before she'd collapsed into the black void of sleep. It had reminded her so vividly of the past, of spending days and nights on Eleanor's sofa after it happened, the three of them in pajamas—Karen's and Bea's borrowed from Eleanor because they'd both left home in such a rush—that on waking the next morning she had resolved to snap out of the fug she was heading for if she wasn't careful and get on with her life. She'd dropped the book off at Eleanor's on the way to the gym—no sense in wasting a perfectly good book, after all—and attempted to forget ever opening it.

When it had first happened, all those years ago, Bea had thought about nothing else but getting the justice she deserved. She'd fantasize about him being dragged from his warm, comfy bed in the middle of the night by SWAT teams and sentenced to public castration or hanging by the neck until dead like in the good old days. Sometimes she dreamed that they were standing on a cliff in the dead of the night and Bea was the only thing between him and the rocks below. Live or die—she decides. When she woke from the dream, screaming and crying, she could never quite bring herself to tell her friends which decision she'd made.

Karen and Eleanor had been amazing, but the one thing they'd never managed to do was convince her to go to the police. As much as she wanted to see Kieran Ressler suffer, the thought of everyone at university, her mum, her sister, and, worse still, her dad knowing what he had done—what she had let happen—was a nightmare beyond the one she had been living. The fact was that it would be her word against his, and there would be plenty of people to attest to the fact that she had been in the kind of state where plenty of women had done things they regretted.

The other thing that scared her, even more than telling the police, was that one of these days, in one of these dreams, she would remember what had actually happened after he'd taken her home. Which would be worse? If he'd done what he'd done after she had passed out unconscious, or if she'd been awake the entire time, so terrified that her inebriated mind had chosen to blank it out? And—something that haunted her waking moments as well as her sleeping ones—what if she'd said yes? What would happen to her on the day it all came screaming back? How would that memory rewire what had become of her life since that night? Her entire existence had been split into two—before the night and after. Going out into the night with her friends, dressed in a black playsuit that skimmed the ample cheeks of her ass and with a neckline that ended at her navel, as someone who firmly believed that bad things only happened to other people—stupid women who were careless and walked home on their own after dark, dragged into bushes with knives held at their throats; and waking up the next day in her own safe, comfortable bed, her naked body bruised and aching, as a victim.

Now, sixteen years later, she could think of nothing worse than the truth coming out, or justice being served. These days, even the thought of him walking into a police station (though that wasn't really possible, was it?) and confessing his sins, dragging up the past, letting everyone know what a stupid little girl she'd been, could stop her heart in her chest. She'd spent a long time, after all, cultivating her tough-cookie, good-time girl image; no one could ever know that she'd been acting her way through life ever since that night.

Bea wondered sometimes what it was like to live without despising yourself. To know exactly who you were and be proud of that person. It was funny; people automatically assumed that what her life was missing, what she must desperately be in need of—after all, wasn't every woman?—was a husband. When in actual fact she wasn't desperate to be loved by another person; all she wanted was to feel the slightest bit of affection for herself.

Bea wanted to be a success at something. Anything. When people talked about Eleanor, they always spoke with awe about how much she loved her family, and how lovely Toby was, and now she was thinking about starting her own business with a three-month-old in tow. Karen had her own beautiful home that she'd mortgaged without Michael's help, and a career that was only headed upwards. What did they say about Bea? How much fun she was, always up for a laugh and a joke, another pint or a glass of wine. How her shoes were always killer and she never left the house without makeup. How was it that all she had to show for more than three decades of living was an ability to match the right shoes to an outfit and drink the same volume of alcohol as a seventeen-stone rugby player?

She didn't blame her whole life on him. It would be easy to think that what had happened to her that night had made her incapable of giving or receiving love, or that she would have been head of some corporation or other if she had never met Kieran Ressler, never let him walk her home, but she had no way of knowing how things would have turned out, so what was the point? What had happened was so much a part of her life that it would be like wondering daily what it would be like if she'd been taller, or skinnier, or blonder. It wouldn't change anything, and anyway she might have screwed up just as royally as a tall skinny blonde.

When she'd found out about the accident, she hadn't known how to feel. Karen and Eleanor had both told her he'd got what he deserved, but she found it hard to reconcile the pitiful creature in the hospital bed on the news with the monster she'd seen so many times in her dreams. He seemed smaller somehow, shrunken and pale, with all those tubes keeping him alive. He certainly didn't seem dangerous anymore, and for that she should feel grateful, but all she felt was numb. His living hell didn't seem enough, and yet had she felt sorry for him? The thought repulsed her, but she was only human and she couldn't bring herself to feel glad that anyone should be trapped in that existence for the rest of his sad life. Cognitive dissonance, wasn't that what Karen called it? This feeling that two separate people existed inside her, constantly fighting to take control of her thoughts.

She'd done so well not to think about him lately, not to even google his name. Now she was going to have to relearn how to forget all over again.

Her mobile phone began to ring. Karen was calling, somehow sensing after all these years exactly when her friend needed her most.

-18-

KAREN

I've got an idea, about this weekend." Karen was at the cooker, checking the early dinner she was making, some fancy recipe involving far too much attention, considering Michael was leaving in just over an hour and she should be spending every last second stuck to him like his shadow.

"Hmm?" Michael wandered over to the cooker and reached around her with a fork to stab at a scallop in the frying pan.

"Stop it, you'll ruin my swanky supper!" Karen swatted at him with the fish slice and he wrapped his free arm around her waist while trying to shove the hot scallop in his mouth.

"What's your idea?" he asked when his mouth had recovered from the pain.

"How about you don't go? Say there's been a problem, you can't make it. We can spend all weekend here in bed. Naked."

Michael groaned and let go of her waist. "Don't, Karen. You know I'd love nothing more."

"Would you?" Karen fixed him with a look, even as she heard her head voice telling her to stop. Don't send him away on a bad note. Don't be that person. The neurotic girlfriend.

"Of course. But I have to go. You know I do."

"I told the girls you were going to Doncaster," she said, turning back to the cooker.

"Doncaster? Do I have to come back with a northern accent?"

When she didn't laugh, he put the fork down and turned her

around, pulling her close to his chest. "I don't know why you don't just tell them the truth. They're your best friends."

Karen put her head on his shoulder and sighed. "I just don't want to. Not yet. Let's not talk about it anymore. Let's just eat."

"I have a better idea. I have an hour until I need to go. Now, what could we do in an hour?"

Karen forced a smile onto her face. If she had to watch him go, she could at least give him something to think about while he was away.

"I can think of a few things," she said, reaching round to unhook her bra.

———

She sat on her bed in just her dressing gown, knees up to her chest. The smell of sex and aftershave was still in the air, even though it had been two hours since Michael had showered and left. She couldn't bear to get on with her evening the way the girls would be imagining she was, so she reached over and pulled her laptop from her bedside table onto her knee. She booted up, clicked on the Internet Explorer icon, and typed "F" into the address bar. The computer filled in the remaining address, and the familiar blue band loaded, already logged in.

When Facebook had first arrived in their lives, Karen hadn't bothered signing up. Bea laughed at her and told her she was the only person she knew who hadn't been on Myspace and now she would be the only person on the planet without a Facebook account, but Karen had replied that her life was far too boring to subject other people to it, and if she wanted to know what Bea had had for breakfast, she could always call her and ask her.

It wasn't that she felt she had anything to hide. She could have joined Facebook, posted random rubbish that had no bearing on her real life. She could have pretended she had a perfect life even on days when she wanted to scream, or moaned about trivial grievances like the entire Western world seemed to do. It was nothing to do with hiding things; she just didn't feel like pretending any more than she already was.

But Bea and Eleanor thrived on it. Karen thought they might as well have printed out timetables and stuck them up at random bus stops around town—along with a miniature map powered by Google and pictures with blurred backgrounds and faded edges. A sepia-tinted Instagram lifestyle. Bea couldn't go from the living room to the kitchen without checking in. *Bea Barker is eating toasted sandwiches and drinking wine . . . classy! With Eleanor Whitney and Karen Browning at My Pad.* Drove Karen crazy.

None of her friends knew about her secret Facebook account. It had no picture, a fake name, and no friends. It was locked down so tightly that to anyone who came across it accidentally, it probably looked like a defunct account that Julie Sparrow had all but deleted. There was only one name in the search history, and she clicked it now, waiting the few painful seconds it took to load. She did this so often when she was alone, it was like second nature. Like picking at a scab that you know will be painful but your fingers do it automatically. You know it'll never heal if you keep picking, but then the scab works free and there's that instant satisfaction, followed by a sting that lasts much longer.

Emily Lenton is feeling excited!

That was all it said, but that was all it needed to. She was happy, and that was what caused Karen's pain. She flicked through recent posts, pictures of Emily and her family, smiling, beautiful creatures who looked to Karen like the children she herself would never have. She carried on through their family holidays and birthdays until she found the one she was looking for: a Christmas dinner, the whole family beaming. Karen had first seen it on Christmas Day and had cried for hours until Michael had found her asleep on the sofa, worn out by exhaustion, the remains of her own Christmas lunch splattered over the wall of her living room.

And there it was. The pain of working the scab free, only this pain wasn't physical. It was the pain of her heart breaking.

- 19 -

KAREN

Karen worked all day Saturday, distracting herself from the constant ache in her chest that set up camp every time Michael went away and stayed until he was back in her bed. In the evening she called friends, not Bea and Eleanor, but her pie-crust friends, easily made, easily broken, people just out for a good time. People who didn't even know she had a boyfriend.

During the week she wore her long dark hair pulled back from her face, wore two-piece suits of navy, black, or gray. Her shirts were fitted and showed barely any neck, let alone—heaven forbid—cleavage. The little makeup she put on was neutral, professional. During the week she was the consummate professional. But not on the weekend.

Her red lip gloss glistened wetly, and she smiled to get her blush just right. She combed out her hair and ran the straighteners along it, spraying on shine to accent the luster. Her black jeans and low-cut red V-neck clung to her lithe frame like a second skin. Karen had no real curves, not like Bea—or Eleanor, pre-baby—but she was slim and athletic and never failed to turn heads. It might sound vain, boastful even, but at her age she was incredibly proud to pass for a woman in her twenties.

She met her friends outside a bar in town, three girls she'd worked with during her training at the hospital in her twenties, all still unmarried with no children to worry about rushing home for. These were professional singletons who loved to drink and flirt with every man in the bar while moaning about how much they hated the opposite sex. Tilly, blonde, plump, with breasts that entered a room five minutes before the rest of her; Erin, tall and willowy but plain faced and painfully shy; and Catherine, with yellow tiger-striped highlights and a too-tight black dress, who insisted on being called Cat even at their age.

They hugged without embracing and air-kissed without anyone smudging their makeup. A counterfeit greeting for counterfeit friends pulled together by grim circumstance.

"So what about you, Karen?" Cat asked, following thirty minutes of bemoaning her latest victim, some bloke whose name evaded Karen instantly but whose penis she could now describe as well as her lover's. "Anyone special in your life?"

She shook her head and they didn't fail to hide their glances. Of course not; if she'd had anyone worth being with, she'd be with them right now. If only they knew. "I just don't have time . . . I know, I know," she cut Cat off while her lips were only just parting. "I work too much. That's why I'm here."

Cat smiled, obviously satisfied with her justification for her spinster lifestyle. "Well, tonight might change that. Hawaiian by the bar has been eyeballing you since you walked in."

Karen glanced over. The man Cat was referring to—wearing a T-shirt emblazoned with "Hawaii Nights" and a backdrop of the ocean—looked no older than thirty, possibly slightly younger. He was in a group of five or six men who were taking it in turn to shoot pool and frequent the bar so often, she couldn't tell exactly who was in the group and who wasn't. None of them looked familiar. They were exactly the right age group to have missed Karen and her friends at school, and it was unlikely even in a town as small as this that she'd know one of them from elsewhere. Perfect really.

"He's a bit young," she murmured, even as she tipped her glass slightly in his direction. He smiled, tapping the side of his pint, and she gave a small nod. Erin caught the exchange but said nothing.

"Anyone want another?" Karen asked, swilling down the last of her wine and glancing at her companions' nearly full glasses. Erin shot another look at the man at the bar and threw her a small smile that Karen got the feeling was aimed at letting her know she wasn't as green as their friends.

"Rosé?" At the bar, Hawaiian slid the glass towards her, clearly pleased with himself that he'd noted what she was drinking. She smiled and nodded in thanks, her back to the three girls behind her so they wouldn't see that she hadn't bought her own drink.

"Where are you headed?" she asked, taking a sip and noting the fact that he hadn't just plumped for the cheap house wine.

"I'm not sure. We're not from round here." Even better.

"Do you know the Bellstone?" It was amusing to watch realization dawn in his dark eyes. He smiled, not the lazy, sensual smile that Michael gave her when she hinted at sex, but an eager grin, attractive all the same. It made him look even younger, and she resolved not to ask his age, certain the answer would change her mind. "It's a bar just off the square. With rooms above."

"I think we passed it on the way up here."

"I have a room booked there tonight. If you want to join me, escape your friends at eleven and come and meet me there." She raised her glass. "Thanks for the drink."

"Wait." He kept his voice low enough not to attract attention, and she wondered if he was hiding their conversation for the same reason as her. She half turned back. "Which room is it?"

"It's under Mrs. Jones."

He grinned.

"What's wrong with him, then?" Cat asked as she sat back down at the table. "Married? Gay?"

"Both, I think," she replied, and sipped her wine as the hyenas cackled.

The room was, by Shrewsbury's standards, quite posh. It wasn't the Marriott, or one of the more exclusive hotels she'd stayed in with work or in the early days with Michael, but it was clean, and had a wide-screen TV they had no use for, and a king-size bed with huge pillows, far more than a normal person could sleep on. The bathroom was the dazzling white of an operating theater and boasted a stand-alone bath that had been placed against the wall, ruining the effect.

Karen arrived at ten to eleven, having cried off from the singles' night. No one had questioned her, but Erin had raised her eyebrows and checked her phone for the time. On the way to the Bellstone, she'd had the strangest feeling she was being followed, and spent the entire walk checking behind her surreptitiously, as though she had her gran's antique silverware in her bag instead of a packet of Durex.

She didn't have to wait long for the rap at the door of the suite. She glanced at her phone: three minutes past eleven. Had he spent the last three minutes waiting downstairs, not wanting to appear too keen? Her heart hammered a hole in her rib cage as she opened the door, half expecting to see Erin and that irritating presenter of *You've Been Framed*. But no, there he was, Mr. Hawaii, that eager smile fixed to his face.

"I wasn't sure you'd be here," he said. "Thought you might have been having a laugh, a bet or something with your mates. They looked the type." His cheeks colored. "Sorry, I didn't mean to slag your friends off."

"'S okay," she said, opening the door wider to let him in. "They're not real friends. I barely know them anymore."

"So what were you doing out with them?" He stepped into the room and she saw him clock her handbag, no luggage.

"I'm sorry, did you come for a chat?" She stepped closer to him, watched him try to swallow without being obvious. She hooked her fingers underneath his T-shirt and began to lift it slowly, revealing the waistband of his jeans and a canvas belt.

"No, I just . . . Don't you want to talk or something first? I mean, before . . . ?"

"You can talk if you want." Her lips were inches from his now, her hands working to unclip his belt buckle. "But I hoped our mouths would be too busy for that."

She leaned up to kiss him, breathing in the faint smell of lager and cigarettes that he'd tried to mask with chewing gum before he arrived. She closed her eyes, drawing the smell inside her, the fingers of her free hand reaching up to lace through the short dark hair at the back of his head. She moaned slightly into his mouth, just the smallest of sounds but enough to make him stiffen against her. The belt buckle released and she flicked open the top button of his jeans and unzipped his fly as their kiss grew more urgent, more intense. He pushed her away slightly and pulled the hem of her top from inside her jeans, lifting it over her head and letting out a groan at the discovery that she'd already taken off her bra. He pushed his jeans down over his hips and yanked at the zipper of hers, both of them stumbling backwards towards the bed in a waltz choreographed over the years by lovers everywhere. His lips were on her breasts, his tongue circling her nipples and his fingers tracing the path of moistness it left behind. She pulled at his shirt and he lifted it over his head, what had started slow and unsure now urgent and feral.

"You are fucking gorgeous," he murmured against her breast, flicking his tongue against her nipple and sending flashes of desire to her groin. "You are so beauti—"

"Ssshhh." She grabbed his hair, not roughly, but hard enough to pull his mouth away from her skin. "You don't have to keep saying that. Just fuck me."

He didn't seem offended, or if he was, he was too turned on to let it stop him. He pushed her underwear down to her knees and they fell the rest of the way. Grabbing her hips, he turned her roughly around and shoved her forward so she was leaning over the bed, then spread her legs with his knee and shoved himself inside her with a moan of ecstasy. Now he was getting it.

The harder he thrust, the more she moaned, gasping out for breath when it felt like he was as deep as he could get. He wrapped her hair around his hand and pulled her head backwards so she could feel his breath on her face as he fucked her, his thumb rubbing her clitoris in slow, rhythmic movements, then faster and faster as he struggled to hold back.

"Not yet," she whispered, her voice urgent. "I'm not ready."

He rose to the challenge, thrusting faster and deeper inside her until it hurt, beautiful pleasure born from pain. She took his other hand in hers and placed it on her breast, his thumb and forefinger instinctively finding her nipple like a baby rooting for its mother.

"Harder."

He grabbed, more fiercely this time, and pain shot through her, exploding into that familiar burst of pleasure between her legs, spreading upwards into her chest and neck. Seconds later she felt him get harder, and he let out a guttural cry of release, then they both slumped forward onto the bed, sated.

They had fallen into bed in a blissful postcoital haze and she'd fallen asleep instantly. When she woke, Mr. Hawaii was snoring gently and her phone told her it was 2:43 a.m. Four missed calls from Michael, and a text: *Tried to call to say goodnight. Miss you. Speak tomorrow. Xxx*

She gathered her things as quietly as she could and pulled the door closed with a click behind her, then stole down the stairs and out into the street. The room was prepaid; she'd used a false name and never mentioned her real one to the man she'd just screwed. It would be as if she'd never been there. There was still the odd Saturday-night straggler on the dark street, stumbling about trying to prolong their evening and avoid going home to the hangover and alcohol paranoia that awaited them tomorrow. It was a little while before the only nightclub on the main drag would let out and the last revellers scrambled for a way back to their beds.

The black cab rank was full of hopeful-looking taxi drivers. Even the drunkest good-timers were reluctant to pay three times the normal fare to avoid the wait.

"Rangart Gardens," she instructed, climbing into the first one in the line. He swung himself into the front seat and pulled the door closed, pressing the meter and putting the car into gear.

Ten silent minutes later, they pulled up to the curb down the road from her house. Karen paid the man his extortionate fare, added a couple of pounds as a tip, and climbed out with little more than a "Thanks."

The house was vast and empty, as it always felt when Michael was away. The silence was almost unbearable, mocking her stupidity. There was no one waiting in bed for her to ask if she'd had a good night, no one to be worried that she was so late or demand to know where the hell she'd been and why she smelled of another man. She felt exhausted, emotionally and physically, and wanted nothing more than to climb into bed and wrap her arms around the love of her life, but she couldn't, and without him the bed seemed cold and uninviting. Instead she turned on the shower full blast until the water ran scalding hot, stripped off her clothes and stepped in, welcoming the searing-hot spray that cleansed her of her sins.

She stood there for what seemed like hours, her tears mixing with the water and swirling away down the drain. When she finally got out, she toweled herself dry, wrapped the towel around her hair, and took her book from the bedside table into the huge comfy armchair in her office, where she woke five hours later with a stiff neck, freezing cold and alone.

There was a chill in the wind that blew through the trees lining the river. Even the murky-brown water looked dull and discontented with its lot in life today, although I knew that tonight would be a different matter. At night this particular stretch of the river was lit up by the colored LEDs adorning the theater beyond, and streetlamps on the bridge offered a warm amber haze, the effect of both of these coalescing on the surface of the night-blackened ripples almost making it possible to forget that you lived in a backwater town, one road in, one road out. You could be in Sydney or Vegas; you could be walking the banks with a lover, about to embark on an illicit affair, or you could be the loneliest person alive, waiting to throw yourself from the bridge into the calm, still blackness below. In the stark light of day, though, it was clear who you were. People in this town were defined by the clothes they wore, the cars they drove, the side of the river they drove them on. Everything painted a picture of you as surely as if it were laid out on a canvas in oil.

I held up my camera and fired off shots, each one quietening the voice in my mind telling me that I'd better get back to work now, *click,* that I was screwing up my job and everyone was going to be saying I'd lost it, *click,* that I was never going to be able to manage a normal life, *click, click, click.* And with each click the pictures of those women faded from my mind, taking up less and less of the space they had occupied all morning—all weekend, in fact.

The pictures, when I downloaded them onto my computer that night, were disappointing. Most of them were faded and out of focus, not quite managing to capture the elusive double nature of the river and the chameleon-like quality that I'd imagined it to have. That second side lay just out of reach, locked in my imagination and failing to translate to the screen. I refrained from deleting them, each one a reminder that something intangible lay beyond the image, something that wasn't there to the untrained eye but remained very real to me.

"Mum, is everything okay?" I threw on my bright and breezy voice like a silk scarf, but my body was tense, braced for the reply. Within seconds I would be able to tell if it was a good or a bad day—before my mum had spoken even. I had long been used to listening for the ragged breaths that signaled a bad one.

"I'm good, darling, how are you?" Her words were crystal clear, with a forced casual tone that made it sound as if we had this kind of conversation all the time. Her meds must be set to the right dosage, and she obviously hadn't washed them down with too much whisky today. I could usually tell exactly how many glasses she'd had as soon as I picked up the phone. Today must be a one-glass day; there weren't any zero-glass days, hadn't been for years.

I had to bite my lip to keep from asking why she was calling; even on a good day she was hypersensitive, and the smallest perceived slight could send her spiraling towards bad before I'd realized what I'd done.

To the outside world, she was a reputable widow with a daughter to be proud of—the picture of respectability. But just like most pictures, the image she presented was a still life, a snapshot of what her marriage, our lives might once have been, frozen in time. It didn't show what happened even moments before everyone plastered on their fake cheese. Careful lighting and heavy makeup hid the lines on my mother's once-youthful face, carved there by years of loss. Did I want that for myself? No, that was a pain I could live without.

"I'm fine, Mum, just a bit busy at the moment."

Despite my breezy tone, I heard her sigh. This was the part where our conversation would go one of two ways—neither particularly appealing. It was a toss-up between abusive or suicidal. Sometimes it would be both. I suppose that's the one thing I had in common with *her*, both of us with screwup parents we so wanted to admire but couldn't. I closed my eyes and braced myself for what was to come.

- 21 -

ELEANOR

Eleanor hadn't sat down since Karen had walked through the door; she'd flitted from room to room, throwing toys into boxes and bundling laundry into piles on the kitchen floor. It was a mark of their friendship that she didn't feel the need to give her guest her full attention—with Karen it hardly felt as though she was a guest at all. Lesley, Eleanor's cleaner, was fantastic, but the idea of it being just a case of wiping the surfaces between visits had been slightly optimistic.

Karen had boiled the kettle and made them both a cup of coffee, moving around her friend's kitchen as though it were her own, knowing exactly where to go for cups and spoons. As she waited for the kettle to boil, she'd busied herself washing breakfast bowls and sweeping up crumbs. If anyone else had presumed to start cleaning her kitchen, Eleanor would have lost her shit, but with Karen she just felt grateful. Her friend helped without fanfare as she'd always done, ever the mother, looking after her friends in all the ways she was needed, sometimes without them even knowing.

"Shall I pop this recycling out back?" She had pointed at the last few days' worth of plastics—everything that had accumulated since Lesley was last in.

"Great, thanks, the back-door keys are on the sofa. Or the TV table maybe."

Now she sat on the sofa with Noah snuggled into the crook of her arm.

"He's getting so big," she said, gesturing for her friend to sit down and relax.

Eleanor picked up her cup of coffee—black, no sugar, and as strong as a caffeine injection directly into her veins—and folded herself into the chair.

"It's all those bloody feeds he has." She smiled without complaint. "I feel like an all-you-can-eat buffet. So much for me stopping breastfeeding."

Karen smiled briefly, then her face grew serious. "How are you doing? Honestly?"

"Honestly? It's hard," Eleanor admitted. "Don't get me wrong, it's rewarding and wonderful, et cetera, but it's bloody tiring. Half the time I feel as though my senses have deserted me. I'm losing things, forgetting things . . . My keys went missing for a week, I got new ones cut, and do you know where I found them? In my underwear drawer. God only knows how they got in there. It's enough to make you question your sanity."

"And Adam? Does he help?"

Eleanor sensed the change in her friend's tone. Were they about to get to the reason she was here? It was unlike Karen to drop by midweek without a million texts arranging times and synchronizing schedules. And without Bea. It wasn't that Karen and Eleanor weren't close, but it was rare for them to be missing their third; if anything, it was more usual for Bea and Eleanor to meet for a casual catch-up. Karen's job kept her busy, and with Michael working away on the weekends, it was rare to see her during the week.

"He's just Adam, you know. He'll do what I ask him to. It's not like he's lazy, but it's almost as though he's yet to notice our lives have changed. He just expects Noah to fit into our schedule. And then there's the fact that I'm home all day—I swear he thinks I just sit around drinking coffee." She looked at her cup and laughed. "Which I usually don't."

Karen didn't laugh. Her brow furrowed and her eyes stayed trained on Noah. Eleanor got the distinct impression she was avoiding looking at her.

"We could carry on making small talk if you like," she offered. "Or you could tell me what you came here to attempt to say."

Karen grimaced. "It's not that easy, Els. . . ."

"Is it Michael?"

"No, it's Adam."

Eleanor felt her stomach churn at the words. Karen wasn't one for drama—whatever she was about to say, she'd thought about it a lot and it was clearly concerning her.

"Spit it out, then." She tried to sound unconcerned, but the wobble in her voice gave her away. "What about Adam?"

Karen switched Noah to the other side, prolonging Eleanor's unease for a few more seconds. When she spoke again, it was in a low voice, but her words might as well have been an assault.

"I saw him with another woman."

Although she'd been half expecting it—what else could have been so important and yet so hard for her friend to say?—Eleanor felt sick. When she said nothing, Karen continued.

"They were in a jewelry shop in town. He had his hand on her arm; they were obviously, um, together."

"Obviously?" Eleanor repeated, almost feeling the moment the denial kicked in. "Why obviously? Did you see them kissing? Were they holding hands?"

"Well no, but . . ."

"But what?" Eleanor's voice went up an octave. "What else is there?"

Karen shook her head and for the first time looked straight at her friend. She let out a sigh. "Nothing. There's nothing else. But they were together, I just know."

"You just know." Eleanor suddenly felt every minute's sleep she'd lost in the last twelve weeks weighing down on her. She just wanted to curl up under a blanket and not have to think about what Karen was trying to tell her. "It isn't like you to prevaricate, Karen. If there's something else, you need to tell me now. This isn't some teenage boyfriend; this is my husband. The father of my children. I need more than just 'I know.'"

Her best friend sat on her sofa, cuddling her little boy and looking as though there was so much more she wanted to say. Why was she holding back? Was she protecting Eleanor? Because if she had solid evidence, Eleanor needed to hear it. She'd never been one for holding on to faint hope—she needed a definitive reason to believe her husband was betraying her, because she couldn't afford to be wrong.

"No, there's nothing else. But it was the way they were together; there can't be an innocent explanation for it. I'm sorry, Els, I know you don't need this now, but I couldn't not tell you. Do you hate me?"

Eleanor couldn't bring herself to answer, the question was so ridiculous. The floor had just been ripped out from under her, and all Karen could worry about was whether she was still going to be speaking to her at the end of it.

She stood and crossed over to take her son from the arms of the other woman. "I don't hate you, Karen, I just don't know what to think. You come in here with literally nothing other than 'the way they were together' and expect me to—what? What should I do now?" She paced back and forth, instinctively rocking Noah on her hip even though he wasn't making so much as a whimper.

"I don't know. I thought maybe you already suspected, that this would be enough to make up your mind." Karen bit her lip. She looked as though she was already regretting her decision to tell Eleanor what she'd seen.

"Well, I didn't. And now I'm supposed to confront him with

'Karen saw you touch a woman's arm'? Let's be honest, even if he were having an affair, all he'd have to do would be to say you were wrong, it wasn't him you'd seen, or that she was a work colleague, and I'd have to believe him anyway. I can't risk throwing away my marriage over your hunch."

"So you're admitting it's possible?"

"No! Look, we might be a bit tetchy with one another, but Adam and I are solid—when would he even find time for an affair?"

Even as she was saying it, her mind was showing her a slide-show of all the times he'd been late home from work recently, or out with friends. She allowed herself to feel the pain of the image of her husband touching another woman, kissing another woman. No, she couldn't let herself go down that road. Not on the basis of him standing next to some woman in a jewelry shop.

Karen sighed. "I'm sorry. I had to tell you what I saw, but you're right, you need more. Maybe I should have followed him, or con-fronted him or something, but I panicked. You know your husband better than me; there was probably a totally innocent explanation for what I saw."

Eleanor knew instantly that Karen didn't mean a word of what she had just said. Something had made her believe unequivocally that Adam was seeing someone else and she was refusing to say what. But why tell her anything if she couldn't tell her everything?

"Look, I appreciate you letting me know what you saw. I know you, and I know you wouldn't have said anything unless you really felt like you had to. Do I believe Adam is having an affair? No, not really. But I also believe that you thought that strongly enough to tell me. So I'll keep an eye on things, pay closer attention to what's going on. But that's all I can do really, without any proof."

Karen stood up, clearly taking the hint from Eleanor's tone of voice that the conversation was over. "Will you be okay? Because I hate to just drop this on you and leave, but I'm guessing Adam will be back soon and . . ."

And you don't want to face him after what you've just accused him of. "I'll be fine," she said, trying to force her face to match her words.

Karen kissed Noah on the forehead and Eleanor placed him in his bouncer to see her friend out.

At the front door, Karen turned. Had she changed her mind about telling Eleanor the full story? "You really haven't noticed anything unusual? Any signs that someone has been in the house, watching you and the baby . . . ?"

"You're freaking me out now, Karen. And no, I haven't noticed anyone stalking me or my family or Adam sneaking anyone out of the back door when I get home. Have I been distracted? Yes. But not enough that I'd let those things pass me by."

"I'm just trying to look out for you, Eleanor . . ."

She nodded briskly. "I know. But I'm a big girl now, I don't need you interfering. Just let me deal with my marriage, okay?"

"Sure," Karen half whispered. "Love you."

But Eleanor had already closed the door.

- 22 -

ELEANOR

Eleanor leaned against the front door and let out the breath she'd been holding. Exhaustion clawed at her eyelids, but there was no way she could let it win. She stood silently for a second or two, listening for the sound of crying that usually accompanied her leaving the room. When she heard nothing, she took the stairs two at a time and crossed the landing to the bedroom she and Adam shared, shoving open the door and cringing as it slammed against the wall.

She didn't know what she was looking for, and whatever it was, she didn't have much time to find it. Considering that until recently she had been the one who did all the cleaning and tidying, there weren't many places Adam could hide things, but there were places she didn't touch—his bedside drawers for a start. She moved with a frantic urgency, pulling out her husband's innocent belongings: a phone charger, a spare light bulb, a remote control for a docking station long taken to the tip. No letters from a secret lover or spare phone, no lacy underwear or receipts from a fancy hotel room. A search of his jacket pockets and under the bed yielded the same result. Nothing to suggest he was anything other than a loving husband and father. Of course that didn't disprove what Karen had told her, but it didn't give her anything to confront her husband with.

What are you doing? she asked herself, sitting back on her heels. *Do you really think Adam is cheating on you?*

She tried to picture her husband browsing for jewelry with an-other woman, placing a hand tenderly on her arm as she chose her consolation prize. Another thought occurred to her. Was he going to leave her? With a sickening clarity she realized that even if she found evidence that Adam was cheating on her, there was no way she could ever confront him. Because that would force him to make a choice. And what if he didn't choose her?

- 23 -

NOW

How did you feel when you realized that Eleanor was the wife Jessica despised?

I think I was just confused, if I'm honest. I'm not saying I don't believe in coincidence, but her choosing me as her psychiatrist by accident was stretching credibility. At first I just thought she wanted me to tell Eleanor so that Eleanor would leave him. There was simply no chance of that—patient confidentiality forbids it.

But not if you believe someone is in danger.

Exactly. At first I wondered if she was telling me these awful things to force my hand, so that I had to tell Eleanor. I never thought she'd act on them. I should have moved quicker.

What happened when you finally told Eleanor what you'd seen?

You know what happened. She didn't believe me.

Did that hurt?

No, she was in denial. Besides, I still couldn't tell her about Jessica being my patient, or the things she'd said. I had no other evidence to give her besides seeing him standing next to a girl in a shop.

So what did you decide to do?

What could I do? I had to wait to see what her next move would be. Are you saying I should have done more? That this was my fault?

I didn't say that. Do you feel like this is your fault?

Of course I do. I should have done more. I just don't see how I could have known after one meeting what she was capable of. I didn't know who she really was. And when I did try and warn them, they didn't listen. They didn't believe me. I did my best. I only wanted to protect them.

Just like you always did.

Exactly. So you *do* understand.

- 24 -

ELEANOR

Eleanor lay on the sofa, her head in her husband's lap, both of them staring at the TV—although if anyone had asked her to name the mindless drivel they were watching, she'd have had no idea. Her limbs were heavy with the exhaustion of everyday life, but her mind hadn't stopped working since the minute she'd woken up to an empty bed and a silent house.

Silent as the grave. That was the saying, wasn't it? She should have been ecstatic. Noah's first full night's sleep since the day he was born meant an entire nine hours' rest for her, and she hadn't even woken in a cold panic in the middle of the night to check his breathing in the way she had on the few occasions he hadn't woken every three hours. She'd obviously needed the rest, and had she woken lazily and reached out to find Adam snoring gently beside her, moved over to snuggle under his armpit—like the days before a tiny demon had infiltrated their lives—it would have been the perfect start to her morning. Instead she'd woken with a start, unable to put her finger on what had disturbed her. It must have been Adam heading to the toilet, but when she reached out to snuggle up to his pillow, his side of the bed was cold and his mobile phone was gone from his bedside table.

She had dragged herself out of bed and cracked open the curtains to see that his car was missing from the drive. Shit—was it later than she'd thought? Her breasts ached with the weight of stored milk, but it was still quite dark outside—though it always

seemed to be dark these days, what with winter making its imminent presence known. Maybe Adam had snuck out to take Toby
for breakfast, leaving Eleanor and Noah to have a well-deserved
lie-in. The thought was so glorious that she'd been gutted to check
her phone and see that it was only 7:05—there's no way they would
have got themselves up and out that early. Gutted, then worried.
Where was Adam? He hadn't mentioned an early start the night
before, and it was so unlike him to be up before his alarm went off
at 7:45. The number of times she herself had still been up at 6 a.m.
from a 2 a.m. feed and prayed he would somehow psychically wake
from his slumber and take Noah while she clawed back an hour
and a half of the night, but not once had he opened his eyes before
that alarm.

She'd thrown on her dressing gown and slippers and padded
across the landing and down the stairs, one eye on the monitor as
the third step from the bottom let out its trademark groan, half
hoping, despite the missing car, to find Adam with a full English
breakfast laid out on the table. But the bottom of the house was as
quiet as the upstairs.

Trying hard to control her rising panic, she had tried Adam's
phone twice while going about her normal morning tasks—making
toast, pouring cereal for Toby, the whole time cradling the phone
between her shoulder and her ear. When she gave up and threw the
handset onto the kitchen counter, she heard grumpy little noises
crackling from the monitor like angry static.

Typically, Adam had called back just as Noah hit full-blown
panic mode at waking and finding himself alone and probably
starving after a full night without milk. Where the bloody hell had
she left the phone? It had been only about four minutes since she'd
last had it . . . Yes, the kitchen. Lugging Noah with her, she got to it
just as it stopped ringing. Immediately her mobile started upstairs.
By the time she'd answered, Noah was puce in the face and Eleanor
was already exhausted and livid.

"Where are you?" She'd tried—and failed—to keep the annoyance from her voice.

"I woke early and couldn't get back to sleep. Thought I'd go to the gym rather than risk waking you and the kids."

"The gym?" Adam hadn't been to the gym in more than twelve months, and suddenly this morning he was Mr. Motivated?

"Well, I told you I wanted to start up again."

He'd mentioned it. Once. Eleanor had told him that if he wanted to start back at the gym, he'd have to go before work—the kids missed him enough in the evenings as it was. She'd just never expected it to actually happen.

"And you didn't think that if you were up early you could have done some of the housework, or got the kids' stuff ready for school like I would have had to do?"

Adam sighed, and she pictured him rubbing his face. "Els, I don't want to argue. I just wanted some time to myself."

She laughed. "Time to yourself?"

"We've been over this before. Time at work doesn't count as time to myself. You get your Fridays—what do I get?"

She'd wanted to ask what was so wrong with time with her—or point out how nice it would have been to wake up together for a change, instead of him going downstairs to find her half-asleep and drooling on the sofa—but Noah's demands for his breakfast had reached a level only dogs could hear, and she could hear Toby banging around in the kitchen and could only imagine the mess he was making getting the milk into his cereal.

"Okay, have a good day at work, babe. Love you."

This was all Karen's fault. If she hadn't mentioned seeing Adam with that girl, Eleanor would never have spent the rest of the day wondering if her husband had really been at the gym, or thinking about all the ways she could find out if he'd been telling the truth, ranging from calling the gym to say he'd lost his pass and had it been used recently (risky—they'd issue a new one and probably mention it to him) to pretending to be a police officer and asking to see their security cameras (she realized they weren't fantastic ideas). The old Eleanor of just a week ago would never have moved practically everything in the house under the guise of cleaning to look for evidence of his affair, and she definitely wouldn't have spent forty minutes on Google looking up phone-tracking software—just in case. She had to forget what Karen thought she'd seen and concentrate on not screwing up her marriage.

Adam had been expecting an argument when he walked in that evening, but Eleanor had been too tired—and too scared of where it might lead—to oblige. The last thing she wanted to do was ask him outright if he was having an affair. What if he admitted it? Everything in their lives would be turned on its head, and she'd be forced to decide what to do about it. She didn't feel ready for that tonight, perhaps not ever. And yet was she really the type of person to ignore her husband's affair? Those women were weak, spineless, devoid of any character or backbone. Eleanor had never been like that. She abhorred people who lied and cheated; if you treated the person you were supposed to love that way, then what kind of person were you? Whenever she'd talked with her friends about cheating partners, she'd been the first to assert her opinion on the subject—if Adam ever cheated on her, he'd be gone. She felt almost embarrassed by that woman now; she'd known nothing of real life and of a marriage under strain. And suddenly life wasn't so black-and-white.

They bathed the children and put them to bed with barely a word between them. As Eleanor left Noah's nursery, she paused by the door of her elder son's room and listened to father and son talking about Toby's day at school. How had it been so easy with Toby and yet so hard with Noah? True, there were differences in their situation, but if anything, their bond after Noah was born should have been stronger than before. Now they had a child who was both of theirs, something they shared together, without secrets and lies. This should have been simple.

The street outside was silent save for the occasional car pulling in and parking up at one of the other houses. Adam seemed more relaxed now that no row had been forthcoming, yet Eleanor felt him stiffen at a noise from outside the window.

"What is it?" she asked, sitting up. Adam's eyes didn't leave the TV.

"What's what?"

"You heard something outside. It was in the bushes; I heard it too."

Adam leaned over and pulled the curtain aside an inch, peered out into the darkness. "No one there. Probably a bird."

"It wasn't a bloody bird. Aren't you going to go and look?"

He pulled a face. "Go and look at someone walking past the house? What's wrong with you?"

The words stung like a slap to the face. Not *What's wrong?* but *What's wrong with you?* As though all their problems could be traced back in a Freudian flowchart to the lunatic mother rather than the absent, possibly philandering husband. *He disappears in the middle of the night and yet there's something wrong with me?*

Did he know who was out there? Was that why he wouldn't go and look? Karen's words came back to her as clearly as if her friend was sitting beside her. *You really haven't noticed anything unusual? Any signs that someone has been in the house, watching you and the baby . . . ?*

Eleanor felt sick at the very thought. She hadn't noticed anyone, but would she? She was always so busy, her attention taken up by one or other of her children. Would she spot someone walking behind her or watching them from afar? Karen must have had a good reason to say it. What did she know?

But it couldn't be anything like that. The noise from outside was like Adam said, someone walking their dog, or kids on their way home from the park. Nothing more. Because if he knew there was someone out there, he would put a stop to it. He would never put their family in danger.

I went to her house.

Afterwards I sat in the cul-de-sac at the end of the street, seething quietly at my stupidity, at my total disregard for the rules I had set myself. Your life, I told myself through gritted teeth, is defined by the rules you have vowed to abide by. If you lose sight of those, you lose everything. It could all come slipping down round you, the snowdrift that is your life becoming an avalanche that will bury you alive. It wasn't the fear that I could have been caught that caused self-loathing to bubble under my surface like tar on a hot road—when you have had the worst possible thing happen to you, that kind of fear is as ridiculous as being afraid of monsters under the bed. I hadn't been caught. But I had lost control.

The house was as different to mine as our lives were to each other. This home welcomed you towards it with a magnetic pull; even empty you could practically smell the freshly baked bread and hear the sounds of children's quickly forgotten squabbles. Sounds that had choked and suffocated him; sounds I craved in my home of sharp edges and vast amounts of fingerprint-free glass.

There were no cars on the drive, but still I approached with apprehension. I had no desire to rush this. I wasn't looking for anything specific here, not like the times I'd crept into the other women's houses with a goal in mind. I just wanted to look.

I'd kept the key in my hand throughout the entire journey, its warmth and the way it sat comfortably in the creases a silent affirmation that I was doing the right thing. That this was long overdue and I couldn't avoid her forever. I'd expected it to refuse to turn in the lock, unwilling to betray its master and let the enemy over the threshold, yet it had slid in and turned without resistance the first time. I stood for a second with my hand on the door handle and my mind stuck in that place between before and after. I was still closer to before; there was still time to walk away from this place with my discipline intact. The minute I pushed open that door it would become after, and I would have to consider at some point what that meant for me, how far I would slip and whether I could pull myself back from where this was all heading.

But I knew myself, and I knew, even as I hesitated, that I wouldn't have come here if I hadn't fully intended to walk through that door. There was a big part of me that had wanted her to be home so I wouldn't have a chance, but now I was here and the house was empty. Better just to get it over with, rip off the Band-Aid without stopping too long to think about the pain it might cause.

The hallway was sparsely decorated—built to be family-functional, with coat hooks that each held one coat and a shelf for the post. I turned my face from the crisp white envelopes ripped open at the top and the letters crammed back in the rush of the school run. The thought of seeing his name on them in this place that felt so unlike him caused my stomach to cramp uncomfortably.

I lifted a man's jacket off the hook. A heavy wax jacket, expensive and functional, the kind of thing you'd wear to walk a pack of dogs across the countryside on a bitter Sunday morning. Dark green, with a black sheepskin trim on the inside of the collar. I raised it to my face and inhaled deeply, the scent pervading my nostrils. Expensive aftershave that reminded me of the cold side of my bed—how I'd spray it on the pillow so that I could smell him when he wasn't there, so I could pretend he was still with me when I closed my eyes. Did she do the same?

Something was missing from my memory of the scent that lingered around him when he was with me. Cigarette smoke. Triumph tugged at my insides—it was a small victory but an important one. Here he was a nonsmoker, here he had to be that better version of himself. When he was with me, he was free to be the real him.

My hunt through the other homes had been fast and purposeful, yet I wandered around this house like a ghost, an echo barely even there, breathing in the very essence of who this other woman was. My head felt as though it was underwater; every move I made carried with it the weight of what our lives had become.

I was in her bedroom, pushing open the mirrored wardrobe doors and slowly flicking through the clothes inside. As my fingers slid through silk and cashmere, thick wool and other expensive-looking fabrics, one jumper in particular caught my eye. A cornflower-blue soft woollen V-neck. I pulled it from the hanger and held it to my face—it smelled of washing powder, and a faint trace of jasmine, but despite the difference in fragrance, it was identical in every other way to the jumper that hung in another wardrobe, in another house far away in distance only.

I slipped the jumper over my head; the fit was perfect but it felt warmer than mine. This whole life was warmer than mine. It wasn't that she was much better off financially; just that her life was richer in color where mine was grayscale.

There was makeup on top of the chest of drawers, makeup I couldn't imagine her taking the time to put on. Who was she making herself beautiful for? Surely not him—if she'd made more of an effort for him, I might not even have been there. I took out one of the lipsticks and opened it: an understated coral color. Understated was the perfect word for her, although she'd undoubtedly have called it "classy" or "demure." Using the mirror, I ran the lipstick over my lips, daubed rose-colored blush on the apples of my cheeks, and flicked mascara over my eyelashes, lashes that had only needed to flutter at her husband for the briefest of moments.

Had I felt superior to her at that moment? Probably, yes. After all, I was the one he had chosen. He wasn't with me through loyalty or obligation to his children; he was with me because of the way I made him feel.

I opened one of the drawers and fingered the satin lingerie tucked way behind the grannie panties. I pulled out a pair of pale pink knickers and laid them flat on top of the rest. My fingers worked automatically, pulling open the button of my jeans, sliding down the zip and pushing them to the floor, shedding my underwear at the same time. Standing semi-naked in that place, I slipped into the satin of this other woman's life. The underwear felt reassuringly loose on my hips, and I watched myself in the mirrored doors of the wardrobe as though I were watching someone else in another house, one in which they belonged.

I sprayed her perfume on my wrists and dabbed them together then onto my neck, taking a breath, inhaling the scent he smelled when he buried his face in *her* neck. I flipped open the jewelry box and lifted out a pair of diamond earrings, slipping them into the holes in my own ears. The woman in the mirror admired them; they suited her. This life suited her. With every second I spent in this house, wearing her clothes, touching the possessions she had touched, it felt as though we were becoming more deeply entwined, almost as though by being here I was rewriting our destiny.

The bed stretched out across the room, the centerpiece of this makeshift theater. I lay down on the clean cotton sheets and stretched out my legs, placed my head on the plush pillow. I curled up into a fetal position as I pictured them lying here together, arms and legs entwined in postcoital satisfaction. A car door slammed outside, but it barely registered in my mind. I knew that any minute now the front door could open and I would be exposed, but still I couldn't move. It was as though every muscle in my body was invested in keeping me in this very place at this very time. Let them find me here. Who would have more explaining to do?

But the door didn't open. No one came in.

The woman in the mirror watched with detached interest as the woman on the bed slid her thumbs into the loose elastic of the satin underwear, hitching it down ever so slightly, enough to slide her fingers underneath, and began to rub automatically, rhythmically. Her lips parted, her breathing quickened as the pressure of her fingers increased. They moved faster now, more urgently, and the woman in the mirror closed her eyes at the same time as the woman on the bed threw her head back and let the climax flow through her, more of a gentle wave than a crash, but exhilarating and exhausting all the same.

When my eyes opened, everything felt wrong. I didn't know how long I'd been there, asleep in the bed they shared in the house he owned, but I knew I shouldn't be there any longer. I wasn't ready to face this situation yet; I wasn't strong enough. But I felt like I could be.

I closed the door behind me, leaving his other life on the inside. I was walking slowly, but my steps were lighter now, as if part of me had stayed there on that smoothed-down double bed. In the car, I lifted a hand to my ear, touched the small diamond. As I put the car into gear and pulled away, I hesitated in the road to let another vehicle out. The woman from the mirror didn't even lift a hand in thanks.

- 26 -

ELEANOR

It had been a bad idea born of desperation: date night. Eleanor had suggested it and Adam had played along, although it had been clear he'd been terrified at the idea of having to sit across a table from his wife and make small talk that didn't include who-said-what-to-whom and who-started-it. They'd arrived home so early that even her mother looked surprised to see them, walking through the door sober and serious rather than falling through like giggling teenagers as they had in the old days.

Adam had offered almost instantly to take her mum home, and Eleanor had allowed herself to think for a second that he might be trying to get rid of her so they could snuggle up on the sofa, maybe put on a film or one of the few programs they both enjoyed. The reality of the situation had hit, however, when he'd announced as he was heading out of the door that he might as well pop into Chris's on the way home; he'd promised to look at his computer and if he was going to be out anyway . . .

Eleanor refused to cry.

She was in bed trying to grab at any sleep she could get before Noah woke in a hungry rage when she heard Adam's key turn in the front door. Fumbling for her phone, her eyes stung at the bright light it emitted, and it took her a few seconds to register the time: 12:45.

More than three hours since he'd taken her mother home and gone to fix his friend's computer. What had taken him so long? She lay awake waiting for him, but instead of coming straight to bed, she heard the bathroom door open and the sound of the shower running. A shower, at this time of night? He'd be up in a few hours anyway, and he usually showered first thing in the morning. When he eventually pushed open the bedroom door, he looked surprised to see her awake.

"Sorry, love, I didn't mean to wake you. How have the boys been?"

"Fast asleep," she replied neutrally. "Computer all fixed?"

There was a slight pause before he replied. "Oh yeah, we got a bit carried away talking—well, Chris was moaning actually. You know what he's like."

She didn't, having only met Chris a couple of times in their six-year relationship, but she said nothing. She didn't want another row tonight.

Adam slipped into bed next to her, and instinctively she moved in closer, snuggling her warmth against his cold body. He responded, letting her into his arms and kissing the top of her head. It had been months since they'd made love—way before Noah had been born. At first it was impractical—Eleanor had still been in pain from the birth and bleeding heavily—but she'd neglected to mention that the doctor had given her the all-clear to resume their sex life nearly four weeks ago. She'd been so exhausted, her breasts heavy and engorged and her mummy tummy permanently encased in unflattering underwear the same size as some of the outfits she used to wear, that it just hadn't been top of her list. Okay, it hadn't even been *on* her list. He'd been patient, not pushing her until she gave him the signal, but now, in the early hours of the morning, suddenly it seemed crucial to her that they made love. She slid a warm hand inside the pajama bottoms he'd taken to wearing and slowly began to rub him, laying a kiss gently on his collarbone. She felt his body respond and all at once felt nervous and excited, as though it was their first time. Then, firmly but tenderly, Adam laid a hand on hers and held it still.

"Not tonight, babe, I'm shattered."

The shock of the rejection was crushing. She couldn't remember a time in their entire relationship—no matter how tired they'd been or however angrily they'd fought—that her husband had refused sex. Tears of shame burned in her eyes and she thanked God Adam couldn't see her in the darkness. She pulled her hand away as though it burned and nodded slightly.

"Of course. Get some sleep and I'll see you in the morning."

"Okay, love." Oblivious to her hurt, he kissed her head again and turned over to sleep. "Good night."

She tried to reply, but the words caught in her throat and she screwed her eyes closed. Before long she heard the rhythmic sounds of Adam's sleep as she lay awake in the darkness.

My entire body felt as though it were alive with a thousand unseen insects, and I raked my fingernails up and down my arms to stave off the itching feeling. I couldn't just sit there wondering what they were doing, the words rolling over and over in my head—*Why can't they see?* Why couldn't they see the danger they were in? Why were they all so shortsighted?

And if they did—no, *when* they did—what would happen then? What would I do? I hadn't really thought that far ahead; I didn't want to waste time ruminating on the consequences my actions might have. Consequences couldn't always be controlled, and my mind didn't—couldn't be allowed to—dwell on things beyond my control.

I'd paced so much my calves hurt from the tension that held my body rigid and alert. Waiting like a coiled spring for something to happen, a trigger, a release. An image of a snake hidden in the long grass flitted across my mind, and I quickly replaced it with an image of them laughing, clinking their glasses together as they celebrated all the minor inconveniences in their lives. They could do this, you see, because the things they lamented week in, week out weren't real troubles. They were minor irritants, fabricated to raise a smile from one another, or spoken out loud to remind themselves how blessed they were to have only these tiny, insignificant worries. They knew nothing of pain and heartbreak, or the kind of demons real people had. Their whole lives were sugarcoated versions of those led by the less fortunate.

And yet as much as I wanted to hold a mirror up to their *I Love Lucy* existence, a part of me still wanted to protect and preserve it. I craved it like nothing on earth, a life in which I could switch off the minute the children were in bed and fold myself into the arms of a husband who was really mine and lose myself in *Celebrity Big Brother* or *The Great British Bake Off.* I longed to pick up the phone and share my petty fears and minor inconveniences with people who had nothing more in their lives than a boss who was a bit of a prick. I desperately wanted my only worry to be forgetting to buy milk or having to change a million shitty nappies from my perfect child in my perfect home. I didn't want the fetid poison that ran through my veins to be the first thing I thought of when I woke in the morning.

But the mind is a wonderful and terrifying machine. I had spent years being made to believe I was a stupid, bad person, that I couldn't be trusted. I had been conditioned to see someone useless and unworthy of love when I looked in the mirror. And like a self-fulfilling prophecy, that was what my life became. A life without a future. So I clung to what I had—is it any wonder I wanted to protect it? You'd do the same if you had to.

The darkness outside was complete and unyielding, and yet I felt a sense of comfort as I stepped out of the back door and allowed myself to be enveloped by the night. This was where I felt most like myself, when I was alone in the dark. My feet moved automatically, my body knowing where I wanted to go better than my mind did. So when I found myself outside Eleanor and Adam's house, staring up at the window where I knew baby Noah lay sleeping, I wasn't even a little surprised.

- 28 -

BEA

It was Saturday night and Bea was stuck at home. Alone. After sixteen years of steely determination to live a normal life, she could feel herself slipping back into that scared teenager who had woken up in her bed in pain and alone, and the thought petrified her.

"Beatrice Barker, you need to get ahold of yourself," she muttered, flicking off the chick flick she'd been watching just before the ditzy female and the extraordinarily white-toothed male realized that it was really each other they'd been looking for after all. No wonder teenage girls had such an unrealistic view of relationships. The girls in these films were always charmingly perfect; even their imperfections were freaking adorable.

The sound of the doorbell cut through her embittered inner monologue. She wasn't expecting anyone, but even Geoff the creepy building maintenance bloke would be preferable to an entire evening where she spoke to no one but herself. God, life wasn't looking great when you were praying there was a gas leak just to get some company.

But when she swung open the door to her flat, it wasn't Geoff the handyman waiting to check her pipes—it was Karen. And she had pizza.

"Special delivery." Karen grinned and handed Bea the box. She held it up to her nose and took a huge sniff.

"What are you doing here?"

"Michael's working away. I was lonely."

Bea eyed her friend suspiciously. "And this wouldn't happen to have anything to do with a conversation I had with a certain Eleanor Whitney the other day?"

Karen had the good grace to look guilty.

"Okay, she told me. Don't give me that look! She was worried about you. She said you were in a bad way. And don't worry, I'm not upset that you told her and not me." Her words were light and jokey, but Bea knew Karen well enough to know she was annoyed. "Although, you two have been spending a fair bit of time together lately."

Bea cringed. She couldn't tell Karen why the pair of them had been getting together without her, and she wasn't quick enough to think up an excuse. It wasn't that they never saw one another separately anyway—Karen was here on her own now, wasn't she? But thanks to the party planning, Eleanor and Bea had been together without Karen more than usual. Luckily Karen wasn't waiting for an excuse, just letting her know she'd noticed, she supposed.

"Eleanor thinks you should tell Fran what happened."

Bea couldn't help but catch the tone. The fact was, Fran hadn't been wrong about Karen. Her best friend had had little good to say about her sister since they were teenagers, and never missed an opportunity to point out Fran's shortcomings in the big-sister department. It had been Karen who had convinced Bea not to tell her sister about what had happened with Kieran Ressler, saying that she didn't want Fran doing anything reckless and getting into trouble because of Bea. It worked both ways, though. Fran always had a certain tone of voice when she mentioned Karen, and the conversation usually involved eye rolling. Karen thought Fran was a loose cannon and Fran thought Karen was a goody-goody with a stick up her backside. Bea had always put it down to the pair of them being jealous of one another, but she couldn't help wondering if it was more to do with the death of Karen's sister when they were just children. Understandable that she should be jealous of Bea having

Fran, but that was no reason to dislike her. Bea couldn't help having a sister any more than Karen could help not having one.

She shrugged in an attempt at nonchalance.

"It was just a shock. I was expecting a book about a woman who finds out the book she's reading is about her, and I pulled out a book about me." She gave a laugh. "Huh, that's ironic, right? I never even thought about the book it was supposed to be."

"Did you get it?" Karen asked.

"Get what?"

"The other book?"

"Oh, yeah, it came the next day. I haven't started it yet, but you can borrow it when I'm done."

"Thanks." Karen was in the kitchen now, pulling out sauces and napkins, but she stopped to look at Bea. "I was thinking, if you got the book you ordered, then it wasn't just a mix-up of the two, was it? I mean, they didn't just put the wrong book in the envelope."

She carried the tray into the sitting area and placed it on the coffee table, then sat down on the sofa, folding her legs underneath her, and leaned over to take a slice of pizza.

Bea paused, her own slice already halfway to her mouth.

"I hadn't thought of that. God, do you think someone sent it to me on purpose?" She had a sickening thought and threw the pizza back into the box. "Do you think it was him?"

"No," Karen said quickly, leaning forward and placing a hand on her friend's knee. "No, Bea, I don't. One"—she sat back again and checked off a finger—"he doesn't know where you live."

"I live in the same town I grew up in, about four streets from my parents. I'm hardly living off the grid."

Karen held up a second finger. "Okay, two, it's been sixteen years and you've not once heard from him. Three," she continued before Bea could interject, "you and I both know what happened to Kieran Ressler. The accident he had left him severely brain damaged. He will never walk again. The last thing on earth he'll be thinking about now—if he even has one cohesive thought a day—is sending you reading material."

It took a second for Karen's words to sink in, although it wasn't so much her words that made Bea relax as the way she said them. She wasn't speaking to convince or reassure; she was stating facts in a take-'em-or-leave-'em kind of way, confident that she was right beyond reproach. When a person was that sure in their convictions, it became much harder to argue with or disbelieve them.

Bea picked up her pizza again, but didn't tuck in the way she'd been desperate to five minutes ago.

"So if someone sent it to me, who was it? There was no note, no 'saw this and thought of you.'"

"Hmmm."

Bea stiffened. "Do you know?"

Karen shook her head, but she was lying and Bea knew it.

"You do. Tell me." That was why she'd been so sure it wasn't Kieran Ressler. Because she thought she knew who it was.

"I don't know, Bea, I promise. But I do have an idea I want to look at. If I'm right, you'll be the first to know about it."

Bea nodded, satisfied. She was used to a certain degree of "don't ask" with Karen—it came with her job. So much of her day she couldn't talk over with anyone. Bea wouldn't be able to keep her mouth shut—not in the admirable way Karen could. She had never been one for keeping secrets.

"Did you keep the packaging?"

They'd finished the pizza an hour earlier—well, Bea had. Despite her initial loss of appetite, she'd never been one to turn down food. Karen, however, had always been a picky eater and had barely touched her half. They'd watched *The X Factor* and now

Karen was in the kitchen clearing away the rubbish and pouring them drinks. Neither woman was drinking alcohol: Karen was driving and Bea didn't much feel like getting drunk and maudlin.

"What packaging?" Bea called back, flicking through the channels. This was why she went out on Saturday nights—the alternative was so bloody depressing.

"For the book. Do you still have it?"

Bea tensed. She'd been hoping the subject was closed, forgotten.

"Yeah, I guess. It's in the bedroom, I think—I chucked it into the closet. Hold on and I'll go and have a look."

Pack rat, her mum had called her because of her minor hoarding habit. Bea preferred to think of herself as resourceful. She only kept things that could be reused—envelopes, especially the boxy cardboard ones books came in, definitely counted as useful.

The floor of her closet, as a consequence of her habit, was a bit of a mess. Bea had thrown the envelope in there only a couple of days ago, and already it was buried under what her mother would affectionately refer to as "a pile of crap."

The dress was on the top of the pile. At first Bea thought it had fallen off one of the hangers, and she pulled it out, ready to throw it in the washing basket—a lazy habit that avoided rehanging. As she did so, she recognized the fabric in her hands. It wasn't a dress. It was a jumpsuit.

BEA

Okay, Bea, breathe. Breathe deeper. Steady, one, two, three, four, and out, two, three, four. Here, drink this." Karen held the glass to Bea's lips and she sipped greedily, then gagged, the cold water making her nauseous. When she felt her breathing returning to normal, she slumped back against her bed.

"What happened?" Karen asked.

The jumpsuit was lying off to one side where Bea had dropped it when she'd begun to scream. She didn't trust herself to speak, but her eyes fell on the piece of material and Karen picked it up. Bea looked away; she never wanted to see it again, let alone so close.

"What is it?"

"It's what I was wearing that night." Her voice cracked and she fell silent again.

"Bea, why would you keep this?" Her friend's voice was low, trying to soothe her, but her question was forcing back memories Bea didn't want to let through.

"I didn't. I threw it in the wheelie bin outside the halls of residence the next day. I couldn't bear to ever put it on again."

"But you bought another one the same?"

Bea shook her head. "I never would have."

Karen was inspecting the material without holding it up or opening it out. "It doesn't look sixteen years old."

"It's not the actual one." Bea forced her eyes to stay open. She wanted more than anything to lie back and let them fall shut, just rest them for a minute, but she couldn't stand the thought of her mind betraying her, picturing her wearing that other jumpsuit, in that other life. "The straps were thinner, they were spaghetti straps, and the neck was looser, more like a cowl than a V."

Karen said nothing, and for a while they just sat there on the bedroom floor, frozen, as though the slightest movement might trigger another panic attack. After what seemed like an hour, Karen crawled forward and sat in front of her, concern clouding her deep brown eyes.

"Bea? I'm going to ask you something and I want you to not be afraid, and not feel upset, okay?"

Bea nodded, instantly afraid and upset even though she had no idea what Karen was going to ask.

"Has there been any time lately that you can't account for? Maybe you've woken up and not known where you've been, or what you've been doing."

Bea stared at her, not sure at first what her friend was asking. Or maybe she knew and just couldn't believe she was being asked the question.

"Of course not."

"You're sure? No periods when time has seemed to pass faster than it should? When you've looked at the clock and wondered where the hours have gone?"

"Well, that's a different question." Bea attempted a smile, but the result felt alien to her face. "Every time I need to get something done at work, I look at the clock and wonder where the last few hours have gone."

"I'm serious, Bea."

"I know you are, and that's what worries me. Surely you don't think I'm going crazy? Come on, Karen, you can't think that." She meant it to sound like she was joking, but she wasn't, and it showed.

"I'm not saying you're crazy, Bea, I would never say that. It's just the book, and now this . . . this was in your closet. You're the only person who could have put it there. Maybe it's your mind's way of forcing you to remember because you never really dealt with what happened to you back then."

The thought raised goose bumps on Bea's forearms, but as quickly as she entertained the theory, she dismissed it.

"The whole idea is ridiculous," she told Karen quietly. "There has got to be a simple explanation. I just don't know what it is yet."

- 30 -

ELEANOR

Eleanor's morning had been a complete write-off and it was only 8 a.m. Noah's arrival had brought out the absolute best in Toby as a big brother—he had grown up in so many ways and was wonderful with the baby. But he had regressed in so many other ways, it was almost unbelievable he was the same child. Refusing to get dressed without her help, not wanting to go to school. Everything was taking twice, sometimes three times as long as it did before Noah came, and it was driving Eleanor crazy. She was impatient all the time and hated herself for snapping at Toby, often ending up crying at the bottom of the garden.

That morning was environmental studies day. For the last three days Toby and Eleanor had worked on his project, Adam actually taking care of Noah long enough for her to spend some quality time with the boy. After ridiculous amounts of googling, they'd come up with the idea of making a 3-D dolphin picture from recycled materials. It was adventurous—the type of thing they'd done together before Noah had come along—and they had spent their evenings covered in craft glue and tissue paper. Eleanor was more than a little pleased with the finished article, and she couldn't wait to hear how it was received by his teachers. But first they had to get it to school.

"A little help, Toby, please," she'd yelled, trying to heft the dolphin out to the car. In his car seat Noah let out an impatient squawk.

"Just a second, darling. Mummy is a little busy right now."

"Yeah, Noah, you're not the only one in this family."

Eleanor cringed, Toby's words making her hideously aware of how often she'd said them to him. He was used to being an only child, and since Noah had been born had been struggling to adjust.

They got the car loaded up, and after what seemed like an age they were all in and ready to go, fifteen minutes later than usual—usual at the moment being ten minutes late to start with. Luckily, being late meant they had missed the traffic, and she was soon pulling into the school car park.

"Have a good day, darling." She kissed Toby on the cheek out of sight of any other children as per normal, and he pulled a face.

"I can't carry this in on my own, Mum."

Of course he couldn't. She'd struggled to get the bloody thing to the car; she could hardly expect Toby to haul it across the playground by himself. She shot a quick look at Noah in his seat. He'd obligingly fallen asleep the minute they'd left the house, drunk on milk and exhausted after his four forty-five start to the day (weren't they both?). His one full night's sleep had been a cruel fluke, making the broken nights even more unbearable now she'd had a glimpse of what normal life was like.

"Okay, mate, let's do this." She closed the car door as gently as possible, checked that Noah was still fast asleep, and clicked the locking system. The school doors were two hundred yards away, there was no one around, and she could see the car. Parents did this all the time, she told herself. She checked again. Still no one.

Toby laughed as they both struggled to pick up the dolphin, Eleanor pretending that her end was heavier than it was.

"Come on, kid, let's see if we can find you someone to help you get this to class."

There was no one around at the entrance either—probably owing to the fact that they were really quite late by now. Shooting a guilty look at the car, Eleanor nodded at the door.

"We can take it inside, and then you'd better run to registration. Someone will help you get it later."

"What if it gets broken?" Toby asked as they hefted it into the gap under the stairs that led to the head's office. "What if one of the big kids steals it?"

"No one will steal it, Tobes." Eleanor's stomach lurched at the sight of her son's crestfallen face. "I tell you what, you get yourself to class and I'll see if Mrs. Fenton will keep it in the office for you."

Toby grinned. "Thanks, Mum!"

She kissed the top of his head. "They're gonna love it. Remember how hard you've worked and it'll all be okay. I love you."

"Love you too," Toby mumbled, presumably in case there were hidden recording devices on the stairs.

Eleanor hauled the project over to the reception, careful not to knock any of the pieces off. There was no sign of Mrs. Fenton. She wanted to leave the bloody thing there and get back to Noah—what if he'd woken and was crying? But she'd made a promise to Toby, and their relationship was fragile enough as it was at the moment. Plus experience told her that Noah would sleep soundly now until the minute they walked through the front door at home and she wanted to put her head down for a bit herself. He only ever slept in the day when they were out of the house; anytime she wanted to work on her business plan or, God forbid, rest, he was wide awake and needing something. She'd never experienced this with Toby; by the time she'd become part of his life, he'd been sleeping through the night, even the loss of his mother not unsettling him for long. He'd been such an easy baby that this had been quite a shock to the system.

After what seemed like an hour—in reality a few minutes—Mrs. Fenton strolled in, the smell of cigarette smoke trailing behind her like a line of ducklings following their mother. Eleanor took a deep breath, savoring the smell for a minute. Something Adam didn't know about her was that until they had got together, she'd been a casual smoker. He'd made it clear on their first date that he hated smoking with a passion that only came from having lost a parent to lung cancer, so she'd decided not to mention it, and had gradually given up altogether. Until she'd had Noah, she'd never considered taking it up again, but lately she'd been craving the feel of that rolled-up nicotine-filled paper between her fingers like she hadn't in years.

"Mrs. Whitney, is there something wrong?" Mrs. Fenton appraised her casual Monday attire: black leggings covered in formula fingerprints where she'd wiped her hands down the sides and a loose navy smock thrown on to disguise the fact that her stomach still hadn't completely made it back to pre-baby proportions.

"Toby has this project for his environmental class this morning—is there someone who could help him get it there, please? I didn't have a chance to walk it with him to his classroom; we were, um, running a bit late." She resisted the urge to go into a lengthy description of how stressful her morning had been. Mrs. Fenton didn't have children, and Eleanor doubted she'd understand how long something as simple as a shower and getting dressed could take when accompanied by the howls of a small human and the trials and tribulations of a slightly bigger one.

"No problem." Mrs. Fenton waved a hand at the dolphin. "Just leave it there."

She swung to pick up the paperback she had hidden in her desk drawer, and in that second Eleanor truly believed she hated her and her simple day, and her ability to make herself a cup of tea without cringing when the kettle clicked too loudly or to flush the toilet after a wee.

"Thank you, I have to get off." She barreled back out of the school doors and instinctively looked over to the car. Or where the car had been, because now it was gone.

PART 2

- 31 -

KAREN

So how have you been feeling since our last session?"

Jessica Hamilton raised her eyebrows at Karen. Was it just her imagination, or were they a bit less bushy than the last time she'd seen her? And was she wearing lipstick? Karen instinctively pressed her own lips together. She'd had Eleanor on her mind when she was getting ready that morning and she'd completely forgotten to put any lipstick on. She felt annoyed at herself for going to work without checking her makeup first, and for letting a patient make her feel inadequate.

"Bored of answering these questions. Disappointed that you don't have any insight other than 'how are you feeling.' Stupid that I ever thought this would help." She leaned her elbow on the arm of the sofa and her forehead on her hand and looked thoroughly fed up.

"And what were you expecting to have achieved by this stage?" *Patient is feeling uncomfortable at the new direction her sessions are taking, manifested as frustration at the lack of progress.*

"I thought you might have a little more insight for me, you know, on how to stop these headaches. And the obsessive thoughts. I didn't expect to have to tell you how I'm going to fix myself."

Karen tried not to sound as though she was pressing too urgently for details. "Is the relationship continuing?"

Jessica regarded her with keen curiosity, and not for the first time Karen felt as though the girl was trying to look inside her for answers to questions she wasn't ready to reveal yet. As though she was the one under the microscope and Jessica was here to dissect her.

"If you had the chance to go back in time and kill Adolf Hitler, would you do it?"

Not the answer she had been expecting. Karen hesitated.

"I think most people would say they would, that one act of murder would be justified to save millions of lives."

Jessica smiled, as though she'd already known what Karen was going to say. "It's interesting you avoid giving an answer by talking about what you think most people would do."

Interesting. Like she was an experiment, a butterfly in a jar flapping its wings despite knowing there was nowhere to fly to.

Jessica paused for a few seconds, giving the impression of someone contemplating their next sentence, but even then Karen got the impression that every word she said was already planned. She didn't speak unless she was reading from her inner script.

"What about if you had the chance to go back and kill Hitler's *mother*? Would you do it then? Sacrifice an innocent life so that millions would live?"

"Are you interested in questions of morality in general, or just my position on it?" Karen was trying not to let her see she was rattled, but she could feel her face burning and felt sure Jessica must be able to see it too, hear the sharpness her voice had taken on.

"I'm interested in people." If Jessica could tell she was feeling uncomfortable, she didn't care. "And how they claim to have one set of beliefs but then act very differently. It fascinates me how we can quote our own moral code and yet completely disregard it when it doesn't fit with how we want to live our lives. Talk about cognitive dissonance."

If blood could freeze in veins, Karen was certain that hers would have turned to ice. Those words . . . cognitive dissonance . . . had she mentioned them to Jessica? It was her initial diagnosis of the girl's tension headaches—headaches that she'd yet to see or hear

any evidence of—and yet she didn't believe in sharing early diag-
noses with patients: if she was incorrect, it could send the wrong
impression, and often people took her first answer and refused to
listen to any other possibilities.

Could it have been a coincidence?

Of course it was possible—but that wasn't what it was. Jessica
Hamilton knew the diagnosis she'd already assigned to her and was
using it to taunt her. *I know you,* she was saying. *I'm one step
ahead of you.*

"Tell me what you know about cognitive dissonance."

Jessica smiled as though Karen had read from her script.

"It's the disparity between our thoughts and beliefs and our actions. Like, I might think that sleeping with married men is wrong
in general, but in reality I'm still carrying on my affair."

"In that case—"

"It's like those people who were on an underground cave tour
when the heavily pregnant woman in front got stuck in the mouth
of the cave. The tide was rising, and soon the only person who
would be safe was the woman stuck in the rocks because her head
was out of the water. The cavers had a stick of dynamite and a
choice. They could choose to blow up the innocent woman and
save the rest of the cavers, or let her live and condemn everyone else
to drowning."

Jessica told the story as if it were a real case, when in fact it
was an entirely fictional anecdote Karen had heard a million times—
variations had been discussed in ethics papers since her days at university, a tool to debate utilitarian ethics versus deontological ethics.

"And what did they do?" she asked. She was rooted to the spot,
waiting for Jessica's answer.

"They blew her up."

Karen heard a hiss and realized that she was sucking air between her teeth. Jessica smiled at her discomfort, then lifted her
feet onto the sofa and tucked them underneath herself. It was

usually a classic sign of self-comfort, but not with her. With her it was dominance, and Karen had never known someone to feel comfortable enough to do it in her office before. She felt a flash of irritation at the thought of her patient's filthy pumps grinding into the fabric as she shifted around. Would she put her feet on the sofa in someone's home?

Jessica spoke again.

"Let's talk about Adam."

Adam? This was it. This was where Jessica admitted the real reason she was here. Karen attempted to plaster on a poker face.

"Adam?" She was getting so good at keeping her tone neutral in these sessions, she was starting to sound like the speaking clock.

"Huh?" Jessica looked confused. "Who's Adam?"

"You said 'Let's talk about Adam,'" Karen reminded her, but Jessica looked so genuinely puzzled, she wasn't so sure anymore. She could just as easily have been hearing things. *Or losing my mind.*

Jessica shook her head. "I said let's talk about *him.* You asked about my relationship. If anything, it's become more intense. It's like my life with him is real life now, and when he's with his wife, they are the ones having an affair."

Karen couldn't speak; Jessica's words had hit so close to home. And she got the distinct feeling that was exactly how the girl wanted it. She wanted Karen's mind spinning like the last sock in the tumble dryer, barely able to recover from one heart-stopping revelation before she slammed it up a gear.

Karen struggled to regain her composure. It felt as though she was in an interview in which the other person in the room knew exactly what question was coming next but she didn't even have a clue what subject it would be on. She wasn't going to let Jessica make her feel that way—*she* was the one in charge here; Jessica was just a girl. *Just a girl.*

"Have you thought much about his wife since you began talking to me?"

Jessica fixed her with steely eyes. "All the time."

"And what do these thoughts involve?"

She shifted around on the sofa, making Karen feel uncomfortable just watching her.

"Different things. Sometimes I imagine that she grows a backbone and leaves him. Sometimes I imagine she comes to where I work and confronts me, hits me or screams at me or something. Other times I imagine confronting her. Telling her what her husband has been doing just to see the look on her stupid face. Last week I fell asleep at my desk and imagined taking that screaming bundle of shit and puke away from her and hiding him, just to watch her panic."

Karen was less alarmed at these statements than she was at the rest of Jessica's behavior. It wasn't uncommon for her to hear similar things on a daily basis. Most people had some kind of disordered thoughts: that fleeting image of punching your boss in the face because he'd just called you an idiot, or screaming at the woman who'd just pushed in front of you in the supermarket queue. What separated them from the Ted Bundys of the world was the knowledge that they wouldn't act on such thoughts. Jessica Hamilton was trying to scare her. It was the why she couldn't figure out.

"And how do you feel after these thoughts?"

Jessica looked down at her thumbnail, picked at the loose skin around the cuticle. "Guilty. I mean, who has those kinds of thoughts? I felt terrible after that last one, really I did."

And that's what separates us from the psychopaths, thought Karen. Guilt. Fear that our thoughts define who we are, when in reality it's only our actions that matter.

Jessica glanced up suddenly, looking Karen dead in the eyes. "And something else."

"What else, Jessica?"

"Excited. When I thought about hurting her, I felt excited."

- 32 -

ELEANOR

Eleanor froze, her mind taking a few seconds to process what her eyes weren't seeing. The space where she'd left the car just a few short minutes ago was empty, as though she'd never been there. Panic rising in her chest, she scanned the other vehicles; they were all still there, exactly as they had been when she'd pulled in. No traffic wardens stood waiting to write her up for parking in the wrong spot (a spot she'd parked in a million times previously), no police officers crowded around her silver people carrier ready to quiz her about why her child had been left alone in a car park. Not one other person was anywhere in sight.

Her legs refused to move, torn between running towards where her car quite clearly wasn't and running back inside and screaming the school down. Her heart threatening to pound through her chest, she stood helplessly on the spot, praying this was some kind of joke or a stupid mix-up. At last she turned towards the school.

"My car!" She threw herself through the door of the office. Mrs. Fenton looked up from her book. "My car's been stolen. Call the police!"

"Calm down, Mrs. Whitney. I'll call them. Why don't you sit down and I'll make you a cup of tea."

"My son is in there! Noah . . . he's in the fucking car!"

Mrs. Fenton's smile froze on her face and she grabbed for the phone, punching at the nines so fast she nearly knocked it flying. As she spoke to the operator, Eleanor paced the office, panic obscuring her thoughts. What should she be doing? Should she be outside, running around the streets screaming?

"Mrs. Whitney, they need to speak to you. Stay calm, the police are already on their way; they just need more details. I'm calling the head teacher now and activating our missing child procedure."

Eleanor nodded numbly and took the phone. The operator asked her various questions and she answered without thinking, things she'd have struggled to remember that morning suddenly surfacing as though she had them written in front of her. Town & Country van, silver, seven-seater, only five in use, DU54 FUP, all doors locked, only one spare key at home. They kept her on the phone until she saw two police cars pulling through the front gates of the school, the way she'd done herself only twenty minutes earlier, two officers in each. As she placed the receiver back in the cradle, her shaking hand misjudged it and it fell to the floor.

The head teacher, Mr. Newman, a small, bald man with his spectacles on his head, was at her side in seconds. He motioned to the police officer who had trailed in behind him. "This is PC Edwards. I was just telling him we have people scouring the perimeter of the school looking for anything or anyone suspicious. There are two people in the car park taking down number plates that don't match the ones we have on record for staff in case the perpetrator dumped their own car to return to later. It's more likely—"

"Thank you for your help, Mr. Newman." PC Edwards looked at Eleanor kindly. "If you could just take me through exactly what happened, Mrs. Whitney."

He listened patiently as Eleanor spoke, the words practically falling from her mouth in a verbal machine-gun spray.

"I was only in here five minutes, maybe slightly more, but definitely no more than ten."

"So which was it, do you think? Five, or ten?"

"Well, probably closer to ten, by the time I'd seen Toby off and waited for Mrs. Fenton to return to the reception."

Georgia Fenton had the good grace to blush, but Eleanor didn't much care about her embarrassment at that moment. If she'd been in the fucking office, instead of having a fag . . .

"Wait, weren't you outside?" She turned, taking a step towards the now-frightened woman. "Did you see anyone there? Was there anyone around my car?"

"I . . . I wasn't out the front," Mrs. Fenton stammered. "I was round by the kitchens; I came back through the school . . ."

"Sir?" The female police officer who had arrived with PC Edwards gestured with her head for him to follow her.

"What, what is it? Have you found him?"

"Yes, ma'am, we've found your car, with your son inside. He looks fine; he was still fast asleep and very much unaware of the fuss he's caused. We had to smash your front window to get to him; he woke up then."

Relief coursed through her so fast that her knees gave way and she leaned back against the wall for support. "Where is he?"

"Well . . ." The woman looked between Eleanor and the other officer. "It was still in the car park, ma'am, parked around the side, just out of sight of the doors. One of the teachers writing down number plates saw it. We would have found it sooner, but we assumed you'd checked the car park yourself. . . ." She looked embarrassed at their oversight, but all Eleanor felt was confusion.

"What? Why would someone steal my car and park it in the car park?"

"Well, that's the thing, Mrs. Whitney, there's no sign the car was broken into. The doors are still locked and no windows were broken."

Eleanor didn't have time to work out what had just happened. She needed to get to her son, to pick him up and never put him down again. Without another word, she ran towards the corner of the car park where a crowd had gathered.

"Noah! Give him to me." She held her arms out for her baby

boy, practically snatching him away from the police officer who was cradling him to his chest.

"Mrs. Whitney, is there someone we can call for you, someone who can come and sit with you while we try and clear up what's gone on here? We need to decide if Noah needs any medical attention, and if, um, if you're okay to . . ."

They needed to know if she was crazy. Hell, *she* needed to know if she was crazy. Right at that moment, all eyes on her, she thought she might very well be. For the first time, with Noah safe in her arms, she noticed the individual faces of the teachers who looked after her son on a daily basis, people she saw every day, laughed with on sports day and parents' evening. They were regarding her with fear and suspicion.

Her first thought was Adam. He was her husband and Noah's father, but she just couldn't face the phone call to tell him how much she'd fucked up. She wanted things to be back the way they'd been when he chose her to be a mother to his precious son. When she was solid and dependable. When she wasn't crazy.

"Karen," she said, pulling her phone from her pocket. "Karen Browning, please."

- 33 -

KAREN

Karen pulled into the car park of Toby's school, the same school that she, Eleanor, and Bea had attended what seemed like a lifetime ago. A police car was parked haphazardly near the front doors, but apart from that, there was no sign that anything untoward had happened. Karen looked around for Eleanor's car, but it wasn't in sight.

"Karen!"

As she walked into the reception, Eleanor threw herself towards her friend, baby Noah in her arms. She looked smaller than Karen had ever seen her look, her face red and puffy, streaked with tears. She folded them both into her arms, ignoring the police officers who were sitting on the visitors' chairs.

"What's happened, hun?" she asked into Eleanor's hair. She held her at arm's length to look at her properly. She looked terrible, her clothes crumpled and not entirely clean, dark purple circles under her eyes.

"Someone stole my car with Noah inside! I mean, they moved it." She dropped her head and fell silent. "I don't really know what I mean, but I think I'm in trouble."

Karen looked over at the police officer who had stood to greet her, a middle-aged woman whose dull brown hair was pulled into a stern ponytail, though her face looked kind enough.

"What's happened here? Have you found out who took my friend's car?"

The woman shot a look at her companion, a young male totally unequipped for dealing with hysterical females.

"Mrs. Browning?"

"Dr. Browning."

"Of course, I'm sorry. Could we maybe talk outside?"

Karen glanced back at Eleanor. "Will you be okay? I'll find out what's going on and take care of this."

Eleanor looked reluctant to let her go now that she had a friendly face in the room, and Karen wasn't surprised. Someone had stolen her car with her son inside! Why were they treating her like the criminal? She touched her friend's arm reassuringly before following the female officer outside.

"Dr. Browning, I gather you are Mrs. Whitney's psychiatrist?"

"I'm *a* psychiatrist; I'm not *Eleanor's* psychiatrist. Eleanor doesn't need therapy. She needs a good night's sleep."

"Okay, well, we're trying to determine if Eleanor is all right to take her son home."

"She's just shocked. Wouldn't you be if you'd had your car stolen with your son inside?"

"That's just it, Dr. Browning, Eleanor's car wasn't stolen. It was found in the car park, where she left it. Just around the corner from where she was looking."

That was when it dawned on Karen the seriousness of the situation Eleanor was in. Not only had she left her son in the car where she couldn't possibly see him from the doors of the school, but she'd then forgotten where she'd parked the car and sparked a manhunt for Noah and an imaginary car thief.

"Okay, so she forgot where she'd left her car and panicked; that could happen to anyone. Especially anyone with a three-month-old baby. And perhaps she shouldn't have left Noah, but if she hadn't forgotten where she'd parked the car, she wouldn't have been out of sight for long."

The policewoman sighed. "Look . . ." She hesitated.

"Karen," she offered.

"Look, Karen. We're not worried about Eleanor's safety, or the safety of her son. It's an easy mistake to make, and as you say, she panicked—I'm sure I would have done the same." Looking at her, Karen thought that probably wasn't true. "We just wanted to make sure she wasn't going home on her own in a state, to dwell on what's happened here and make herself feel worse."

Karen let out a relieved breath. "Thank you. I'll take her home; I'll look after her."

"But . . ." Oh Christ, Karen hated that *but*. "I wouldn't be doing my job if I didn't inform someone at social services what happened here."

"Is that really necessary? You said yourself it was an easy mistake."

"Yes, and I do believe that. However, if something were to happen to Eleanor or her son, it'd be my neck on the line. They're going to want to have a quick chat with her, just to check everything is okay. She needs to be prepared for that."

"Fine." Karen turned to look back at where Eleanor was sitting, clinging on to Noah as though someone might walk in at any second and take him away from her. "Of course you need to do your job. Just let me take her home and prepare her."

"That's exactly why we called you. Support your friend, Karen. I get the feeling she needs that more than anything at the moment."

"What did they say?" Eleanor asked as they walked across the car park to her damaged car. "Are they going to take Noah?"

Karen shook her head. "They said it was a simple mistake, but they have to let someone at social services know. It's part of their job."

Eleanor looked as though she might burst into tears again. "I knew it. I knew she hated me, that female one. She looked at me like I was shit on her shoe."

Karen stopped and turned to face her full on. "She doesn't hate you; she was worried about you. Why did you park so far away, Els? When you had to leave the car?"

"I didn't park there." Her voice was low and urgent. "I had to pretend I did to get them to stop treating me like I was mad, but I know, Karen, I parked exactly where I always park. Toby will tell you. I could see the car from the school."

"But you didn't see anyone move it?"

"I was waiting for that bloody secretary to finish her fag. I went into the reception, but I was only gone for a few minutes! Someone did this to make me feel like I was losing my mind. I swear, Karen, you've got to believe me."

"I do," Karen promised, and the look of relief on her friend's face told her it was the right thing to say. "I'll look after you. I promise."

- 34 -

ELEANOR

O h, come on, Eleanor, who the hell would want to steal your car to move it fifty bloody yards? It doesn't make any sense! And how could you be so fucking stupid as to leave Noah unattended? What if the car really had been stolen?"

"It *was* stolen, Adam; you're not listening to me!" Eleanor tried to keep her voice low to avoid waking Noah, but she could feel panic rising in her chest again. "You heard Toby! He told you we'd parked close to the school!"

What he'd actually said, under close questioning from both Eleanor and Karen, and with a shrug of his shoulders, was that he was "pretty sure" they'd parked in their usual spot. But it had been a long day, his friends had all been talking about the police coming to school to arrest his mum, and the shine had been taken right off his amazing project. Once again Eleanor was the bad guy, and she could tell he was in no mood to jump to her defense.

"Toby doesn't remember what he had for breakfast," Adam snorted. "Assuming you remembered to give him breakfast."

"What's that supposed to mean?"

His face was bright red from the effort of not yelling, but despite his quiet tone, his words tore at her chest. "You've not exactly been yourself lately, Els. You always seem so frazzled; you lose things on a daily basis; you don't know if you're coming or going. And now this . . ." He waved his arm. "We need to decide what we're going to say when social services turn up."

"What do you mean, what we're going to say? I'm going to tell them the truth. Someone moved the car, Adam, whether you believe me or not."

He sighed. "I'm not saying I don't believe you, sweetheart; what I'm saying is that it sounds pretty unbelievable. And if it sounds unbelievable to me, it's going to sound crazy to them."

She flinched, and to his credit, he noticed.

"I'm not calling you crazy, Els, I just think you should tell them you made a mistake. Surely that's going to sound better than some conspiracy theory that someone's out to get you?"

Eleanor nodded, defeated. He was right. What she was saying sounded crazy. And she believed it a hundred percent, which meant *she* was crazy. But there was no way she was going to let anyone else know that.

35

Tell me about the day Eleanor lost Noah . . .

I've told you what happened. She insisted afterwards that it was a mistake. That she'd forgotten where she parked.

Did you believe her?

It didn't seem like her. And she was so insistent when I first got to the school that she'd parked in her normal space—I believed her then, so I didn't know what to believe when she changed her story. She'd been so distracted, so unlike her usual self.

Where were you when the police called you?

I was at work.

The police said you arrived very quickly.

They said it was urgent. Are you going to arrest me for speeding?

It was important to you to get to Eleanor quickly. To be there for her.

Is that a question?

Would you disagree?

No. Wouldn't you want to get to a friend who had lost her child?

But you didn't know that at the time.

I knew it was urgent. That was enough.

Didn't you ever worry about putting your friends' needs before your own? Leaving work at their slightest call, getting embroiled in their squabbles?

Not at all. They needed me. It's what any good friend would do.

At your age? Some would say they are adults now, old enough to take care of themselves . . .

Well, they aren't. They needed me.

And now? Do they need you now?

I think we're done for today.

36

From my vantage point behind the large tree outside the gates I watched Eleanor's car enter the school. I waited as it came to a stop in its usual spot and watched Eleanor climb out. Toby got out of the front passenger side, then hauled his project out, nearly letting it topple to the ground under its own weight. I'd considered moving it close to the log burner in their front room when I'd spied it through the window last night, letting the heat melt the plastic tubes and rendering the hours they had spent on it useless, but I was glad I hadn't now. Toby's disappointment at his mother's carelessness would have been nothing compared to Eleanor's confusion at losing her car, the panic I could imagine in her eyes when she returned with the baby to find they had no way of getting home. But it turned out better than I could have imagined. Because when Eleanor left the car to help Toby carry the project into the school, she gave a furtive look around before locking the car door with Noah still inside.

For a second I considered abandoning the plan. Stealing the car was one thing—I had Eleanor's spare keys and it would only take me a few seconds to move it once she was safely out of the way—but stealing Noah . . . that felt like it was going too far.

But I might not have to actually steal the car for the plan to have maximum effect. What if I just moved it? Even if Eleanor spotted it straightaway, those few seconds when she realized it wasn't where it was supposed to be would be enough, all the more so now she'd been stupid enough to leave her son in it. I had to move fast, though; if she just dumped the project inside the front doors, she might return quickly and I'd be seen. I had no explanation ready for that eventuality, but crossing the car park and slipping the key into the lock, I knew I would think of something.

Sliding into the driver's seat and turning the key in the ignition, I could feel the adrenaline surging through my veins. All I had to do was ease the car slowly around the corner of the school to the far side of the parents' parking. I threw a glance at the corner of the school. No sign of Eleanor anywhere. I should get out, make my escape now, but my attention was drawn to the sleeping baby in the back, his breathing gentle and silent. He looked so still and peaceful—how was it that this tiny human being was able to reduce a grown woman to the blubbering, stressed-out mess that Eleanor was becoming?

I reached out a hand to stroke his cheek. It would be so easy to uncouple his straps and lift him from his seat. I could hold him close, snuggle into that warm body. I could show him what a mother should be like: not a resentful, harried shell but someone who would give him everything he needed; someone who would never let a man control her life so completely that she would become useless without him; someone who had no need of another person's love to make her feel real, rather than a ghost who disappeared when her husband wasn't looking.

My fingers fumbled with the clasp of the straps, a big red button that was damn near impossible to push in all the way. I knew in that instant that my mind was made up. I was taking him away from all this negativity and betrayal. He wouldn't grow up a spineless, cheating worm of a man like his father, or married to a needy control freak like his mother. His future would be defined by who he was, not by his fucked-up family.

And that was when he started to stir, his eyes fluttering, his eyeballs rolling back and forth in their sockets, fighting wakefulness.

From beneath his pacifier came a low moaning noise. I froze. It was like waking up from a dream, one that you desperately wanted to fall back into but you knew the moment was gone. My senses returned. I'd been too long as it was; my luck had been stretched thin, and if I wasn't careful, it would snap like overloaded elastic.

Without waiting to see if he woke, I shoved open the car door and jumped out, throwing it shut behind me. Clicking the central locking system and cramming the key back into the pocket of my hoody, I jogged back to my tree to wait and watch.

- 37 -

KAREN

How did it go?"

Karen had put her next client on hold to sneak in a phone call to Eleanor between sessions. She'd had her visit from social services that morning, and as far as Karen could tell, she seemed a lot less anxious about it than she had the other day.

"It was fine." Eleanor sounded distracted but calm. "I told them the truth: that I'd made a stupid mistake and I'd learned my lesson. There's no way I'll let Noah out of my sight again. Adam has offered to cut his hours down for a few weeks and help out a bit more here, let me get a bit of rest. Things will be back to normal in no time."

"Do you really believe that?"

"Of course, why wouldn't I? It was a stupid thing to do and I won't let it happen again."

Karen tried not to sound too judgmental, but she failed to keep the tone from her voice. "Because the other day you were convinced that someone had moved your car to try and make you think it had been stolen. Now you're saying it was all your mistake."

"That's because it was. I didn't want to admit it the other day, not even to myself, but I made a stupid decision because I was tired. I must have thought I was parking in my usual spot but parked in a different space. When I came out and couldn't see the car, I panicked, overreacted. It's not a big deal."

It had certainly seemed like a big deal when she had been

hyperventilating into a brown paper bag while Karen had held Noah and tried desperately to calm her best friend down.

"Okay, that's great." There was no point in arguing now that Eleanor had made her mind up. If she wanted to believe it was a misunderstanding, that was fine—it made more sense than the wild story she had concocted on Friday about it all being an elaborate scheme by persons unknown to drive her crazy. "Let me know if you need anything. I have patients all day today, but if you leave a message with Molly, I can call you again between sessions."

"Thanks, and thank you again for the other day. Sorry I was so mental." Eleanor tried to keep her voice light, but Karen heard it crack slightly as she said, "See you Friday."

"Love you." Karen signed off with their usual good-bye, but Eleanor had already hung up.

Karen's last client that morning had been one of her more interesting ones. At the age of forty-two, he'd undergone hypnotherapy to try to find the cause of his issues with food, only to find out that when he was four years old, his mother would alternate between force-feeding him and starving him as a punishment for the smallest slight. Given that his mother had died three years previously, he had no way of knowing if this was a real or false memory, and no way of getting closure. The hypnotherapist had panicked at the implications of the discovery and swiftly referred him to Karen, and they were making slow progress. These were the types of cases she had always wanted to deal with—ones where she could really make a difference to a person's life. That was all she'd ever wanted to do.

Michael arrived after that session to take her to lunch. Karen still wondered how he managed to turn up at the most perfect times, exactly when she needed him, like the proverbial lucky penny. He'd looked amazing, as he always did, and as she leaned into his dark gray suit she inhaled his aftershave, trying to imprint the scent on her mind for when she had to let him go again. The weeks went so much slower than the weekends; it felt like the twelve-month wait for one day of Christmas.

"How's work?" he asked, trying—and failing—to look suave as he wound noodles around his chopsticks and they fell off for the third time in a row.

Karen laughed, motioning to the woman behind the Chinese takeaway counter. "Can we get a fork, please?"

The place had only three tables for a handful of eat-in customers, and the other two were empty, so she had no concerns about being overheard as she answered his question. Michael knew she couldn't go into specifics about her patients, so they had code names for them and their situations. Her professional ethics allowed this game on the grounds that it wasn't any different from all the scholarly articles she was permitted to publish as long as identities were concealed.

Karen nodded. "Mmm, okay. Travis is still referring to me as 'boss' in every other condescending sentence, even though I'm not going to start my training until after Ken's retirement. The high-class Hail Mary was a bit intense this week," she continued, keeping her voice neutral as she referred to Jessica Hamilton. A high-class Hail Mary was a woman who didn't have a real problem; usually they had done something they wanted to get off their chest and used therapy as a confessional rather than a way to explore why they behaved the way they did. Changing their behavior was usually not in the cards.

"She still coming?" Michael nodded his thanks to the pretty young waitress who brought his fork.

"Yep. And she's no closer to figuring out that the reason she hates her lover's wife is because she feels guilty that she's screwing a married man with children." Karen longed to mention Adam's name. *You don't have any evidence. Remember your ethics. Remember your promotion.*

"She sounds like a charmer. I've said it before, Karen, I just don't get your profession. You know the exact reason this woman is beating herself up. Why can't you just tell her?"

"Believe me, I'd love to." She managed to inhale the rest of her beef noodles without any slopping down the front of her beige shirt. "But people refuse to believe that they might be responsible for their own disordered feelings. If I tell her straight, that means admitting she'd have to break up with him in order to fix the problem. Which she has no intention of doing. So she'll come to her sessions and go away convinced that it can't be her head that's screwed up, because she saw a psychiatrist and it didn't fix her." *Or she'll try to find another way to break up Adam and Eleanor.*

"Which works out better for Robert, I guess. How would he make his money if you fixed all his clients after one session?"

"And how would you cope with me having to be a kept woman?"

Her voice was lighthearted, but Michael's face darkened and neither of them said any more.

"How's Eleanor doing after the other day?" he asked when he finally spoke again.

Karen grimaced. "I called her this morning. She sounded weird."

"Weirder than usual?"

"Ass. You don't have to be so mean about them, you know; they love you."

He smiled. "Who doesn't? You know I like them; I just think it's weird how they depend on you so much. I mean, you're all in your thirties; shouldn't they be grown up by now? Eleanor's got two kids of her own and she's still dragging you out of work at the slightest problem."

"You don't get it because you're a man. Men don't have these kinds of friendships. They rely on me because that's what they've always done, since we were five. I'm the stable one. The sensible one. The one they can depend on."

"And what happens to you when they don't need you anymore?"

"That's not going to happen," she replied confidently. "They will always need me."

- 38 -

BEA

Her eyes were closed but she could smell cut grass and river water. The breeze cut through her hair and she pumped her legs harder to push herself farther out over the water. The branch that the rope was twisted around creaked dangerously, and Bea's fingers gripped the swing until her knuckles turned white. She hadn't thought too much about how she was going to get herself back onto the riverbank, not stopping to consider when she pulled the dirty old tire swing towards her that her thirty-five-year-old body might not be as supple as her sixteen-year-old one had been. Not to mention that it was long summer days she and her friends had spent down here rather than cold autumn ones, and their forays onto the rope swing had nearly always ended by plunging into the refreshingly icy water. These days the water just looked filthy and scum topped; it was a wonder none of them had caught E. coli.

She often came back here—although she didn't tell the others—to relive those carefree teenage days, the days before any of them realized that bad things could happen to them.

They had found this stretch of river, with its mud platform reaching out into the water and hidden by trees and bushes higher up the bank. You had to climb or slide down a narrow gap in the greenery to where half a dozen teenagers lounged on the dirt platform passing around two-liter bottles of cider and lemonade bottles filled with whatever concoctions they could steal from their parents' alcohol cupboards. The sun cast leafy patterns on their denim shorts as they took turns boosting each other onto the rope swing—it had been a branch back then; no sophisticated tire setup back in the old days—screaming as they tried to make the leap back onto dry land and failed.

And then there was the last time . . .

They hadn't visited the river in years; they had grown up, moved on. All three of them were at university, and the boys they used to try to impress had long moved on to other girls, less educated and more fun. Adulthood had grown on them like a tumor, almost undetectable at first, and by the time they had noticed, it was terminal. They had returned home for the summer after their first year—the year Bea's life had veered so far off course it had formed a permanently new track—with an urgency that none of them could explain. It was as though with the knowledge that bad things could happen to good people the veil had been lifted from their eyes and they were fighting it with everything they had. That summer they reverted to their adolescent selves: they took Saturday-evening jobs in bars and spent their days sunbathing in Eleanor's parents' garden or down by the river. The nights they had off work were passed in an alcoholic haze, just the three of them this time, wearing jeans and Doc Martens rather than as little as they could get away with. It felt to Bea as though her friends knew she was spiraling out of control and they had two choices: try to pull her back, or stick as close to her as possible while she fell.

"Who's going to boost me?"

The sun had begun to push its way through the clouds now, and Bea let her legs stop pumping and leaned back gently. She could hear the words as clearly as if she'd spoken them out loud only seconds ago, pictured herself stumbling to her feet, dusting off her jeans, and attempting an upright position.

"Come on, we can't come to the river and not swing. Who's going to boost me?"

Karen had opened one eye lazily, looked at her, and closed it again.

"Don't be ridiculous. You can't go swimming with the amount you've had to drink."

"You're wrong." Bea poked a finger in the direction of her friend, despite Karen not being able to see her. "That's eating. You can't go swimming until two hours after you've eaten. There's no law against drinking."

"Karen's right, Bea."

But Bea wasn't listening. She was already wrapping the rope around her wrist, wedging her foot against the tree to boost herself up. She'd grown taller since the last time she was there, slimmed down a bit too, and it was easier than she'd expected to pull herself onto the seat without any help. It wedged uncomfortably between her legs, and the branch above groaned almost theatrically, but she'd consumed too much alcohol to notice, or maybe just too much to care. She kicked her legs against the tree, sending herself spinning out over the river, closing her eyes to stop the alcohol surging back up into her throat. When she opened them again, the world was a blur of green and brown, the trees, the bank, the river itself all merged together so completely that she couldn't pick out what was what anymore.

That was how her whole life felt, the days blurring into night, alcohol blurring the edges until every day seeped into the next, indistinguishable from the last. Even Karen and Eleanor didn't know the extent of how much she'd been drinking, how her tutor had told her that if she came back in the same state she'd left in, then she might as well not bother. The nights of meaningless sex with faceless strangers—anything to block the face of the one person she couldn't erase. Sex to her had become a sport, a game of control. You couldn't steal something that someone was giving for free. If her friends knew what she'd been doing, they'd have staged an intervention, pulled her out of university, forced her into counseling, or worse, reported her to the police. But she'd become very good at hiding the pain.

The crack of the seat had sounded to Bea like a gunshot echoing out over the river. She was falling almost before she'd registered what was happening, the force of entry and the temperature of the water sucking the air from her lungs. Instinctively her legs kicked towards the surface, and she pulled in gulps of air. Shock gave way to relief and she was about to wave to the two women screaming on the bank that she was okay when the current yanked her under.

Every time she'd thought about the incident since, it was with humor. She and Eleanor laughed—remember when you were so wasted, you almost drowned in the river?—but Karen refused to talk about it ever again. Karen had never gone back to that stretch of the river after Eleanor had waded in to drag her friend onto the bank, pounded on her chest weeping until Bea had coughed up half of the river and half of her stomach contents at the same time. Maybe it was because she'd frozen—capable Karen frozen stiff in an emergency. She'd never been in the river all the time Bea had known her, but after that she treated it almost as an enemy, a physical being that had conspired to remove her friend from the world. In time, as they realized, they stopped talking about the episode in front of her.

Bea herself had been scared enough to spend a few days off the alcohol, and then it had seemed less necessary to get blasted every day. She'd gone back to university more or less sober and spent her Saturday nights catching up on what she'd missed the year before rather than searching for something she couldn't put into words and trying to prove to herself that she was unaffected by her experience. She had allowed herself to heal. So in a way the river had been the third best friend she'd ever had. It had saved her life once and maybe it would work again, she thought now as she pulled herself upright and launched herself into the water.

- 39 -

KAREN

The café was practically empty when Karen arrived. She was surprised to find that she was first—normally the other two were already there, heads together conspiratorially, when she walked in. She ordered them a pot of tea and three slices of chocolate cake and pulled out her iPad to check if any emails had come through in the fifteen minutes since leaving the office. It might sound crazy, but she had to keep herself busy—unfilled time was thinking time, and she couldn't bear too much of that. There was nothing new in her inbox, so it was a huge relief when she saw Bea walk in, dragging a handbag the size of her car. She wore tennis shoes with her fitted pencil skirt and frilly-necked blouse and still looked unsteady on her feet. Her face was pale and her eyes dark rimmed.

"Jesus, Bea, you look like crap," Karen remarked as Bea threw her bag on the seat next to her and sat down opposite.

"Thanks." Bea scowled. "Like I needed telling. Four people have asked me today if I need an ambulance. Do I seriously look like I'm about to drop dead?"

"You look a bit like you already dropped dead and someone propped you up in your chair. Still not sleeping?"

Bea ignored the question. "Has anyone ever told you that honesty isn't always the best policy?"

The waitress came over with their cake and Karen pushed a slice in front of Bea, who looked as though she might throw up at the sight of it.

"You have got to be kidding. Can I just get three pints of blood and an IV, please?"

The poor girl couldn't seem to figure out what the joke was or how to respond. Looking like a deer trapped in headlights, she stared at both of them in turn before muttering, "I'll just bring your tea," and scuttling off towards the kitchen.

"Seriously—no patience for the flat-earth society today," Bea grumbled, pulling her phone out of her bag and placing it on the table. "And enough with the living dead comments, you're not exactly looking sparkling yourself. What's up? Were you and Michael up all night doing the horizontal tango?"

Far from it, although she was right about Karen not looking herself. She didn't feel it. She'd been thinking about Jessica Hamilton every quiet second since their last session, her words, her animosity towards the woman she prayed wasn't Eleanor filling her head like honey in a jar, sticky and unyielding with no room for anything else to seep in.

"I wish," she muttered. She didn't want to mention Jessica to Bea. Her friend didn't have Michael's gift for discretion—she'd want to know every last detail, and Karen wouldn't even know where to start.

"Where's Eleanor got to?" She was relieved when Bea changed the subject so she didn't have to. "Have you heard from her recently? I didn't know whether to keep my distance and all that; I didn't want her to think we were interfering . . ."

A convenient excuse for Bea to forget about Eleanor and her problems the minute she was out of sight. It wasn't that Bea was intentionally selfish; she was a good person—the best—and when she set out to be thoughtful, she excelled at it. It was just that thoughtful wasn't a journey she set out on very often these days.

"Did she tell you about what happened with Noah?"

Bea grimaced and nodded. "Yeah, what do you reckon social services will do? Are they going on a list?"

"Most definitely on a list. What did she tell you?"

"That she'd forgotten where she parked the car and called the police. Poor thing must have been out of her mind."

Karen nodded but didn't mention the part about Eleanor swearing blind that someone had moved the car. If Eleanor hadn't told Bea, there was a reason for it and Karen should respect that— although she was dying to ask what Bea thought of the whole idea. Maybe Eleanor was just embarrassed.

"I'm a bit worried that she's showing signs of—"

"Oh God, Karen, you're not going to start the psychiatrist stuff on us again, are you? We agreed."

They had agreed. They'd sat down early in her university days, when she'd perhaps been a little overzealous with the psycho-analysis and got carried away with the jargon. It was hardly something she could help. Psychology excited her: the way the past could account for much of the present, the way people's actions could be examined and understood. People were literally textbook. There was rarely a problem that couldn't be explained by careful assessment of the factors.

But unsurprisingly, Bea hadn't taken well to hearing that her constant need for attention came from being the youngest female child of an overbearing mother and an emotionally absent father. In her own words, she was quite happy with her "fucked-up child-hood" and the person it had made her into, and she'd balked at talking about why her relationship with men was so unhealthy. Equally, she had warned Karen never to mention to Eleanor that her constant mothering of Adam and need for control over every aspect of her life stemmed from the insecurity and lack of control she'd had over her weight issues as a young child. They'd agreed then that Karen wouldn't use her newfound knowledge on her friends, their families or boyfriends—potential included—and they wouldn't tie her to a bag of rocks and throw her in the river Severn.

"Okay, fine. Once she calmed down, she was all right."

Bea scoffed. "I don't believe that. It's more likely that she was as uptight and highly strung as ever, which is hardly surprising given that she has a newborn baby and gets no help from her feckless husband—" She broke off as Eleanor walked into the café and cast a look in their direction. "Jesus, look at her. Remind me never to have kids. Ever."

She plastered on a smile as fake as her nails as Eleanor approached the table. She took one look at the cake and managed a weak smile of relief.

"Thank God for chocolate cake."

There were no two ways about it, Eleanor looked terrible. And not in a frazzled, new mum, "I forgot to put any makeup on this morning and my knickers are inside out" kind of way. This was much worse. A picture of Jessica Hamilton flashed into Karen's mind. *When I thought about hurting her, I felt excited.*

"What's up? Are you okay? Did something happen?"

Eleanor sighed and sat down, putting her elbows on the table and her head in her hands. Her hair was scraped back into a knot secured with elastic bands. Stray strands had escaped and stuck out at right angles to her head, giving her a slightly "nutty professor" look. She lifted her head, and Karen couldn't help but notice the rash of pimples on her chin and the redness under her right eye as though a sty might be forming.

Eleanor made a groaning noise, and for a minute Karen thought that was all they were going to get out of her. After a few minutes of silence, Bea reached out gently and touched her arm, the way you might approach a tiger at feeding time.

"Els? Tell us, we might be able to help."

Eleanor shook her head and put it back in her hands. "I doubt it." Her voice was muffled, but Karen could still hear the exhaustion. And something else, something that sounded like defeat. A knot of panic formed in her chest.

"Try us."

Eleanor looked up, her eyes struggling to convey a message Karen couldn't quite understand.

"I just feel as though I'm not in control of my life right now," she said slowly, as though she was choosing her words very carefully. "I realize I'm probably just being paranoid, baby blues or whatever, but it feels like there's something going on, some outside force that I'm not aware of controlling things. I don't know how to put it, but the more I think about it, the more it explains things. I keep feeling like there's someone watching the house . . ."

Karen fought to control the gasp that threatened to escape from her lips. She understood now the look Eleanor had given her before she started to speak. She was thinking about what Karen had told her about Adam, and her warning to be careful, but she obviously wasn't ready to tell Bea about it yet. Karen didn't know why, but if she were to hazard a guess, she'd say that Eleanor didn't want to say the words out loud in case acknowledging that her husband might be having an affair made it real somehow.

"And then there was my car being stolen. . . . I just feel as though I'm going crazy."

Bea leaned over and lowered her voice. "You're sounding pretty crazy right now. I thought you said you forgot where you parked it."

Eleanor sighed. "I convinced myself at the time that it must have been that, but now I'm not so sure. Or maybe I'm trying to convince myself there's someone else involved because I can't bear to think that I might just be screwing things up on my own. Me and Adam barely talk to each other, we're both so tired; Toby thinks I only care about Noah. Everyone seems to be irritated by me all the time and all I wanted to do was my best. My stupid business idea has gone out of the window and my house is only clean one day of the week. I don't know how to fix things, so maybe I'm blaming someone else so I don't have to shoulder the responsibility."

Karen took a breath. If she was going to tell them her suspicions about Jessica, she had to do it now, but she'd never broken patient confidentiality before and it was a big thing for her. Yet she could hardly ignore what Eleanor had just said.

"Look, Eleanor, I don't think you're crazy. I'm going to tell you something now that you cannot repeat to anyone." She glanced around the café to check there was no one close enough to over-hear. "I have this patient. I can't tell you her name, but I think she has developed some kind of fixation on me, which might extend to one or both of you as well. I can't say any more, really I can't, but I think you should both be very careful, keep an eye out for anything unusual happening."

She sat back to gauge their reactions; both of them just looked confused.

"But I thought you said . . ." Eleanor stopped. "Why would we be in danger if she's obsessed with you?"

"Obsessed how?" Bea asked.

"I really can't say any more. Anything more specific could get me into real trouble. But you don't have to worry; I'll fix this. I'm not sure how yet, but I'll deal with her."

"You two are nuts," Bea announced. "Obsessed stalkers, car thieves— you sound like you're in a soap opera." She turned to Eleanor. "Shit stuff happens all the time. Do you remember when you first had Tobes and you went into town to do a ton of stuff and came home and had forgotten to do every last thing? Was someone stalking you then, whispering forgetting spells in your ear?"

"Well, no . . ."

"And you filled the car up with petrol instead of diesel, and you had that break-in, and—"

"All right," Eleanor interrupted. "I get it, you don't have to de-tail every time I've failed in my life."

Bea turned to Karen. "No offense, Karen, but if you had any evidence this girl was dangerous, you'd have done something about it by now. So obviously you don't have any. Now, I don't know about you two, but I don't fancy spending my days looking over my shoulder for someone who is going to hide my toothbrush and use up all my loo roll just to make me think I'm losing my mind. I have enough going on to keep me awake as it is. Don't give me that look, Karen. I love you, but you're dramatizing and poor Eleanor is sleep-deprived enough to take you seriously. You should know better. I bet you a hundred quid this girl is totally harmless."

- 40 -

KAREN

My patient today, the one who is sleeping with the married man?" Karen had tried to say it casually, but Michael had given her that look, the one he got when she was obsessing over something he didn't understand. He let out a small sigh, one you'd barely notice unless you knew it was coming. After the reaction she'd had from Bea that afternoon, though, she desperately needed to speak to someone about what was going on. For a minute it had looked as though she had an ally in Eleanor, but after Bea's little speech, she'd shut down and hadn't wanted to talk about it anymore. She'd texted Karen after they'd left to ask if her crazy patient had anything to do with what she'd told her about Adam. Karen had just replied, *As soon as I can tell you more I will. Xx*

"Yes?"

"She let slip the name of the guy today. I don't think she even realized she'd said anything and she denied it straightaway but I know I heard it."

"But you're not allowed to tell me. Patient confidentiality and all that, yes?"

"Well, she didn't say his last name, so I don't see how you could identify him."

"Then what's the newsflash? There must be something in this or we wouldn't be discussing it instead of . . ." He gave her the look, and she knew exactly what he'd rather be doing.

"No, you're right." She snuggled in closer to him and he ran a warm hand over her hip. "It's just a bit weird, because his name is Adam."

"And that's weird because . . . ? Wait, let me guess, *Cosmo* voted men with the name Adam least likely to have affairs with mentally ill young women?"

"Stop being an ass. I just thought it was strange because, y'know, Eleanor's Adam?"

Michael grinned, and she knew that he wasn't about to agree that Jessica must be sleeping with her best friend's husband based on his name.

"Well, you do know that Adam is one of the least common names in the UK, don't you? For example, when I was growing up, there were only three Adams in my whole year group, only about eight or nine in the entire school. With odds like that, I can understand your suspicion."

Karen was sure she was supposed to feel silly at his acute observational humor, but all she felt was annoyed. *Tell him the rest . . .* "His wife has just had a baby. Eleanor has just had a baby."

"In that case I really don't know what to say." Michael tried to keep his face straight, but she knew he wasn't being serious. "Because I feel like I just used up all my good sarcasm on the name thing."

She wanted to tell him about seeing the two of them together, but Eleanor hadn't believed her and she couldn't be bothered to try to convince Michael as well. He clearly couldn't care less about her concerns over Jessica Hamilton. She knew unequivocally what she'd seen and what was going on, but it didn't seem that anyone else was going to take her word for it.

"Oh, piss off." She tried to turn away, but he grabbed her arm and pulled her into his chest.

"Hey, don't be like that. You're not going to huff off over some patient. I've told you before, you need to let go once you leave the office. That place will be the death of you."

"Okay, you're right." She knew she sounded sulky. She felt sulky.

"Come on, don't be grumpy." Michael lifted his feet up onto the sofa and pulled her in close to him. *Clean, socked feet,* she thought, grimly picturing Jessica Hamilton's dirty pumps. She leaned back and let herself relax into the solid warmth of his chest. "She just sounds like a woman scorned to me."

"Scorned?" She lifted her head and turned to look at him. "Why would you say that? Like a loser in some kind of battle?"

He gave her a look that told her she was putting words in his mouth and about to start an argument with herself over them.

"I shouldn't be talking about her anyway. I've already said more than I usually would. This one freaked me a little, I suppose."

"Well, you shouldn't let it. She'll use you as her sounding board for a few more weeks and move on. You can't let it leave the room with you."

He was right. She'd had plenty of other patients who had issues far greater than Jessica Hamilton's, and she'd never let them bother her before. The rule of the practice was that they did not get involved personally. If they started to feel like they couldn't maintain a professional distance, then they brought it up at the weekly meeting and someone else took the case or counseled them through it. It might sound weird, psychiatrists getting counseling, but in their field everyone had regular sessions to ensure their minds were fit for purpose. But this just didn't feel like something she could bring up with the other partners. She imagined they would feel as Michael did: that this woman was no different from any other patient—less threatening to her mental well-being in fact—and she should be able to handle her. They might even suspect she had another reason for being so uncomfortable with the way the sessions were going, a deeper meaning behind her misgivings. They were professionals, after all.

There was perhaps one person she could talk to—Robert. She

had to speak to someone; if they even suspected someone might come to harm from one of their patients, it was professional suicide to stay silent. Plus there were her notes. Notes she couldn't amend after the fact; all their documents marked the time and date of any amendments, in the interest of full disclosure should any . . . *problems* arise.

She didn't know why she didn't tell Michael about how she really felt—as though Jessica knew her. Like it was personal between them. Maybe she was still denying the possibility; maybe saying it out loud would mean she had to act on it.

"You're right," she murmured, not wanting to continue the conversation anymore. "I should make dinner."

- 41 -

ELEANOR

The screaming hadn't let up all morning. Every time Eleanor had put Noah down for even a second, he'd turned into a wailing siren, desperate to alert the authorities to his abandonment. Toby hadn't helped; he'd eaten so slowly, she was certain his cereal bowl was getting fuller every time she checked, and it was seven forty-five and neither child was dressed.

The problem was that she just didn't feel as though she could concentrate on anything. The wheels in her head were turning in slow motion, the hamster on strike. It was almost as though her brain had been scooped out and someone had filled her whole head with Bubble Wrap. Every now and then she would just find herself unmoving, staring straight ahead with no clue what she was trying to achieve.

She should have prepared everything last night, she knew that. She'd promised herself that when Noah came along, she would prep the school runs the night before, be organized. That was almost laughable now. Adam was out nearly every night, and by the time both boys were settled, all she wanted to do was fall into a Xanax-induced sleep. Thank God for her magic pills.

She'd put Noah into his bouncer to try to figure out which day it was and what Toby needed to take with him, the things she'd have to get done while she was out of the house, Toby's birthday presents to buy and party invites to write, but the baby just wouldn't stop screaming. Toby had the TV turned up loud to try to hear his programs over the din, and the drums pounding a rhythm in her head hadn't let up since she'd woken at six.

"Mum . . ." Toby started. Fearing that she might just sit down on the floor and start screaming herself, Eleanor held up a quivering hand.

"Just a sec, Tobes, Mum's popping to the loo." She disappeared through the door and took the stairs two at a time—the fastest she'd been able to move all morning. Closing the bathroom door behind her, she sank down against the wood, Noah's wailing still audible from downstairs but at least at a tolerable volume.

Pulling out the bottle of pills that had been rattling invitingly from her dressing gown pocket all morning, she palmed two and pushed them into her mouth greedily, swallowing them without any water. She leaned her head back against the door and closed her eyes.

Okay, come on, she told herself silently, it's just a school run. Noah doesn't even need to be dressed; just shove his coat on and he's ready to go. As long as Toby has his lunch money and last night's homework in his bag, he'll be fine. Does he need his gym clothes? What day is gym? Send it with him anyway, better to be safe. . . .

She willed herself to stand up, but her legs were so heavy and it was so comfy there on the floor, so much quieter than downstairs. If only she could stay there, even for five minutes . . .

The banging on the door was urgent, followed by cries of "Mum! Mum! Mum!" so loud that Eleanor's eyes flew open. Had she fallen asleep? How long had she been sitting there? Not more than a few moments, surely, yet Noah's cries sounded more anguished and Toby's voice was desperate. She pushed herself to her feet, firecrackers going off inside her head, and threw open the bathroom door.

"Noah's fallen out of his bouncer!" Toby shouted, and ran down the stairs before she could respond.

It was pure panic that moved her legs to follow her son. She was on autopilot—get to Noah and she could deal with what had happened later.

As she flew into the living room, Noah's cries turned to hysterics. He was lying on the wooden floor, facedown, unable to push himself up, legs flailing wildly. She dashed to his side, scooped him up, and pressed him tightly to her chest, terrified to look at the damage he'd done.

"What happened?" She turned to Toby, desperate to have someone to blame other than the real person responsible—herself. The stricken look on Toby's face halted her in her tracks.

"He just fell," Toby said. "He wasn't strapped in. You were ages."

"I wasn't age—" Eleanor glanced at the clock: 8:13. She'd been in the bathroom nearly half an hour. "Oh Jesus. Come on, Tobes, get your uniform on. Don't look like that. Your brother's fine and you're going to be late for school."

She prized a calming Noah from her chest and checked his head for bruising. An angry red mark that would surely produce a lump the size of a golf ball was forming, but his eyes were alert and he was no longer crying. She'd just have to keep an eye on him for the rest of the day.

How had she allowed this to happen? Holding back tears for the sake of Toby—who to his credit had gone upstairs to dress without another word—she smiled at Noah and jiggled him around a little on her hip to calm him down. Now she just needed to calm herself down. Her heart was pounding so hard, she was surprised it hadn't come through her pajamas, and she was shaking uncontrollably.

How she managed to get dressed and both of the children in the car she didn't know, but she didn't feel in any fit state to drive anywhere. Should she call Adam? Karen? Bea? Both women would be on their way to work now, and her mum couldn't drive. Calling Adam would mean admitting to the Xanax, admitting that their children had been in the care of a zombie for days.

"Mum, are you okay? We're going to be late."

Eleanor slid down the window and let the cool air hit her in the face. There was a refreshing autumn bite to the morning that made her feel more awake, more alive. She turned on the motor and put the car in gear. She was fine, she could do this—she'd driven the route a thousand times before.

"No problem, dude, we're on our way." She pulled away from the curb, paying extra attention to the road, muttering instructions to herself to compensate for the fuzzy emptiness where her brain should be.

- 42 -

BEA

On her birthday last year, Eleanor had sent Bea a card that had a black-and-white picture of two women talking. "There's this new machine at the gym," one was whispering. "It does everything. Kit Kats, Mars bars . . ."

That was pretty much how Bea felt about the gym. The vending machine was the only machine she had a meaningful relationship with, and yet still she was there, night after night, her mother's words shoving her forward more effectively than any hand would.

"Us Barker women have to watch what we eat, or we have to exercise, and I haven't seen you do either lately. Unless you want to end up with thighs like Auntie Gemma, you need to stop the take-outs and junk food."

But that hadn't really been an option, given that Bea was the type of person to eat a Mars bar on the treadmill, so she'd upped her workouts to four times a week and had been pleased to notice a difference. Now she had less time to eat.

"That's just Mum's way." Fran laughed when Bea told her what their mother had said. "You're lucky you're the baby. If I'd told her to bugger off like you did, I'd have been up shit creek and she'd be chasing me with the paddle."

Bea grinned at the thought of her mum chasing her thirty-nine-year-old sister around the garden with a paddle. Fran was right, though: the house rules had relaxed somewhat by the time Bea had come along, or maybe it was that her mum had just been too busy to notice how many of them she was breaking. The disparity in their upbringing had been part of what had stopped them becoming close until they were old enough not to care anymore. Bea had always felt that her mum showed more interest in Fran than in her, and Fran had complained tirelessly that her little sister was the golden child who could do no wrong. Nowadays, though, sibling rivalry had given way to the kind of friendship you only got from sharing bath times and meals every day for the first ten years of your life.

"You know damn well Mum loves you more." Bea continued the age-old joke they'd both become accustomed to. "Otherwise why would I have been named after Nanny Beatrice when you get to be named after Nanny Frances? I could have totally rocked a Frankie. The cool name was wasted on you."

"Well, if you've finished sweating, I was thinking maybe I could pop over. Rich and Lewis are at football, Maisy is at a friend's, and I don't have anything better to do."

"Gee, thanks, Fran, how can I resist an offer like that?"

Talking to Fran these days was easy. Sometimes easier than talking to her friends. Bea wasn't sure if it was her or them, but sometimes it just felt as though they were finally outgrowing each other. When she was with Fran, she didn't feel like some kind of failure because she wasn't settled down with 2.4 children and an amazing job. Fran was older, and the fact that she'd had kids before her baby sister was to be expected—plus her children were little shits and made Bea glad to be a lonely old spinster. Bea loved her friends like sisters, but whenever she saw them, she was just reminded of her fledgling career and total lack of a serious relationship. So many times she'd thought about telling Fran what had happened to her all those years ago, and yet she still couldn't bring herself to say the words—to relive it all again, or worse, to find she was wrong about her sister and see the judgment in her eyes.

"So Eleanor is a bit mental recently because of all the baby hormones and something to do with feeling like she's losing her identity." Fran had barely made it through the door before her sister had started to let off steam. "And Karen's been talking about a patient who creeps her out. She's taking it too seriously, I think. I'm sure she knows me and Els are hiding something from her—we're so rubbish at this whole surprise party thing. Plus she's been going on at me about this guy at her work. I let her give him my number ages ago but he hasn't texted yet. Maybe he thinks *I* sound like a loser."

Fran raised an eyebrow. "Still trying to set you up with boring misfits?"

Bea grinned. "Yup. I've tried telling her I'm happy how I am, but it's like she doesn't believe I can be satisfied and single at my age. . . . She's only looking out for me. She just wants me to be happy."

Fran shrugged. "Hmmm. I'm sure she is, it's just . . ."

"Just what?" Bea's tone of voice was sharper than she'd intended.

"Forget it," Fran replied quickly. "Sorry."

"No, seriously, what?"

"Well, it's just that Karen's looking out for you always sounds a bit like trying to change you. I know she's your best friend, but is there seriously anything wrong with you being single?"

It was normal that Fran didn't understand; it was a mystery to everyone how the three women were still friends after so many years. Despite the fact that they were from a relatively small town, most of the people they'd gone to school with had nothing to do with people they knew from back then, let alone still counted them as their best friends in the world. Their history was the cement in their walls. Still, with how she'd been feeling lately, her sister's words struck a chord.

"Karen doesn't mean anything by it. It's just what she does. She likes to feel that she's helping in some way. And this guy doesn't sound too awful. . . ."

"Okay, point taken. So he's a psychiatrist?"

"Um, no. He works in IT."

Fran's head snapped up and Bea laughed. "Don't give me that look. Michael works in IT and it hasn't done Karen any harm."

Her sister frowned.

"What? What do you have against Michael? You always make that face when I mention him."

Fran shook her head. "I don't trust him, Bea. I can't put my finger on it, but I just don't trust him at all."

- 43 -

KAREN

Karen knocked twice on the door and waited. She didn't think she'd ever been this nervous about speaking to her boss in all the years he'd mentored her. She liked to think that Robert liked and respected her, but the practice had and would always come first with him, which made what she was about to tell him particularly difficult.

"Yes?"

She pushed open the heavy oak door and stepped in, letting it close quietly behind her. Posh doors; there were too many jumpy people in this building as it was without loud bangs causing hysteria.

"Karen, hey. How are you? I couldn't help noticing how quiet you were at yesterday's meeting."

She walked over to his sofa and sat herself down like a patient, despite the fact that Robert was behind his desk. He took his cue, and got up and went over to sit opposite her. His sharp, manly scent followed him; expensive, the kind that made a woman's blood pump regardless of the man wearing it. Not hers, though. He'd worn it for years; she'd become immune to it. It reminded her of late-night study sessions, cramming for exams she was sure she would fail despite looking confident to the outside world. She could honestly say that Robert was the only person who'd seen her panic; she'd let down her defenses and he'd seen the real her.

Now he sat back, watched her in silence. She wondered what he saw. Did he notice her hair, splayed out around her head in frizzy waves, a stark contrast to her usual glossy straight style? She'd been up so late the night before that she was certain her eyes held dark purple shadows, stark against her too-pale complexion. She must have looked a complete mess, but Robert didn't pass comment.

"I think I have a problem with a patient."

She watched him stiffen slightly, a movement that most people would have missed.

"What kind of problem?"

"A conflict of interest."

He relaxed a little, leaned forward, placed his elbows on his knees. "You know them personally?" This was a problem he could deal with. She knew he was just going to suggest they move her patient to another psychiatrist, shuffle things around. As if it were that straightforward.

"Not exactly. She's conflicted about an affair she's having with a married man. It's possible that her feelings are a manifestation of a deeper issue involving her experiences of relationships, but that's not the problem here. I believe I know the husband. And the wife, actually. It's Eleanor."

"Eleanor the super-mum?"

She smiled. "More like Eleanor the harassed these days. Did I tell you she'd had another? Noah. He's just a few months old."

"And you say her husband's been having it off with one of your patients? Ouch."

"Don't say 'having it off,' Robert, it sounds bloody awful. But yes, I think he's the one Jessica is referring to."

Robert shifted in his seat. "You think? She hasn't told you outright?"

"No, that's the problem. She came to see me about an obsession she has with the wife of the man she's sleeping with. She's been messing with her. Her words."

He was starting to look uncomfortable again; clearly his hopes of a quick fix were fading. Any minute now the vein in his neck would start twitching.

"Messing with?"

"Just little things, she says, making life difficult for her. It sounds as though the poor woman is going to go crazy. And that's the thing: you should see Eleanor. She's a mess, missing appointments, losing things . . ."

Robert frowned. "That just sounds like every new mum I've ever met." Noticing her raised eyebrows, he added, "Yes, I have met a few in my day. Therapy was all the rage for the yummy mummy crowd at one point."

"This is different, Robert."

"It doesn't sound it, Karen. Unless you've got some hard proof that this woman is causing your friend harm, you absolutely cannot take this any further. I know I don't need to remind you of patient confidentiality. I don't think anything you've said suggests a serious threat. Unless there's something you're not telling me?"

She wanted to tell him more, but in truth she didn't have more to tell that didn't make her sound crazier than most of the people they saw every day. Eleanor losing her car with baby Noah inside and swearing blind that someone had moved it. The letter she herself had received. The idea that someone had been outside her house in the dead of the night and a strange *feeling* about this girl, the feeling that she was playing with her, that she had no intention of using her therapy sessions to improve her mental well-being; she just wanted to toy with Karen's. She had nothing concrete on Jessica Hamilton. Should she mention seeing her with Adam? Then he'd ask her if she'd told Eleanor, and she'd have to lie to her boss, or admit breaking the rules. Had she been wrong to tell her friend her suspicions?

"No, nothing."

"I'm not saying you're wrong about this, Karen, but you're

reaching here. You're seeing associations that don't exist and you'll end up doing more harm than good, to your patient, your friend, and yourself."

"You're right." She made to stand up to leave, deflated, let down. She'd expected Robert to tell her that her fears weren't unfounded and to help her find some way through what was going on. She was so sure she'd been doing the right thing. It was like in those movies when you screamed at the helpless woman to get help, *just tell someone!* And the strong male character was supposed to fix things, yes? Liam Neeson didn't tell his daughter it was unlikely she'd been kidnapped and it was just a coincidence those men had put a hood over her head and shoved her into a car. He didn't make her feel like a hysterical female. He bloody helped her.

"Don't go." She froze an inch off the chair and lowered herself back down. "I need to ask you, Karen, is everything all right with you?"

Had he not been listening? Of course she wasn't all right; couldn't he see the state of her? He was the only person in her life—including her lover—to whom she'd admit not being okay, and he'd basically told her she was imagining things. How long had he known her? She'd never been inclined to dramatic overreactions. She'd never tried to find drama where it wasn't. God knows, she'd had enough of the real thing.

"Not really, no," she said. "I've been conflicted about this since I began to suspect that Jessica Hamilton was using me to inflict further damage on my best friend. I'm worried about Eleanor; she's an absolute mess."

"And you feel like this is your fault?"

"I suppose I feel guilty that I'm not there enough for her."

"But if her problems are being caused by Jessica Hamilton and her cheating husband, then there's no way you could be responsible for that."

"No, I'm not responsible for her husband's actions, or Jessica's if that's truly what's going on, but I could . . ."

Oh, he was good. She'd entered her own little therapy session without even realizing. She supposed that was why his name was above the front door.

"I see what you're doing. You're intimating that I'm transferring my feelings about not being there for Eleanor onto my patient in order to assuage my own guilt."

Robert opened his hands in a gesture of surrender. "I should know better than to try and out-psych a psychiatrist. But do you think that might make sense? Don't you think that by assigning blame for Eleanor's inability to cope to an external source, you're absolving yourself of the need to act?"

"You sound like a bloody textbook, Robert, not a friend. And your theory has one flaw."

He raised one eyebrow—something she'd never been able to do and had always been a bit in awe of. Michael said it made him look like the Rock.

"A flaw? Never." He smiled.

"If I'm trying to absolve myself of action, then why is action all I can think about? Why am I constantly wondering what to do for the best?"

"Because you can't bear to leave a friend in need. You are determined to be the one who helps everyone, the one everyone turns to, even when you can see what it's doing to you. Look at yourself. You have a good relationship, your own home, a career that you're set in for life, promotion imminent, and you're falling to pieces worrying about the fact that your friend can't make her doctor's appointments."

"I—"

"You nothing. As your boss and your friend, I'm telling you to go home, take a bath or go for a run or do whatever it is that you do to destress these days, and come back tomorrow with your mind on your patients and nothing else. Do you think you can do that?"

His voice had a warning tone to it, one she hadn't heard before. One that said she'd better be able to do that, or the next step wouldn't be an afternoon off work.

"Of course I can," she lied. But even as he smiled and told her he was there if she needed him, she realized he knew she was lying as much as she did.

- 44 -

KAREN

Karen put down her book, too agitated even to lose herself in someone else's story. There was the usual noise from outside: the shouting of teenagers excited about something and nothing, enjoying themselves and not even contemplating that at 8 p.m. there might be children trying to sleep or shift workers grabbing their precious catnaps. It made her think of her own selfish teenage years, nights on the playing fields with Bea and Eleanor, actually managing for full hours on end to be a normal teenager, happy, unencumbered by her past. She got so good at it that sometimes there would be moments when she'd even forget what had happened altogether, until the tinkling sound of a girl's laugh would shove her back there.

Then they'd discovered cheap cider and she could practically obliterate her memories completely, searching for absolution at the bottom of the plastic two-liter bottle. The only time she wouldn't dream was when she'd been drinking—the only nights she could guarantee not to see *her* face imprinted behind her eyelids. Then there was just the comedown the next day to deal with. Not the normal alcohol shakes—mouth like a moldy sock and mild paranoia—but the screaming reel of memories like a ghoulish episode of reality TV. A punishment for the blissful hours during which her emotions had been numb. She spent so many days locked in her bedroom, tears flooding down her cheeks and the TV so loud that her head pounded to the beat of whatever daytime junk she was using to stop her parents hearing her cry. And every time she would tell herself that the short reprieve wasn't worth the pain she would go through the next day. That it was getting harder and harder to pull back the Karen she was trying to be.

But she never stopped. Not until the evening it had all gone wrong. The evening that had brought her past rushing up to meet her present. The others, Eleanor and Bea, laughed about it now, albeit nervously, with the giddy hindsight of people who had never had the worst happen to them, but she couldn't bring herself to join in, because to her it was more than just a silly near miss. To her it was fate trying to send her a message: *Look what happens when you try to be normal. Look what happens when you try to forget. You can never forget, because when you do, people die.* She stopped drinking.

She lifted the remote and flicked on the TV, her fond memories tainted now, like a child who had picked up a pretty stone to find a wood louse stuck to the bottom. It seemed to her sometimes that on darker days, usually when Michael was away, she couldn't allow herself to think about the past at all. And she definitely couldn't allow herself to contemplate the future. So it was easier to distract her mind with trashy TV and sudoku. Those things were much less painful.

- 45 -

KAREN

Karen prepared for her next session with Jessica Hamilton as though she were going into battle. Her conversation with Robert yesterday had rattled her—if she was honest with herself, his comments about how she was dealing with things scared her. Every time she closed her eyes she could picture Jessica sitting with her dirty pumps on the sofa and the look on her face when she'd been talking about the pregnant woman stuck in the rocks. *"They blew her up."*

Well, if Jessica thought she was going to get the better of her, she could think again.

She checked the clock: fifteen minutes to go before their session, plenty of time to pop to the toilet. Nerves. *Get a grip,* she told herself.

Molly was at her desk when she passed, and Karen smiled a greeting without trusting herself to speak. The toilet was empty, but as she sat in the stall she heard the door swing open and someone throw themselves into the cubicle next to hers. Seconds later there was the sound of sobbing.

Unable to ignore what was obviously a woman in distress, she spoke.

"Molly?"

Their PA was the only other woman on this floor, and Karen's assumption proved correct when she heard her squeak a reply. She flushed the toilet, washed her hands, and waited for Molly to appear. When she did, her eyes were red and her face was glistening with tears.

"What's wrong?" Karen asked, putting out a hand to touch her shoulder. "Has something happened at home?"

Molly shook her head and looked embarrassed.

"It's Joe," she said, not meeting her eyes but instead pretending to fix her hair. "I think he's going to break up with me. He says he needs space."

Karen couldn't help thinking that it wouldn't be a terrible thing if Joe did break up with her, but that wasn't going to help the situation. The only time she'd met Molly's boyfriend he'd been sprawled in the waiting room and had barely looked up when she'd opened the door and introduced herself. He spoke in a language made up of single syllables and grunts, and Karen wondered how this weedy, barely literate man could be the cause of so much grief for pretty, clever Molly.

"Men always say that," she said instead. "Then they almost never want it when they've got it. If he loses you, he loses the best thing in his life and you get to demand an extra-large bouquet of flowers when he realizes his mistake. And jewelry."

It sounded like something Bea would say, which was a lot more helpful than what she herself usually came out with at times like this. She would always snap into psychiatrist mode, start talking about defense mechanisms and the primal need for men to spread their seed to as many women as possible in order to increase their chance of procreation. Molly seemed satisfied with the Bea answer, and Karen excused herself before she was expected to hug her.

The waiting room was empty. Jessica's session was still five minutes away and she hadn't arrived yet. Grabbing herself a cup of coffee, Karen pushed open the door to her office, ready to assume her poised, "in control" position before Molly brought her client through.

Jessica was standing behind Karen's desk, studying the only

personal photograph Karen had in the entire room. The shock that reverberated through her almost forced the coffee cup from her hand. Black liquid sloshed over the side, dripping down onto the carpet.

"Jessica."

Jessica hadn't looked up as Karen had entered, but she did at the sound of her voice. She smiled, not looking the least bit embarrassed at being found in Karen's office, touching her personal things.

"Dr. Browning. There was no one outside, so I came straight in. Nice photo."

She held it up to indicate what she was talking about, then replaced it on the desk. It was a four-by-six photograph of Karen and her friends, linking arms and beaming widely at the camera. They'd been on a hen weekend in Ireland, and shortly after the picture was taken, they'd argued about no one booking a taxi and had to walk the two miles to their hotel, getting lost twice on the way.

"I'd rather you didn't let yourself into my office, Jessica. And please do call me Karen."

She gestured to the sofa, hopefully looking much more composed than she felt. How did this girl always manage to get her on the back foot? Jessica shrugged and sat down without apologizing.

"How have you been since our last session? Any more headaches?"

She braced herself for a reply about her obvious and boring question, or an interrogation into her feelings on prisoner-of-war camps, but Jessica just shook her head.

"No, they seem to be gone at the moment. I'm feeling much better. Maybe these sessions really are helping."

Karen couldn't imagine how. They'd gone around in circles avoiding talking about the real reason Jessica was here and seemed to have made no progress on her feelings towards her affair. In fact the only thing they appeared to have achieved was to turn each session into a sparring match, Jessica trying to goad Karen into losing her composure and Karen trying not to scream.

"Is there anything you'd like to talk about today?"

Jessica looked down at her feet, and Karen felt sure she was about to lift them onto the sofa again.

"Maybe I could talk about my past? Isn't that what I'm supposed to do? Explore the reasons for my screwed-up relationships with men?"

This was territory Karen was familiar with. "If that's what you'd like. Is there anything that comes to mind?"

She nodded. "My father cheated on my mother a lot when I was younger."

No real surprise there. Daughter following mother into an unhealthy relationship with the opposite sex, repeating patterns of destructive behavior, sabotaging attempts at a real relationship by choosing someone inappropriate. Textbook.

"Do you remember how you felt about that? As a child, it must have been hard to see your mother going through that kind of pain."

"I guess. I think I blamed my mum more than anything. If she'd just been prettier or funnier or made more effort, my dad might have wanted to be at home a bit more. It was almost like she gave up trying to keep him."

Karen almost felt like shouting "Aha!" but stopped herself in time. The suspicious part of her told her this was too easy, almost as if Jessica had come in here ready to reveal the reason for her problems. She shook away the feeling, desperate to cling to the thought that they might be having some kind of breakthrough.

"And why do you think your mum reacted the way she did to the affairs?"

"I have a sister. Had . . . had a sister." She gave a nervous little laugh. "I never know whether I'm supposed to say have or had— you know, like when a woman's baby is stillborn and she still says she has a child. As if it belongs to her even though it isn't alive any-more. It's like that. I used to have a sister. She's dead."

Karen's hand froze halfway to her coffee mug and she could have sworn she actually felt the blood stop pumping through her veins.

There's no way she could know, she told herself, desperately trying to keep her composure. There's no way she could know what happened to Amy. It's a coincidence. Lots of people have sisters who die. When she looked back on the session, she would be furi-ous at herself for letting her guard drop, for believing Jessica was just another patient, even for a minute.

"What happened to her?" Her voice didn't quaver, didn't give away any of the thousand emotions she was feeling. And yet Jessica Hamilton studied her as though it had.

"I don't want to talk about it," she said, her own voice devoid of any emotion. "Do I have to talk about it?"

"No, not if it's too difficult for you," Karen replied, the voice inside her head screaming, *Yes! Yes, you do have to talk about it!* She wanted to know what had happened—needed to know what had happened to Jessica's sister. If there was a sister. Everything that came out of Jessica's mouth seemed to be aimed straight at Karen's heart.

"Good. Let's talk about him, then," Jessica said. "Or more im-portantly, her."

"Your lover's wife?" Karen was spinning again, her mind strug-gling to deal with the constant change in direction.

"Yes, her. I think she's going mad."

Karen managed to successfully pick up her coffee cup and bring it to her lips. The coffee was cooler than she'd have liked, but she needed the pause to slow the pace of the session, bring it back under her control. By making Jessica wait for her reply, she was giv-ing herself time to appraise the rapid turn in the conversation while hopefully making her patient feel a little less like she was running the show. The fact was that she couldn't manage to separate in her mind the woman Jessica was talking about from Eleanor. Now that the idea had entered her head, it was as clear as if she'd come straight out and said it.

"What do you mean by mad?"

Jessica frowned. "You know, crazy. Batshit. Lost it. Mad."

"And what makes you think that?"

She threw her an "I thought you'd never ask" smile. "She lost the baby."

Karen couldn't help the sharp intake of breath as Jessica finished the sentence, and the iron ball of dread that had been forming since this morning seemed to grow in size and roll over in her stomach.

"What do you mean, lost?" she asked. "As in 'I can't remember where I put my keys' lost?" She winced inwardly at her flippancy—an annoying habit she'd picked up from years of friendship with Bea. In reality she was in no way feeling flippant.

"Exactly like that. She was at the grocery store and she forgot where she'd parked the car. She phoned the police and everything. He told me about it, said she was losing her mind."

Forgot where she parked the car. Called the police and everything.

"At the grocery store?" This was it. This was where she came right out and asked her if she was talking about Eleanor, demanded to know why she was targeting her like this. What was the worst that could happen? Jessica would deny it was her husband's best friend she was sleeping with and they would carry on with this game of cat and mouse. Only then she would know Karen was onto her. That she was winning.

"And you didn't have any part in what happened to her son?"

Jessica scowled. "How could I? She forgot where she parked the car—I can't make the stupid bitch forget things. Can I?"

It was a challenge, daring Karen to suggest she might have

moved the car—daring her to ask more questions. Except Karen didn't need to ask; she knew that Eleanor hadn't forgotten where she'd parked the car. She knew it had been taken. What she didn't know was why Jessica was here, taunting her with talk about madwomen and dead sisters. What did she know?

Karen leaned forward, her elbows resting on her knees, and looked Jessica square in the face.

"Let me ask you, Jessica, if you could speak to this woman, if you could just walk up to her on the street, what would you say?"

Jessica considered this for a second—this question she hadn't planned for or rehearsed, this break from "How does that make you feel?"

"I'd tell her that she doesn't deserve any of it, any of what she has. And that I'm going to take it all away from her, and there's nothing she can do about it. That she will know what it feels like to lose everything she holds dear. And when she asks why, I'll tell her that someone did the same to me once upon a time, and this is my revenge. This is my turn to be someone people remember. And by the time I'm finished, she will never forget me."

Does that strike you as strange now, now that you have some perspective?

I don't think I understand your question.

You were certain that Jessica Hamilton was sleeping with your friend's husband. She had changed calendar entries to mess up Eleanor's appointments, she had stolen her child and had her investigated by social services. Yet you were convinced that this woman was out to ruin your life.

Touché. Maybe at that point I was internalizing the problem. Making it all about me as Bea would sa—would have said. But given what's happened since, what we know now, I'd say I was pretty accurate in thinking Jessica Hamilton's grudge was with me.

Would you? I mean, considering what happened, I'd say you got off lightly.

I'd say you know jack shit.

I'd like to talk about your relationship with your mother.

I bet you would. That's what we do, isn't it? Look for where the problems begin; start with childhood.

Do you have a problem talking about your childhood?

I just don't see the point. We both know what happened.

Do you speak to your mother now?

Occasionally. We don't have the closest of relationships, if that's what you want me to say. Not everyone does; there's nothing unusual about that.

Your phone records show you spoke to your mother the night before your first session with the woman you call Jessica Hamilton. The call lasted thirteen minutes. What did you talk about?

I can't remember. Can you remember every call to your parents? That was a long time ago.

And yet you've only spoken to her once since, and only for four minutes. Did you argue with her the night before your session?

Maybe. Like I said, I don't remember. All families argue.

Not like yours, though, do they, Karen? Not all mothers say the things yours said to you. The things she's been saying to you since you were a child.

My mother is troubled. You can understand why.

I can, certainly. Can you?

I'd like to take a break, please.

- 47 -

KAREN

She was still shaken up by the session the next day, so much so that she canceled her other patients and declared it a "personal growth" day. She knew it sounded a bit tree-huggy, but they were encouraged to take these days often, although they were never encouraged to ditch patients for them. She put it in her calendar and hoped no one would realize it was a new development. In the last month she'd started to take more days off, and longer lunch breaks, and it was only a matter of time before one of the others noticed and started questioning her commitment. Ten years of dedicated, devoted service, working through lunch and writing notes at weekends, would count for nothing if one of the others made a complaint—her money was on Travis.

They were present in the office for their personal growth days, although they were encouraged to use their flexitime to take longer lunches, come in later and leave earlier, to set up a relaxed atmosphere while they reflected on their professional development, any challenges they were confronting, and any goals they were setting for the future. They were expected to keep diaries of their time over these days for a development portfolio. Needless to say, on this particular day she did none of that. What she did instead was spend the entire morning searching the Internet for any sign of Jessica Hamilton.

Her absence was what made her so conspicuous. There were

plenty of Jessica Hamiltons on Facebook, Twitter, and LinkedIn, but none of them resembled her Jessica. When she drew a dead end at every avenue she tried—Google Images, even Myspace in case sixteen-year-old Jessica had been more Internet savvy—she searched their patient records for more information.

She'd already read the referral notes before their first session and not come up with a whole lot of information, but now, given Jessica's behavior and her unusual fixation on Karen's personal life, the lack of detail in her records was alarming. What they did have, however, was an address. She was so shocked to see it there, a nice, normal-looking address, just as you would expect to see in patient records, that the first time she skimmed through she missed it completely. Once she'd seen it, though, it was impossible to unsee. A quick Google search told her nothing except that the house was not in the phone book and belonged to a Mrs. Beadle—probably a landlady, as she didn't expect Jessica would own her own home at her age. It had been purchased in 1996, when Jessica would have barely been out of nappies.

You are not going round to a patient's house, she told herself even as she was picking up her pen to write the address down on a pad next to her computer. It would be madness. Career suicide if Jessica complained. Which was probably exactly what she wanted. Karen had no idea why, but by this point she was utterly convinced that Jessica Hamilton was trying to ruin her life.

By a quarter past twelve, she couldn't stand being in her own company anymore. There was no one at work she could talk to without risking them thinking she wasn't fit to do her job; Michael didn't want to know about some whining rich girl who thought she had a right to complain about a situation she had brought on herself—besides, he thought Karen's problem with her was more than just an issue with a creepy patient, and the last thing she needed was someone psychoanalyzing *her*. She needed to talk to someone uncomplicated, someone who would just listen, maybe crack the odd inappropriate joke, but who knew her well enough to know that if she was concerned, there was a good reason for it.

When Karen walked into the office, Bea was surprised to see her. Maybe she thought something had happened to Eleanor, because the first words out of her mouth were "Is everything okay?"

"Everything is fine," Karen replied, trying to stop her hands working over each other, straining not to pick at the skin around her thumb the way she knew she did when she was agitated. "I just wondered if you wanted to go to lunch? My treat?"

Bea's brows rose in suspicion. "Shouldn't you be at work?"

Karen tried a smile, forcing a casual air she didn't feel. "Even psychiatrists have to eat."

Bea nodded and checked the time on her computer. Then she turned to the girl at the desk next to hers. "Do you mind if I head out for lunch? I'll only be an hour or so. I'll divert my phone to reception."

The girl nodded without even looking at them, and Karen knew this show was for her benefit: Bea wanted to make it look as though it mattered if she was in the office. The sad truth was, she could have left and not returned for the rest of the day and it only would have been noticed when it was her turn to make the tea. That was the problem with big organizations: no one was as indispensable as they liked to believe.

"So, where are you taking me?" Bea grinned as she slid into the passenger seat of Karen's car, but she looked nervous, on edge.

"Let's get a sandwich and park," Karen suggested, ignoring the disappointed look Bea threw her.

Karen stopped outside a park across the road from Subway and they collected their lunch in tense silence, like lovers after a jealous row. When they were back in the car, Bea unwrapped her sub, then turned to look Karen in the face.

"What's this about? Is it Eleanor? Because I can see how stressed she is at the moment. I just don't know what to do to help her."

"It's not about Eleanor." Karen picked at the corner of her wrap, not feeling like eating in the slightest. "Well, I suppose it is, in a way. It's about Adam. I think he's having an affair."

Out of the corner of her eye, she saw Bea's hand freeze halfway to bringing the sub to her lips. "Excuse me?"

"I think he's been sleeping with one of my patients."

Bea had always known never to ask about Karen's patients. She knew she was working with Susan Webster, one of the most high-profile cases their county had ever known, but she'd respected the boundaries of her work and her professional and personal ethics and never asked for a single detail of any case. She would know that for Karen to be even saying as much as she already had, she wasn't messing around.

"Has your patient said that? Has she said 'I'm sleeping with your best friend's husband'? That's weird, right?"

"It's not that simple." Through the windscreen Karen could see the whole of the park. She watched as a small boy, wrapped up against the elements, hauled himself up the steps of the slide and sat stubbornly at the top, refusing to move until his mother laughed and clapped at his achievement. Then he threw himself down, his mother still acting as though it was the most amazing thing she'd ever seen. Had her mother been like that, once upon a time? Had she thought that every step Karen took, every slide she climbed, every new word she uttered was some amazing feat? She was sure life must have been like that once, but she had no memory of it. No recollection of a time when she wasn't someone to be either snapped at or ignored.

"You know you can talk to me about anything, Karen."

"It's not that I don't want to tell you, Bea, it's that I don't know where to start. I've already spoken to Robert about this and he basically said I was losing my mind. Michael thinks I'm overreacting. I don't want to tell you just for you to think the same."

Bea looked as though she was going to put her hand on her knee but thought better of it. Karen had never been one for physical contact between friends; she always used to make jokes about her personal space that weren't jokes at all, but now she wished she was the type of person people felt comfortable hugging. Or someone who felt comfortable asking to be hugged.

"I'm not going to think you're crazy. You're one of the most levelheaded people I know. You've met my family, right? Now *that's* crazy."

Karen smiled for what felt like the first time in weeks.

"And I don't have to remind you how confidential this is? You can't tell Eleanor anything, not until we've figured it all out."

"Absolutely."

Karen knew that Bea broke confidences, because she'd broken other people's to tell her juicy bits of gossip countless times—she just had to trust that she wouldn't break this one.

"Okay." She took a deep breath in through her nose. "This client—the one I told you both about the other day who I think has a fixation with me—well, it transpires that she's been sleeping with a married man."

Bea nodded but didn't interrupt—probably in case she changed her mind and stopped speaking.

"Well, like I said before, she said a few things that concerned me." It occurred to Karen suddenly that she couldn't actually tell Bea the things Jessica had said, because Bea didn't know what she herself had done. "Some personal things that led me to think they were a dig at me specifically, rather than at psychiatry and psychiatrists in general."

"Like what?"

Karen went for a "don't push your luck" look and must have hit it, because Bea shrank back slightly and didn't ask again.

"Anyway, she mentioned that she was fixated on the wife of this guy, and that she'd been doing things to make her life difficult. Things like changing diary appointments and hiding letters to make her think she was losing her mind."

"She sounds charming," Bea snorted. "But I'm still not sure why you think it's Eleanor. Just because she missed a couple of appointments . . ."

"There's more. She started talking about the kids. After that thing with Noah, she practically admitted she'd taken this woman's child."

"Whoa." Bea held up a hand. "She said that? Then shouldn't you be speaking to the police instead of me? Even if she's not talking about Eleanor, she sounds dangerous."

Karen sighed. "She's clever. She hasn't said anything that I can use as strong evidence that she's a danger to anyone. It's all so abstract that it's like she's goading me, like she's picked me personally to tell her story to. Then she slipped up and I'm almost certain she said his name, even though she denied it afterwards." She paused, still not a hundred percent sure that she was doing the right thing, giving Bea this much detail. "It was Adam."

Bea let out a breath. "We have to tell Eleanor."

Karen had been afraid she would say that. As much as Bea pretended to understand patient-psychiatrist confidentiality, she wasn't invested in this situation the way Karen was. If she was wrong . . . well, even if she was right, there wasn't a good enough reason to break privilege.

"I tried to tell her Adam might be seeing someone, but she didn't believe me. I couldn't tell her all the details," she added at Bea's frown. "Unless there's a real and proven danger to Eleanor or her children, I can't give her the evidence she needs. That's probably why she was paranoid the other day, and I don't want to make that worse without proof. . . ."

"That's ridiculous! This is your best friend's life we're talking about. Her child and her marriage. You might not understand that—"

The insinuation that none of them understood lives they weren't living angered her instantly.

"What, because I'm not married, I don't know how important a husband is? Unless it's escaped your notice, Bea, you don't exactly have men lining up to sweep you down the aisle either."

Bea looked crestfallen. The remains of her sub fell from her hand and landed on the paper in her lap, a piece of lettuce dropping into the footwell. It was testament to how wound up she felt that she didn't pick it up straightaway.

"I'm sorry." Karen sighed. "That was a horrible thing to say. I've just been driving myself crazy over this. Of course I know how important it is to Eleanor, but the fact is, she said she didn't believe me. And then if J—if my patient found out I'd told her, I'd lose my job. It's probably exactly what she wants; that's why she's telling me all this. I can't believe it would be a coincidence that she sought me out."

"So what can we do? If Eleanor won't believe you and you can't give her the proof you think you have now?" Bea's voice was harder now, with a weary tinge that told Karen she didn't really want to be involved in any of this—or she still didn't completely believe her either. She knew Bea had issues of her own and she didn't court drama the way some people did. This wasn't a sport for her.

"You could try and find out for yourself. Don't look like that, Bea. If you found evidence that Adam was having an affair, then you could tell Eleanor without breaking any client confidentiality. You wouldn't even have to tell Eleanor; you could just tell Adam you knew and he'd probably break it off with this woman himself."

"Wouldn't that just put Eleanor and the boys at more risk? If this woman gets dumped? I mean, if she's obsessed with Eleanor, then getting cast aside in favor of her might push her over the edge of crazy."

"That's where I come in. I'll carry on working with her, and if her mental health deteriorates, I can take the case for breaking confidentiality and going to the police back to Robert. He just needs something concrete to ensure the practice doesn't suffer. This will all be fine. I promise."

The look on Bea's face told Karen that her friend didn't believe her. And perhaps she was right not to.

- 48 -

BEA

Today had started out as a good day. Then Karen had turned up and blown her good mood to pieces with her weird ramblings about Adam having some affair with one of her patients, and now she was confused and worried about the mental health of both of her friends. And the two people she would usually talk things through with were the two people acting strangely.

Throwing her handbag onto the sofa, she made herself some dinner—sausage and beans on toast with a sprinkling of grated cheese and Worcester sauce (food of the gods, her granddad used to say)—and was just about to settle down to season two of *Orange Is the New Black* on Netflix and forget everything for the evening when from somewhere inside her bag her mobile rang.

"Fuck sake," she muttered, her mouth full of hot melted cheese. She'd pretty much made up her mind not to answer when she checked the name on the display. Eleanor. She had only exchanged the odd obligatory *Ru ok?* text message since following her out of the café last week, and given her conversation with Karen today, she really couldn't ignore her now.

"'Lo." She swallowed her food. "What's up?"

"Bea, it's me, Eleanor." Bea smirked. Eleanor did that every time she called, despite the fact that she knew very well that her name would flash up on Bea's screen.

"Is everything okay?"

Eleanor hesitated. "I'm not sure. Look, you didn't send me an email earlier today, did you? From a new address?"

"Nope. I haven't got a new email address." Bea clicked the TV on with the remote. "Why? Is it an RSVP? I thought we were having all those sent to that party email?"

"No, it was from you and it wasn't anything to do with the party."

"But I didn't send you any emails today. What did it say? And if it's not my email address, what makes you think it was from me?"

"It had your name on the account," Eleanor replied. "So it looked like it was from you at first glance. I checked the address and it was slightly different; the E in Barker was a three."

Bea stopped scrolling through the program list. "So what did it say? Penis enlargement? Viagra advert?"

"Have you got your laptop there? I'll send it to you."

Bea resisted the urge to sigh. Eleanor could be so melodramatic sometimes—why couldn't she just tell her what the bloody thing said? All this cloak-and-dagger, and her melted cheese was going claggy.

"Here, let me stick it on now." She booted up her laptop. "So how are the kids?"

"Fine, thanks. Do you have it?"

"It's still starting up. What's up, Els? You know me and Karen have been worried about you the last few weeks. Is there anything I can help with? Can I have the boys more for you so you can get some rest?"

"What's Karen been saying? Don't you think she's been acting a bit weird?"

Bea stayed silent. She knew exactly why Karen had been weird around Eleanor, but there was no way she was going to talk about it now, and especially not over the phone. Eleanor hadn't told her personally what Karen had said to her about Adam, which meant she either didn't believe it at all, or she did believe it and didn't want to talk about it.

"Has she said something to you?" Shit, she'd been quiet too long. "About what happened with Noah? About what I'd thought happened?"

"Huh? I'm just getting my email up. What did you say?"

"It's okay, I'm just rambling. Do you have it?"

"Yeah, here, I've got two from you." Bea's cursor hovered over the first email.

"I only sent one. When was the other one sent?"

She checked the time stamp. "Midday. The second one's from your AOL account and the first one's from your Hotmail."

She double-clicked on the second email and a new window opened.

"I don't have a Hotmail account. What does it say?"

"Calm down. I'm opening the one you just sent."

The picture appeared bit by bit on the screen. "It's Karen coming out of the Bellstone. Why would anyone send you this?"

"Look at the time stamp on the photo," Eleanor instructed. Bea looked at the digits in the bottom left-hand corner of the photo.

"Two forty-five a.m. Doesn't the Bellstone close the bar at eleven? I didn't think they did lock-ins."

"They don't. She must have had a room. Why would she book a room twenty minutes from home?"

Bea almost shrugged before she realized Eleanor couldn't see her. "I don't know; maybe she and Michael had a sexy night away."

"Look at the date. Two weeks Saturday. Michael was working away that weekend."

Bea blew out a breath between her teeth. "You think she's having an affair?"

"I don't know, but it looks odd, right? And if you didn't send it, who did? What does the other one say? The one that's supposedly from me that I didn't send you this afternoon from a Hotmail account I don't have."

"Just a sec . . . it's loading . . . Jesus, this computer's been slow lately."

The picture on the email downloaded. *Shit.*

"Eleanor? I'm going to have to call you back."

She hung up before Eleanor could protest and stared at the screen, where their friend's boyfriend stood with his arm around another woman on what was clearly their wedding day.

It was after our first session; that was when I knew. She thought she had the measure of me, that she could hide who she really was, but there isn't any hiding, not from someone like me. A killer in plain sight—what do they say? A wolf in sheep's clothing. When you wear a mask yourself, you see others more clearly, you know what to look for, the signs that someone is imitating. We were more alike than she would ever be willing to admit, both so desperate to be normal and loved for who we really were, not who the world thought we were. The only difference was that I was onto her. I knew how dangerous she was.

I don't know when I realized I was going to have to kill her. It wasn't a conscious decision, contrary to what they think now. I don't know what surprised me more: the realization that I was going to have to kill again or finding that the idea didn't completely repulse me.

- 50 -

ELEANOR

Humming to herself, Eleanor made sure the bathroom door was fully closed before turning on the shower full blast and cranking up the heat. The video monitor rested silently at the side of the sink, Noah's tiny frame filling the screen. He looked so angelic when he slept—which was mainly in the day—no trace of the demon child who emerged every night between the hours of eleven and two, screaming relentlessly until his face was so red it was almost purple, and Eleanor didn't think she could take any more.

He'd been asleep for only ten minutes, which meant Eleanor had at least twenty minutes to have a shower and make herself a cup of tea, maybe even some toast if she was lucky. As she stepped into the bath, the warm spray hitting her exhausted body, she groaned with pleasure. This was one of the small luxuries she'd taken for granted before she had children, and had come to take for granted again as Toby had got older.

As she relaxed against the warm water, she thought about the email she'd received, the photo of Karen leaving the Bellstone. Was Karen cheating on Michael? If she was, it certainly wasn't any of her business, but the part of her that needed to be involved in every aspect of her friends' lives was dying to know. It wasn't like she could come out and ask her. And it wasn't as though she wasn't busy enough with her own life to worry about how Karen spent her Saturdays, or to think too much about why Bea had slammed the phone down on her and not answered her calls since. Instead she considered what she had to do next week. Tuesday—credit card bill and Target catalog to be paid. Thursday—was that the twenty-seventh or the twenty-eighth? She picked up the shampoo and took her time rubbing it into her scalp, enjoying the luxury of lather, rinse, repeat.

Definitely the twenty-eighth. Which meant Noah had the health visitor at eleven and Tobes had football after school. She didn't have to pick him up until four thirty, but she had to remember to have his uniform ready in the morning to save having to make a mad dash to the school with it like last week.

She reached for her leave-in conditioner just as she heard Noah stirring in his crib. Bugger. Washing the soap from her face, she scanned the instructions:

Comb through damp hair from root to tip. Leave for two hours and rinse. Repeat once weekly. If anything needed some TLC, it was her hair. Pregnancy had given it a new lease on life, making it shinier and thicker than ever, but since Noah had been born it was finding its way down the plughole more often than not, and she often went a week without remembering to wash it. The baby was barely moaning; plenty of time to lather this in, and she could have it rinsed and dried before picking Toby up from school. The other mums would probably report her for kidnap, she'd be that unrecognizable.

She finished rubbing it through just in time for the full-scale crying fit to begin. Looked like tea and toast were off the menu until her mini waste disposal unit had had his fill. At least she had her wonder pills.

"Okay, baby, Mummy's coming." She wrapped her hair in a towel and grabbed her dressing gown. Water had pooled at the side of the bath and her foot went skidding out from underneath her, nearly sending her ass over tit onto the bathroom floor. She grabbed at the glass shower screen, steadying herself. "Good save," she muttered.

Noah stopped screaming the minute she picked him up and snuggled into her bare shoulder. She managed to pull on some pajama bottoms while still holding him and lay down on her bed, guiding him to her breast with one hand and turning on the TV with the other. Her eyelids fluttered; she struggled to keep them open while Noah suckled, but they felt so heavy, and closing them felt so good. On the TV she could hear the talk show host introducing their guest, a woman who was being plagued by ghosts. As she drifted off, she heard the woman talking about her life turning into a living nightmare.

She woke with a start, freezing cold and her scalp on fire. The show's theme song was playing its closing notes—she must have been asleep more than an hour. Horrified, she looked down at Noah. His eyes were closed and she placed a hand on his chest to check his breathing. *Oh, thank God,* she thought when she felt his tiny rib cage move. He snorted against her bare breast and she moved gingerly, turning herself to the side and swinging her legs off the bed, placing Noah in his crib as though he were made of glass.

She checked the time on her phone: 12:34. This hair stuff had only been on half an hour longer than it said on the tube—surely it shouldn't sting this much?

Stepping back into the shower, she flipped on the water and stood under it before it had even warmed up. She ran her hands through her hair, desperate to get the conditioner off. When she lifted them away from her scalp, she reeled in shock at the clump of hair stuck to her hand.

Flicking it into the bath, she watched as it swirled into the plughole, too big to go down. She'd been losing hair for weeks—it was normal after pregnancy, apparently—but never this much in one go. She ran her fingers through again and the same thing happened, another thick clump of blonde hair coming away in her fingers. Frantically she clawed at her scalp, watching her once-beautiful hair falling away and powerless to stop it. Feeling her knees go weak, she sank to the bottom of the bath, the water beating on her head, and burst into tears.

- 51 -

BEA

Shiiiiiit, what did you do?" Bea could picture her sister loading plates into the dishwasher, cradling the phone under her chin, and trying to decide what to cook for tea. She felt a little thrill that she was sitting on the grass outside the local library enjoying some rare autumn sunshine.

"Nothing. Absolutely bubkes."

"What, you didn't tell Eleanor? I definitely thought you'd tell her when you found out."

"God, no! She's very clear on what she thinks about women who sleep with married men. Wait, what do you mean, *when I found out*?"

"Oh. Um, well . . ."

"You knew! Didn't you?"

There was a silence that screamed guilt and then a small squeak from Fran. "I suppose I did."

"How? And why didn't you tell me?"

"Rich had a job at a house. Turned out it was Michael's. He didn't realize until he saw pictures of Michael with his family all over the place—wife and three kids. He recognized him straightaway; it wasn't long after we'd been for that meal with you all. I didn't want to tell you because if Karen hasn't told you, then she doesn't want you to know. I have tried to warn you. . . ."

"Why would Karen tell me? You're not suggesting she knows, are you?" A thought occurred to her. "Did you send me those pictures?"

"Oh yeah, because I have time to go undercover as Joey Greco. If I'd wanted you to know, I'd just have told you. I was waiting for Karen to do it."

"You keep saying that; what makes you think she knows?"

"She's not stupid, Bea. He's probably got a dent in his finger where his ring usually sits. Rich said you should have heard his poor wife. Talking about her wonderful husband who sacrificed so much working away all week so they could afford nice things. Made him feel sick, he said."

The hairs pricked up on Bea's arms, despite the lack of any breeze. Her phone beeped in her ear, and she held it up so she could see the screen:

Where ru? Need u. Please come. Xx

"I gotta go, Fran, Eleanor has just texted."

"Do you think she knows?"

Bea shrugged. "God knows. Guess I'm about to find out."

- 52 -

KAREN

When Karen pulled up outside Eleanor's beautiful mid-terrace house, Bea was just getting out of the taxi. She hung back as she waited for Karen to pull on the hand brake, jump out, and click the central locking.

"What's going on?" Bea eyed her somewhat suspiciously, as though she was surprised to see her there; maybe she'd expected that Karen wouldn't be able to leave work.

"No idea. Got a 'get here now' text. You?"

"Same. You don't think it's to do with Adam, do you? You know, what you were saying about that woman you've been treating?"

Karen had wondered exactly the same when she'd received the text message, and had left the office straightaway, telling Molly that she was taking an early lunch and hoping desperately it wouldn't be a problem. Her next patient wasn't until 3 p.m.—that gave her two hours to find out what the hell was going on with Eleanor.

"God, I hope not. It'd break her."

"Karen, I . . ." Bea started, her face creased in a frown.

"What? What's wrong?"

Bea stopped walking and looked from Karen to the house, obviously trying to decide whether to say what she wanted to say.

"Nothing," she mumbled. "Just that Adam's car's here." She thumbed down the street.

"I didn't see that. Let's just go in and find out."

Bea seemed as reluctant to go into the house as Karen was, although she wasn't sure what either of them was dreading. Adam opened the door before they had a chance to knock. Noah was draped over one shoulder, eyes wide open but quiet and not visibly hurt in any way. That was one thing, she supposed.

"What's going on, Ad?" Bea asked as he stepped to one side to let them in.

"There's been an accident." His voice was grim and Karen's heart sank.

"Eleanor? Is she okay?" Her mind swam with possibilities.

"She's not hurt. It's . . . well, it's her hair."

"Her hair?" The nauseous feeling that had plagued Karen since she'd received the text half an hour ago gave way to mild annoyance. She forced her voice into a light joking tone. "Please don't tell me she called me out of work because she got a bad haircut?"

"She didn't text you; I used her phone. She didn't want anyone here, but I've got to go to a meeting, then I'll have to pick up Toby . . ." He lowered his voice and shot a look towards the closed living room door, as though his wife might have materialized there. "I don't want to leave her on her own. I'm afraid she might do something . . . stupid."

"Postpartum depression?" asked Karen. He shrugged.

"I don't know. She doesn't seem depressed, but there are all these little things going on. That thing with the car, for Christ's sake. We managed to convince social services it was a huge misunderstanding, but now I'm starting to worry I did the wrong thing. She looks like she's taken something."

When they entered the living room, Eleanor was sitting on the sofa in her dressing gown, her knees pulled up to her chest and a towel wrapped around her head.

"I told him not to call you," she said, without looking at either of them.

"He didn't, our Spidey senses were tingling," Bea quipped. Eleanor didn't even raise a smile.

"I suppose he's been telling you I'm going mad. He might be right."

"Don't be silly, Eleanor, you're not mad. You're tired, under a lot of pressure. Why don't you tell us what's gone on? Adam was very cloak-and-dagger about the whole thing." Karen sat on the other end of the sofa, Bea on the floor next to Eleanor. They looked at each other while Eleanor sat in silence, unmoving. After a few minutes she reached up and unwrapped the towel from her head, pulling it onto her lap.

Bea let out a tiny squeak from inside her throat. Eleanor's hair, usually shiny blonde and beautiful (although admittedly less shiny and beautiful lately), was missing big clumps where it looked as though she'd taken a razor to her scalp. What was left was still wet and clung to her head in rat's tails.

"What did you do, Els?" Bea asked quietly after a few moments' shocked silence.

"It was an accident." She reached up to touch the straggly strands that still hung down limply, but her hand didn't make it all the way up. "There was hair removal cream on the windowsill next to the leave-in conditioner. Adam thinks I did it on purpose. He doesn't think anyone could be that stupid."

"Oh God, sweetheart, how long did you leave it on for?"

"I fell asleep," she said simply by way of an answer.

"Right." Bea stood up. "This is bound to be fixable. You've plenty of hair left to do something with while the rest grows back. Adam, fetch me the hair dryer, I'll see what I can do."

Eleanor sat motionless while Bea busied herself plugging in the hair dryer, getting out a comb and shine spray, and generally faffing around trying not to show her panic.

"Excuse me a second." Karen slipped out of the living room

door and up the stairs to the bathroom, which was still in disarray. The tube of hair removal cream sat on the windowsill next to the conditioner. Aside from the fact that they were both in tubes, they couldn't have looked more different. The hair removal cream proclaimed *Veet* in large pink letters. Karen squeezed the bottom, and thick white cream oozed out onto the palm of her hand. She washed it off, then placed the tube back on the windowsill and picked up the conditioner. Beads of water ran down its surface and the tube was squeezed in. There was no way Eleanor had used the other one by mistake; Adam was right, she was neither that stupid nor that distracted, and the conditioner had clearly been used, whereas the hair removal cream was still dry.

Karen squeezed out a little of what was left of the conditioner. The cream that seeped out of the nib was thinner, but there was a similar sharp, acrid smell. Without thinking too much about why she was doing it, she replaced the cap and crammed the conditioner into her pocket.

"What do you think?" Bea asked brightly the minute Karen reentered the room. "You can't even tell now, can you?"

She'd done a good job, Karen had to give her that. Eleanor's hair was dry now, and styled with a side part to cover the left side where most of the damage had been done—that must have been where she'd been sleeping on it. You could barely tell there was anything wrong, as long as she kept her head perfectly still—and there was no wind.

"It looks great," she enthused, trying desperately to keep her voice from cracking—the last thing she wanted to do was to show Eleanor how bad things really were. Anyone who had seen Eleanor before Noah had come along would know how much pride she took in her hair; that it would be the final nail in the coffin after the diminishing control she had over her household lately.

"Then why does your face look like you're staring at the Bride of Frankenstein?" Tears welled in Eleanor's eyes. "I know you're lying."

And Karen *was* lying. When she told Eleanor it would all be okay. When she told her she could trust her. It was all lies—but she was used to them by now.

- 53 -

BEA

She'd left Eleanor fast asleep on the sofa, Adam barely taking his eyes off his exhausted wife. He'd been paper white since they'd arrived, and Bea had had to assure him a hundred times that it was a simple mistake. Not that she really believed that; it was a crazy mistake to make and she had no idea how tired or rushed off your feet you'd have to be to make it. And yet even as she reassured Adam, all she could think about was Karen and Michael, Michael and his wife. Clearly she'd not been able to talk about it with Eleanor—Karen had been there the whole time and Eleanor could barely string two words together—but she had to speak to someone about it. The whole thing was driving her crazy.

Her laptop was open and asleep; she pulled it over to where she had been sitting and with a tap brought the screen to life, then typed "Michael Lenton" into Google. Thousands of results, none of which looked promising. She clicked onto images; none of them matched Karen's Michael. She scrolled further down, watching pictures of gray-haired men and seventeen-year-old boys appear, until at last she saw it. A photo of Karen's Michael, looking very suave in a gray suit, white shirt, and cream waistcoat. He was a fair few years younger, but it was definitely him. And on his arm was a very beautiful young woman in a wedding gown. It was the photo she'd already received.

She clicked on the photograph and it filled the screen. At the bottom was the caption "Michael and Emily Lenton find their dream cars for their dream wedding" and a box that said "Visit website." The website, advertising cars, was no longer available.

Bea opened another tab and typed in "Emily Lenton." The familiar "Find Emily Lenton on Facebook" appeared—there were plenty to choose from, but none matching the picture of the woman standing next to Michael. Bea clicked on a few until she hit upon one with the profile picture of two children, twin girls around thirteen years old. Most of her photos were private, but when Bea came to an old profile picture from Christmas Day 2013, she knew that Fran had been right.

- 54 -

KAREN

Karen woke naturally—no alarm, which meant it was the weekend. The sunlight was warm on her face and bright in her eyes; what time was it? And why were her curtains open? When she tried to lift her head off the pillow, it felt like someone had poured wet concrete inside it during the night, and as she moved her neck from side to side and bent her arms, she discovered that almost every muscle ached.

What had happened last night? It wasn't like it was a total blank—having a glass of wine, going into town, meeting the guy . . . Oh Jesus, the guy.

She turned slowly to the right, hoping to hell she wasn't going to see what she thought was waiting there for her. A tumble of dark hair lay against the pillow, falling over half a tanned face. He was naked—well, his top half at least, and she wasn't about to check the bottom in case he woke up and caught her peeking.

Something must have gone seriously wrong last night. There was no way she would ever bring anyone back here, to the bed she and Michael shared. And how could she feel this rough? She'd barely drunk anything—one glass of wine before she went out, a bottle of Coca-Cola in the taxi on the way into town, and a cranberry juice and soda in the bar. So how was it that everything was so hazy? She could see snippets of the evening like a trailer for a movie—meeting this guy (as usual, she hadn't asked his name, which made things more difficult now) and inviting him back with her—but the point at which she'd decided to take him to her house instead of the room she'd booked in advance was missing from the slide show.

She groped on the bedside table for her phone as quietly as possible. She didn't want him waking up until she'd decided what to do with him. And put on some clothes.

The phone slipped through her fingers and onto the floor with a thud. She winced and checked over her shoulder; he was still asleep. Swiping her finger across the screen, she grimaced at the time: 9:04. What if Michael came back early? She didn't think he'd be too impressed having to maneuver around Mr. Floppy Hair to put his suits back in the closet.

She rolled out of bed and slipped into her robe, pulling it tight around herself to cover her nakedness.

"Hey, psst." She shook the man's shoulder and his eyes fluttered open. He smiled when he saw her standing over him.

"Morning," he murmured. "Ready for round two?"

"No," she snapped. "Sorry, no, you have to leave. Please."

He looked confused and still half-asleep. "Is there a problem?"

"Oh come on." She walked round the room, grabbing at the clothes he'd tossed casually aside the night before. "Don't tell me you didn't notice the men's shoes in the hallway? The Armani watch on top of the jewelry box? The photographs?"

He smiled guiltily. "Okay, I did notice those things. And now I'm guessing that Mr. Armani watch is coming home and that's why you're so desperate to get rid of me. I'm also guessing you won't be calling me."

"You're smart, I'll give you that." She passed him his clothes and turned around. "I'll call you a taxi."

"What, not even any time for coffee?"

"There's a Starbucks ten minutes down the road. Should I call your taxi for there?"

"No, don't worry about it. I'll get myself home. But just for the record?"

She turned to look at him. He was dressed now, and looking at him properly, she could see why she'd chosen him. And she had no doubt that she *had* chosen him. Despite how fuzzy her memories of last night were—and she still had no idea how one glass of wine could have done that to her—she didn't feel as though she'd done anything she hadn't wanted to do. And she certainly hadn't been taken advantage of. She'd have to figure out why she'd screwed up so badly, taking him back to her house instead of the hotel, but she knew he wasn't to blame.

"Yes?" she said impatiently.

"I don't know what kind of setup you've got here," he waved a hand around the room, "but whatever you're mad at your old man for, it's really not right to go around using people to get back at him."

She just stood there, mouth half-open, not knowing what to say. When she found her tongue, all she managed was "Excuse me?"

"Your shit is your own problem, not mine. But if the situation was reversed? If I'd approached you in that bar last night, had a few drinks and a laugh, invited you back to mine and screwed your brains out, then woken you up in the morning and kicked you out on your ass before my wife came home? I'd be an asshole." He swung his coat over his shoulder and stuck his arm in.

Oh God, he was right. She rubbed a hand over her face, letting everything he'd said sink in. How many of the others felt that way? Used and discarded when they woke to find her gone in the night? She'd assumed they were all there for the same thing as she was, but all along she'd been the one in control; she'd been the user.

"I'd like you to go now."

She left the room before he could see the tears spring to her eyes, and shut herself in the bathroom. She heard the bedroom door open, then the front door open and slam behind him and foot-steps crunch up the path, followed by the creak of the gate. He was gone. She knew she had to set about erasing every trace of him and sort herself out before Michael came home, but all she could seem to do was sit on the cold bathroom floor and cry.

- 55 -

KAREN

Jessica and Karen sat facing one another across the low coffee table in the center of Karen's office. Karen had not left the room this morning, not to get coffee or even go to the toilet—when Jessica turned up, she had been ready and waiting. Molly had shown her in in the usual way, and Jessica had seemed somewhat subdued. Instead of asking her how she was feeling, if anything of significance had happened since their last session, or if there was anything she wanted to talk about, Karen had decided that enough was enough.

"What do you want from me?" she asked as soon as her patient was comfortable. Jessica looked at her with those blank, unreadable eyes without so much as a flinch.

"I want you to help me with my headaches. That's why I came here."

Karen shook her head. "No, I think we both know that's not true. So I'm going to lay my cards on the table, although I realize I'm risking giving you exactly what you want by doing so. I'm going to ask you again. What do you want from me?"

Jessica sat back, appraising her in silence. Eventually she replied.

"I'm not sure I really know. I can't say it was planned, me coming to you like this, but here we are."

Karen was momentarily wrong-footed, although she didn't let it show. She had been expecting more of a denial; perhaps Jessica was as weary of this game as she was. She felt exhausted and her day wasn't about to get any easier. Bea had texted her before work imploring her to meet both her friends for lunch. They needed to talk, she'd said. Karen had no idea what had happened now, but lately every day brought a new drama, and she had a bad feeling about this latest one.

"Are you having an affair with my best friend's husband?"

Jessica let out a sharp laugh. "Is that the Adam you mentioned before? No, I haven't been near your friends."

Karen didn't believe her for a second. Maybe Jessica thought that if she admitted it, Karen would have all the evidence she needed to go to the police about the things she had done. No matter; she had all but admitted that she had lied about the tension headaches. This had to be the end of things.

"You know I can tell Eleanor about you? All I have to say is that you pose a threat to her family. I have every right to warn her about you."

Jessica smiled but said nothing.

"Although, I suppose that's what you want, isn't it? For me to tell Eleanor all about what's happened in these sessions. You probably thought I'd do it before now; I realize that's why you came to me. You thought I'd tell Eleanor and break up her marriage for you. That way you get Adam to yourself and you don't risk him being furious at you. You can't be blamed; you thought our sessions were confidential."

"Looks like you've got this all figured out. So what now, Doc? Are you going to call the police on me? Is that what you planned to do all along?"

Karen stood, her physical and mental advantage over Jessica giving her a sense of control that she'd never once felt in their sessions together.

"I'll admit that I haven't had a clue what to do about you. You're young and in love; I can understand how that feels."

"Don't patronize me." A snarl crossed the girl's face. "You have no idea how I feel."

"Maybe I do, more than you know actually. But that's still no excuse for the way you've behaved. You're lucky so far that no one's been hurt. If you stop this now, maybe no one will be."

Jessica stood, grabbed her handbag, and moved to the arm of the sofa as though she intended to leave. Karen felt a surge of triumph, followed by the slightest sense of unease. She hadn't expected it to be this easy—she had elevated Jessica Hamilton to movie villain status, and it was slightly anticlimactic to settle this with a few stern words.

"I know what you're doing," Jessica said. "I've seen the things you're capable of."

Karen thought back to the letter. *I know what you're doing. I know what you've done.* She'd known then it was from Jessica, and it felt good to have her suspicions validated. At least she wasn't going crazy.

"I don't know what you think you know about me . . ."

Jessica leaned forward, closing the gap between them. Karen saw that the redness in her cheeks that had been present in their first session—that she had attributed to the stinging cold—was back, only now she recognized it for what it really was: anger.

"I've seen you, Karen Browning. I've seen your heart and I've seen the person you really are. You act like you're morally unimpeachable and you think no one will ever see the real you, but you're wrong. You are wrong and you will not get away with it for much longer."

Karen's chest felt as though it had been filled with lead as Jessica stormed from the room. She should feel good; she should feel vindicated, but she just felt like this was in no way over.

- 56 -

KAREN

The pair of them sat opposite her, watching, waiting for her reaction to the news Bea had just delivered. They knew Michael was married.

She felt numb. She was certain of how she was supposed to react, shouting, screaming, crying, but she couldn't give them what they wanted.

"But you already knew that." It was a statement, not a question from Bea as she searched Karen's face for signs of surprise, confusion, or bewilderment. Karen was too exhausted to conjure them up. Biting on the loose skin inside her lip, she cast her eyes to the floor.

"Don't be ridiculous, Bea. Karen would never do that with a married man." Eleanor moved towards her, putting a hand on her arm, and Karen felt herself begin to well up. "Are you okay? What are you going to do?"

She didn't know what to say. Eleanor was obviously so desperate for her to be upset, to prove to her she'd been taken in by this awful cheat that she didn't want to tell her the truth: that Bea was right. Karen had known exactly what she was getting into when she became involved with Michael. She knew about his children and his wife, his other life and the home he owned. They weren't separated, and Emily knew nothing about her. She thought he worked away during the week, when in reality he did a job he could do from anywhere—working remotely, they called it—and he easily could have been at home with her and the kids. But he wasn't. He was with Karen.

"She's not going to do anything, Eleanor," Bea said. "She knows about Michael. She knows everything."

Eleanor looked at her like a wounded child, and Karen took a breath and nodded. "She's right, Els. I knew he was married."

From confusion to disappointment, then finally rage, Eleanor's emotions played out on her face as though they were written in Magic Marker. "What the hell are you playing at? How could you get yourself involved with a married man? Does he have a family? Karen? Does he have children?"

Karen knew this situation was bringing into the open everything that Eleanor feared about Adam. She had nightmares about her family being taken away from her by some unknown femme fatale, a woman with no morals who took what she wanted and gave no thought to the other people involved. The woman her best friend had just turned out to be.

"I . . ."

"If you say you love him, I might punch you in the mouth." Karen didn't think Eleanor meant it, but she could be wrong and she wasn't willing to take the chance. Bea was standing silently watching her, and Karen wasn't sure what she wanted from her. She knew what Eleanor wanted; Eleanor wanted her to cry, beg forgiveness from people she hadn't even wronged, explain how she'd had no idea until last week, or even last night and her trustworthy, reliable best friend wasn't a lying, relationship-wrecking cheat. Bea was a mystery.

"Why didn't you tell me?" she asked quietly. "You've been lying to us for years."

"Because I didn't want to see that look on your face," Karen replied, one hundred percent truthfully. "I didn't want you to be disappointed in me."

"Because you wanted us to think you were Little Miss Perfect,"

Eleanor raged. "You couldn't bear us to know that you're morally bankrupt. You're so high and mighty all the time, with your classy job and your puke-free wardrobe and your un-sweary vocabulary. When the whole time you've been breaking up people's lives."

"Don't be ridiculous, Eleanor, and stop yelling, you're causing a scene." Bea's words were emotionless. Karen thought she preferred Eleanor's histrionics.

"Say something, Karen. Please say something."

"Bea's right." Karen's eyes dropped to the table, and now that she could no longer see their accusing faces, the dam broke. The words came flooding out, crashing into one another, each one fighting to get out faster than the one before. "I knew he was married when we met, and it wasn't that I didn't care, I just didn't care enough to not let anything happen between us. When he flirted with me, when he made it obvious he fancied me, I pushed the thought of his wife and family into some black box in my mind and buried it. And every time we met in secret I threw another layer of dirt on top of the box until I forgot it was there completely. We slept together and I felt no guilt whatsoever. I'd never even met her—she didn't exist to me. His children weren't real people and I never let myself think about them long enough for their existence to bother me."

She took a breath and looked up. If it was at all possible, Eleanor's face was more contorted in disgust than it had been before she started talking. Bea was chewing the inside of her lip and refusing to meet her eyes.

"And when I introduced him to you guys, you both thought he was perfect, and he tried so hard with you all. I couldn't tell you then. I didn't want every conversation we had to be about whether Michael was going to leave his wife, or if I was going to leave him. I couldn't stand the thought of what you'd say after I'd left the room, about what an idiot I was, and how the relationship was doomed to fail. Even if you had accepted it—and I knew you never would,

Eleanor—you'd never let me forget that he wasn't really mine. And I've been good at forgetting."

Hot tears burned the corners of her eyes and she blinked furiously to get rid of them. She never cried in front of her friends.

"I don't have to listen to this." Eleanor rose and snatched up her bag so violently the table shook. "This whole thing makes me feel sick. And to think the only reason we were keeping secrets from you was to plan you a fucking birthday party. That's the only thing we've ever not told you in our lives! I'm going. Are you coming, Bea?"

Karen couldn't resist looking at Bea with what she was sure must be desperation. If Bea stayed now, there was a chance she would forgive her. She wasn't going to give up Michael, she couldn't, but maybe she could make Bea see that one bad thing didn't make her a bad person. Surely she would understand that no one was perfect?

But Karen didn't get the chance to try to make her see the situation from where she was sitting, because Bea got up and followed Eleanor out, leaving her completely alone.

- 57 -

KAREN

Karen rapped on the door and pushed it open with her palm. Robert was sitting at his desk, slumped forward, his elbows resting on the shiny oak. The serious look on his face put her on her guard instantly; he looked as though someone had replaced his PlayStation with an abacus.

"Karen." He gestured for her to enter, and she pushed the door closed behind her and moved farther into the room. The pain in her head intensified.

"What's this about, Robert?" She placed a hand on the back of the chair in front of her to steady herself. Her legs didn't feel like they were up to the job of keeping her upright anymore.

"Are you going to sit down? You're making my office look untidy."

"Don't try and make light of this, Robert. What am I doing here?" When he didn't answer, just looked pointedly at the chair, she reluctantly sat down.

"You're right, it's not a light situation, I'm afraid." He rubbed a hand over his face, and the bubble of dread in her stomach grew heavier. "There's been a complaint."

It took her a minute to process his words. The first thought that entered her head was *About who?* But that was a stupid question. She already knew who the complaint was about—she wasn't a senior partner yet; she wouldn't be consulted on an issue like this unless she was involved somehow. The complaint was about her. It was from Jessica Hamilton.

"Who?" He didn't even look at her. "Robert, who complained about me?"

"I can't tell you that, you know I can't."

"So what am I doing here?" She went to stand up, but thought better of trying to force her legs to work and sank back down into the cool leather. "If we're doing this by the book, then why are you even telling me? Shouldn't I be in front of the board right now? Hot coals on the floor, me dancing over them while you lot sharpen your pitchforks?"

Robert sighed. Obviously he was warning her in order to prevent her making a scene in front of the other partners. Not only out of a sense of misguided loyalty; he thought her unhinged enough to put both their careers at risk. Better to have the fireworks here and hope she'd calmed down by the time she got in front of the board.

"I thought I owed it to you to warn you. We have to have a formal meeting before the General Medical Council investigates, but I didn't want these accusations leveled at you for the first time in front of the other partners."

"What's the nature of the complaint?" Her voice didn't waver or crack; she sounded just like herself. The herself she was before she ever met Jessica Hamilton. Before her life imploded.

"They claim you smelled of alcohol during a session."

"That's ridiculous!" And impossible. She never drank alcohol before work—she got to the office at nine, for goodness' sake—and had never even had so much as a sip on her lunch break.

"You must know I'd never drink at work; why are you even entertaining the idea?"

"That isn't the whole complaint. They also said that you called them to rearrange their appointment and then weren't in the office when they arrived; that you let them down in this way on more than one occasion. They said that during the sessions you did make it to you were distracted and appeared to have been drinking. They said you called them at home to comment on something written on their personal Facebook page and that you sent them inappropriate text messages outside of sessions."

"Well, it's all lies, Robert. And easily proved to be lies as well. I don't understand why someone would think they could get away with this."

"If it is lies—"

"If?"

"Okay, let's go with me believing you. Because I want to, Karen, honestly, despite what I've seen with my own eyes these last few weeks. But we have to take every complaint seriously."

"But they are lying. I swear to you, Robert, I've never sent a patient any text message, let alone an inappropriate one. And drinking at work? I don't even drink on a work . . ."

She stopped, knowing that she was about to voice the lie she'd been telling herself for weeks. She never used to drink at all, not for ten years, but just lately she'd been having the odd one or two at night to relax—in fact she'd had a drink every evening this week. But she showered, she brushed her teeth, there was no way she'd still smell of alcohol at 9 a.m. the next day. Would she? Oh God. She put her face in her hands and rubbed her fingers against her temples as she felt the last of Robert's goodwill get its coat.

"I don't drink at work," she mumbled.

"I think you should take some time off," Robert said in way of reply.

Her hands dropped to her lap and her head snapped up in shock. "Is that a joke? If I leave now, I look guilty. I'm not taking any time off."

"It doesn't make you look guilty; it makes you look like you're taking the allegations seriously."

"Well, I'm not taking them seriously. And frankly, I'm furious that you are. They are completely unfounded and you know it! If there had been any proof whatsoever that I'd been sending inappropriate messages to patients, or drinking at work for that matter,

I'd have been suspended the minute I walked in. The fact that it's even got to go in front of the board means you don't have enough to make the decision yourself. I'm not going anywhere, Robert."

He sighed. "I had a feeling you'd say that. You're right, there's no real proof, thank God. I've seen the text messages and they haven't come from any number we have on file for you. Despite how pissed off at me you are right now, Karen, I'm your friend and I don't want this to get as far as suspension. But these things have to be investigated and I'd rather you weren't here while that happened. What I want you to do is take some time off; you and Michael go on holiday or something, get yourself back on track."

She finally found her feet. "We can't just run off on holiday, life isn't that simple for everyone. And anyway, I haven't come off track. I'm not taking time off; you'll have to suspend me." She picked up her bag and moved towards the door, her stride more confident than she felt. Only the thudding of her heart against her rib cage gave any indication of the panic rushing through her. She couldn't lose her job; it meant everything to her. Without it she didn't even know who she was.

"At least take the rest of the day," Robert called after her hopefully. She was on the cusp of saying no when she caught sight of herself in the black glass-paneled door. Her complexion was paper white against the darkness of the backdrop, only the dark purple half-moon shapes under her eyes adding any color. Her hair, usually straight and shiny, had fallen into the natural kinks it got from being slept on wet, and there was a white stain on her left breast—toothpaste. At least she'd remembered to brush her teeth this morning. The pulsing that had been strumming a rhythm in the base of her skull since she'd woken had risen now to a concerto.

"Yes, okay, fine."

"What? Fine what?" His voice was laden with suspicion.

"I'll take the rest of the day off. Maybe tomorrow, too. I'll come back after the weekend, unless you and the other partners feel you have enough evidence of wrongdoing to formally suspend me. What action will you take with the board?"

He gestured to the papers on his desk, and she realized with a jolt that the file outlining the complaint was in front of him. "I'll have to show them the evidence I've been presented with, but I suspect it will be an informal meeting rather than a hearing. We probably won't even need you involved." Robert's voice had relaxed a little; maybe all he'd wanted was for her to realize the seriousness of her situation. Maybe if she'd gone away, taken a break like he'd told her, things would have turned out differently. There was no way of knowing that now.

It was either falling into place or falling apart, and I had no idea which. There had been times over the last few weeks when I'd felt like I'd gone too far—I'm not evil, you need to know that, I just wanted to make them see. I'd thought a lot about that concept of good and evil—what made me any better than her? The things I'd done, I had good reasons, but in the end didn't everyone say that? The prison system is full of "innocent" men. In the moments that I stopped and looked into the distance, I would become terrified of where it would all end, debilitated by the fear of what I was becoming. I could have stopped it at any moment. Couldn't I? If I could—if I had—it would never have turned out this way. They would still be alive.

- 59 -

KAREN

Karen sat staring into the still pool of water, tiny air bubbles bursting against the surface the only indication that an entire ecosystem lived and breathed beneath. It was the same thing that had always fascinated her about the mind—how so much could go on in people's subconscious that even they weren't aware of. So much floating unseen just out of reach until the bubble reached the top and burst.

Suspended. A forty-minute hearing with the board of the General Medical Council and the only phrase she could remember was "suspended pending further investigation."

A big part of her wasn't worried at all. Years of being told what a crucial part of the practice she was, before that being top of every class at university, walking through every exam as if she'd written the questions herself, had left her feeling professionally invincible. She was the teacher's pet, clearly Robert's favorite by a mile. There was no way these ridiculous allegations were going to stick, and Robert was just going through the motions with this formal suspension. He had his practice to think about, and she respected his—and the other partners'—decision. She would have made the same one had it been any of her colleagues in her position.

Then there was the other part of her. The part that whispered words like "ethics committee," "professional disgrace," "suspended pending further investigation." This was always going to be a blot on her copybook, a black mark against her name. Even if she was

cleared of any wrongdoing and kept on at the practice, her colleagues would forever be giving each other sidelong glances when
they saw her, all wanting to sit next to her at meetings to see if
they could smell alcohol on her breath, second-guessing every opinion she put forward as to someone's care. Her cases would be reas-
signed while she was on her imposed hiatus, and it was unlikely she
would get them back even if she was reinstated. She'd be starting
from scratch, all her hard work in the hands of one of the other
psychiatrists. As formal as they all tried to keep their sessions, she
had come to care about her patients; she had a vested interest in
their well-being. Would alcoholic Gerry Young continue to stay on
the wagon under the care of someone else? Would Susan Webster be
forced to relive her experience from the beginning with one of the
other partners? Or would they quit therapy altogether, unable to
face starting again? And what would become of Jessica Hamilton?

The idea sat like a brick in her stomach. Nothing she had tried
to do—not cleaning or reading or watching awful programs with
irritating hosts and guests with more problems than the whole of
their patient list put together—nothing distracted her from the
snowballing idea that she'd been wrong all along. That all this had
been for nothing.

- 60 -

BEA

When the door opened, it was Michael who stood behind it.

"She's not here, Bea," he said, his voice wary.

"I know," Bea replied shortly. "I came to see you. Will she be long?"

"She's gone to get some wine and a takeaway from that place we like in Bridgnorth. She'll only be about half an hour. She's had some trouble at work; she doesn't want to talk to anyone."

"You'd better let me in quickly then."

Michael looked as though he was about to argue, then dropped his eyes to the floor and let out a weary sigh. Without waiting to see if she was following, he walked through into the living room. Bea pushed the front door closed and followed him.

"I assume this is where you question my motives towards Karen, tell me I'm the scum of the earth, and warn me away from your best friend or you'll tell my wife."

Bea's smile was without humor. "And then you tell me your wife doesn't understand you, you haven't had sex for years, and you're only together until the children are old enough for you to leave."

Michael raised his eyebrows: touché. "So why are you here?"

Bea perched herself on the edge of the sofa as though it was alien to her; as though she hadn't curled up on it a hundred times, a bottle of wine at her feet.

"I'm worried about Karen."

"You needn't be. She knows exactly what she's involved in and she can walk away at any time." He rubbed his hand over his chin. "She's a grown-up, Bea, and what we have works. I don't lie to her, and she doesn't lie to me. She's happy."

"Well, if you honestly believe that, then you don't know Karen as well as you think you do," Bea declared. "But I don't mean I'm worried about her relationship status, or whether you're going to break her heart. I'm worried about her . . . well . . ." Suddenly she was unsure she'd done the right thing going there. But she was there now, so she had better get on and say what she'd planned. "Her mental health."

She'd expected Michael to scoff, to remind her that Karen was the mental health professional and she was an HR assistant, not the other way round. But he didn't. To her surprise, he nodded.

"Me too. You know what's going on with her?"

Bea sighed. "I'm not entirely sure, no, but I think it has to do with this patient she has. She's convinced herself, and tried to convince me, that this girl is having an affair with Eleanor's husband."

"She told you about that?"

"That's what surprised me at first. Karen has never spoken about her patients to me. She's the ultimate professional. When she confided in me about this girl, I knew she must have a good reason to think we had a problem."

"Did she tell you her name?"

"No. She wouldn't cross that line unless she had proof there was some kind of danger. The thing is, it all just sounds so . . ." She stopped, searching for a word that wouldn't antagonize Michael. But she didn't have to; Michael said it for her.

"Crazy. It sounds crazy. That this girl is sleeping with Adam and taunting Karen with the knowledge. I know."

"It's not impossible, I suppose, but why? My guess is that Karen has sensed there's something wrong in Eleanor and Adam's relationship and is trying to save them, just like she always does when one of us is in trouble. She's using this girl, projecting the issue onto her."

Michael smiled, and Bea could tell he was impressed at the amount of time she'd spent on coming up with a credible theory.

"So tell me something else," he asked. "Why does Karen have this God complex in the first place?"

Bea reached down to her handbag and opened it. She pulled out some A4 pages and passed them to Michael, who studied them, a frown crossing his face.

"What is this?"

"It's newspaper articles. From thirty years ago. Karen's mother gave them to me."

"You went to see Karen's mum?"

Bea nodded. "I went about the birthday party Eleanor and I were arranging for her. To be honest, I'm not even sure it will be going ahead, but I'd arranged to see her mum to get family phone numbers, so I thought I'd go in case Els cools down and it all still happens."

"I didn't think Karen spoke to her mum. Some kind of family feud over her dad."

"She doesn't, only Karen never told us that, or anything about a feud. She hasn't seen her mum in about six years. And only once a year or so before that. Before her dad died she went quite frequently but when he wasn't there anymore it got less and less, then not at all. She speaks to her on the phone every now and then, but most of the time it ends in an argument."

"Because of this? Because her mum thinks she let her sister die? But that happened thirty years ago, not six."

Another nod. "Nettie, that's Karen's mum, said she tried and tried to get over what had happened, but Karen wouldn't forgive her for being a terrible mother. It became unbearable for them all. Karen moved out when she went to university and never went back.

She never told us any of it. Isn't that weird? I mean, we knew her mum wasn't like ours, she didn't have friends over for tea or whatever, but everyone was always at mine anyway. Our house was like a gathering point for everyone on our street, so it didn't seem that strange."

"And you're sure this is our Karen in this article? Karen is the kid who caused her sister's death?"

"Of course not; her mother caused it. Karen was barely four years old! But I'm sure she blamed herself."

Michael let out a breath and read the article again. "No wonder she feels so strongly about being the protector of the group. She still carries the guilt of what happened when she was four years old. Poor thing."

"Nettie said she'd only left them alone for a few minutes, but it must have been longer. Karen had been playing with her sister, and she'd always been so good with her, her mum said; I think she forgot she was barely more than a baby herself. I suspect Nettie had postpartum depression, although that's not an excuse for the way she treated Karen. She blamed her for what happened to the baby. She told me she tried not to, but she couldn't help it: every time she looked at Karen's face she saw her baby sister. She started drinking, heavily. She wasn't there for Karen when she needed her; she couldn't function enough to be a proper mother."

"And where was her father in all this?"

"He was away a lot with work. Back then the mothers practically brought up the children on their own, remember? After the accident he couldn't bear to be at home—he probably blamed himself for not being there, so he stayed away more and more, became the useless father he thought he was anyway."

"So they were on their own, just the two of them."

"Yes. Both blaming themselves, and blaming each other at the same time. It must have been horrific."

"Poor Karen. But what does this have to do with what's going on now?"

"I don't know. All I know is that this is why she feels like she has to spend her life looking after people. Fixing them. She's making amends for what happened to her sister."

'd spent a whole evening signing up to some of the dating websites I'd found online—okay, not so much dating as glorified Tinder sites. Some of the things these guys opened their conversations with . . . Well, put it this way, I could see why they were looking on the Internet for their kicks. Within minutes of putting a random photograph from Google onto a profile and filling in a few sparse details, I had three messages from blokes looking for hookups. I scanned a few of their profiles, but none of them were quite right. I'd read about this woman online—a catfish, the article called her, after a reality TV show that caught people who lied about who they were on the Internet to trick people into relationships. This woman hadn't been fishing for herself; she had managed to set up a relationship between a model and a famous American basketball player, acting as a go-between so that each person thought they were talking to the other when in reality they were talking to her. A tricky undertaking, but she had proved it could be done, and in doing so had given me an idea.

I had to find the exact right person for this to work. And even then it might not. On the Internet you could be whoever you wanted to be, so it was amazing that so many people chose to be complete idiots.

It took nearly a week and more than seventy messages to find the right guy. He'd started off his message extremely charming, but his profile made it clear what he was looking for.

I find it hard to believe that someone as beautiful as you has to look online for a date, he sent. I waited awhile before replying.

I'm so sorry, but this is a really old profile. I only reactivated it so a friend could take a look at how many normal guys are out there looking for fun.

Shame. You and I could have had fun. Did your friend find anything she liked?

Maybe she has now ;-)

The messages continued in that way for a while, harmless flirting as I explained about my friend Bea and how she was out for a good time, no strings attached. I told him in a roundabout way just how up for it she was, and how she always gave the men in her life a night to remember. How she didn't have time for a real relationship but how I didn't think that should mean she missed out on the benefits. The guy, who told me his name was David, was clearly interested regardless of which woman he was being offered, and when I sent him a photo of Bea stolen from her Facebook page, it had pretty much sealed the deal.

I'd also sent him a phone number, and he texted that night: *Hey, my name's David. Your friend gave me your number—I hope you don't mind?*

I sent an edited version of the message to Bea. Bea responded, and before long I was communicating to the pair of them, keeping the messages as true to the originals as possible, though making the ones to David flirtier and more suggestive, and the ones to Bea wittier and closer to what I was sure her version of the ideal man would be. This was easier than I'd imagined when I'd first come up with the idea; it might just work.

When David's text messages started to take on a more ominous sexual edge, I very nearly put an end to the whole thing. I had to remind myself more than once why I was doing all this, and once I'd pushed it to the back of my mind, I barely remembered my brief guilty conscience.

After only a few days it became exhausting. Playing piggy-in-the-middle between the two of them, making sure neither one suspected they weren't talking directly to the other, took up time I didn't have.

Now the phone bleeped again and I shoved it under one of the sofa cushions without glancing at it. All I felt was irritation. My legs were restless, but I didn't have the energy to go anywhere or see anyone. I knew the feeling would pass, but it had been happening more and more recently, the feeling of dread in the pit of my stomach without even knowing what I was dreading, the weight of my body almost impossible to move. There were so many things I needed to do, so much of my plan still to put in place, but I was exhausted. If only I could rest, just for one day. Forget everything that was going on, go back to trying to live my normal life.

I closed my eyes and imagined a huge white duvet, thick, soft, and bouncy, pulled up high around my shoulders with only my face peering out from beneath. I could almost feel the warmth seeping over me. A lie-down wouldn't kill me. Just until I felt better. Just until I could open my eyes again. It was all so exhausting.

– 62 –

BEA

Bea resisted the urge to glance in the mirror for the fifteenth time before leaving the flat, double-checking the door was locked behind her. Considering she hadn't even wanted to be set up when Karen had first mentioned it, she'd spent a ridiculous amount of time getting ready. Trying to choose the right outfit had been a real pain in the ass: not too much on show (don't want to give the wrong impression) but enough to impress. She'd settled on a dark red fitted dress with a relatively high neck and a silk scarf. No cleavage, but formfitting enough to make her hours in the gym worth it. Hopefully David from IT would be worth it too. The only thing dampening her excitement now was that after her fight about Michael she couldn't talk to Karen about it, pump her for information the way she would have done before. Damn Eleanor and her principles. After tonight she was going to contact Karen herself, try to play mediator and work out some way of making this Michael situation okay.

She'd been exchanging text messages with this guy for just over a week now and was surprised at how funny and charming he seemed. Karen wasn't known for setting her up with the most charismatic of guys; she seemed to think Bea would do better staying away from the charming, good-looking types. But she was more than ready to be proved wrong with this one, and she'd made a real effort just in case. After everything that had happened over the last few weeks, she felt like it might finally be time to give a guy a real chance. Why should she be content to watch everyone around her settle down happily while she punished herself for something that had happened so many years ago? It was time to stop being afraid.

She had done everything by the Just In Case He's A Psychopath Handbook For Girls. They had arranged to meet at a bar in town, a busy place where Bea would be safe and surrounded by people. She'd set up a signal with Eleanor: she would call once and hang up if she needed Eleanor to call her with a fake emergency, although she was pretty sure he would see straight through that one. Not that she was bothered about hurting his feelings. If she disliked him enough to invoke an emergency call, then she probably wasn't going to be too worried about seeing him again. She cringed when she imagined the lecture she was in for from Karen if this blind date ended the same way as the last one—with her popping to the toilet and leaving through the smoking exit, jumping straight in a taxi to Karen's to cordially request she stay out of her love life. Then she remembered the scene in the café, the wounded look on her friend's face as Eleanor had launched into her vicious tirade and Bea had said nothing to defend her. There wouldn't be any lecture this time—Karen might never speak to her again.

The taxi was late and she fired off a text to David to tell him it wasn't that she'd seen him and left without introducing herself. Her phone beeped its reply.

LOL! Thank God for that, I was beginning to regret wearing my Freddy Krueger outfit as a laugh.

Bea smiled. It was possible that tonight wasn't going to be all that bad after all.

"You look great, and not like Freddy Krueger at all." Bea had to raise her voice over the bar's music and lean in close for David to hear her. She hoped she still smelled as good as when she'd left the house.

He couldn't have heard her properly, because his eyes narrowed slightly in confusion, but he smiled in that way people do when they know it's expected of them. They had chosen the worst first-date spot ever; Bea had been so concerned with being safe that she hadn't thought about simple things like being able to hear one another. Not to mention that she was starving—she'd been so nervous about choosing what to wear that she'd forgotten to eat, and now she couldn't risk bar snacks with her skintight dress. Her stomach gurgled unattractively; maybe it was a good job the music was loud.

"Look, do you wanna go for a walk? It's really loud in here."

Bea hesitated. She'd promised Eleanor she would stay at the bar for her own safety, but this guy was Karen's friend. Plenty of people knew who she was with, and it was unlikely he was going to abduct and kill her then return to work with Karen tomorrow. And Bea often walked home from the clubs around here gone midnight, even though she knew she shouldn't, and nothing had ever happened to her. She knew how to handle herself.

"Sure, yeah."

The evening air was milder than when she'd left the house, or maybe the alcohol had taken the chill off the evening, which was lucky because she hadn't worn a coat. David nodded towards the river—it was opposite the pubs and clubs, across a busy main road, but hardly off the beaten track. Plenty of people walked along the path and it wasn't even nine o'clock.

"Sorry about that place," she apologized. "Nightmare trying to have a conversation." She paused and then added wistfully, "Food's good, though."

"Don't worry about it." He shook his head impatiently and reached out to touch her elbow. "Look, I booked us a room at the Bellstone. Why don't we just go straight there?"

At first his words didn't completely register. She assumed he meant a booth, like the ones you could book at a couple of the nightclubs that thought they were classy because they had VIP areas. It didn't seem to make much difference to the people of Shrewsbury that the VIP areas were just a corner with some rope around that absolutely anyone could put their name down for a tenner deposit. Although the Bellstone didn't have a VIP area, or even booths. It was one of those places that was classier because it didn't pretend it was a celebrity hangout. With sickening clarity it dawned on her what he actually meant. What the Bellstone *did* have was rooms upstairs.

"I'm sorry, you mean for a drink, right? At the bar."

He smiled and shrugged. "I'm sure they do room service."

Bea felt the heat rise in her cheeks. Sure she'd dressed up, but she still didn't think she looked like the type of person who would send someone a few text messages and go straight to bed with them. Was that the impression she'd given him? She couldn't think of anything witty or clever to say to defuse the awkwardness; her mind was too busy running through the texts, looking for where she might have given him the impression she was just meeting him for sex.

"Um, David, I'm sorry if I let you think that I was just here for . . . well, that a room would be necessary . . ."

"Oh God, no." He had the good grace to look embarrassed. "I'm not saying we have to jump straight into bed. We can have a drink downstairs in the bar first; it's much quieter than the place we were just in. But it makes sense to be closer to the hotel, right? Are you okay? Did I say something wrong?"

"I just, I don't . . . I don't feel comfortable with the assumption that we're going to have sex on our first date." She stepped away from him in the hope that physical distance would make her point. *This can be salvaged. If he just apologizes, we can laugh about it and maybe get some food. It'll be a running joke: "Remember that time you tried to get me into bed ten minutes after meeting me?"*

"Well, come on. I mean, I came all this way. . . ."

"What, and that means I owe you a shag?" Bea could hear her

voice getting louder, but she wasn't aware of raising it. "Because you paid for a train ticket?"

"There's no point in going all feminist on me now," he hissed. "Karen told me what you're like."

"Oh yes? And what exactly did Karen say?" There was a lump forming in her chest, and her cheeks were burning. She couldn't imagine Karen telling this man anything terrible about her, but suddenly she was afraid to hear what he was about to say. It was as though the person she had been speaking to for the last week had disappeared completely, replaced with a complete stranger. He leaned in closer than was comfortable, and for the first time her embarrassment gave way to panic.

"She said you were up for a good time. I know what she meant."

Bea drew in a sharp breath. Had she really said that? Was that what Karen thought about her? *Well, isn't that what you wanted her to think? Because you'd rather she thought you a slag than frigid and terrified.* And that was the only reason he was here, not because they'd had a connection, or clicked, but because her best friend had told him she was an easy lay.

Hot tears stung at the corner of her eyes. They'd always joked about her single life, and yes, she did exaggerate her sexual appetite to her friends, but she'd never realized she'd caused Karen to have such a low opinion of her. In reality, there had been so few men in her life since university, she could name them on one hand. Part of her was hurt, shocked, disappointed. The other part was furious.

"Karen had no right to say that, and you can tell her so from me, next time you have one of your cozy little chats in the canteen."

David looked confused, then confusion gave way to a sneer. "She told you we worked together? Ha, I think you're the one who needs to have a chat with your 'best mate.' We met online. On a dating website."

She'd only had two glasses of wine in the bar, but now Bea's head was starting to pound, right behind her eyes. A dating website? "Karen has a boyfriend. She doesn't use dating websites."

"I know, that's what she told me when I contacted her. She said it was an old profile and that she wasn't looking for anyone. But she had a friend who was, and she gave me your number. Told me all about you, how you've been single for years. Told me to text you and gave me your number."

How dare she! Encouraging her to go on a date with someone she'd never even met, telling an absolute stranger she was desperate and a sure thing. And this guy was vile. Seriously, who took a train journey to meet someone just for sex? And didn't even offer to buy them a bloody meal first!

There wasn't much else she could say to David, but a whole lot more she wanted to say to Karen. Karen, whose perfect relationship was with a man who wasn't even completely hers, calling her easy! The whole thing would be laughable if it weren't so horrific.

"I'm really sorry that there has been a misunderstanding, but I think it's time I went home. Karen should never have said those things; she should never have set this up in the first place."

David's face darkened, his eyes narrowed, and he stepped closer again, so close that Bea could smell stale smoke on his breath from his last cigarette.

"You must be fucking joking. I came all this way to meet you. I paid eighty quid for a decent hotel room. You're not going anywhere."

Reaching out, he grabbed hold of her wrist before she had a chance to move backwards, and squeezed so tightly, she thought it might break. "Let go of me or I'll scream," she said, sounding more confident than she felt. Pain shot through her wrist as he pinned it to her side and twisted slightly, guiding her through the gate in the railings that led to the river, his mouth close to her ear.

"You won't scream." His voice reverberated through her head. "Because if anyone comes near us, I'll tell them you came on to me and then cried rape. And it won't be the first time, will it, Bea?"

Bea's chest tightened at his words. There were only two people who knew about what had happened sixteen years ago, and they were her best friends. There was no way either of them would tell a complete stranger. Was there? Karen had already said more to this man than Bea ever would have imagined she would.

He yanked at her arm and she had no choice but to follow him down the bank to the riverside. It was deserted down there, but in the lights from the theater on the other side of the river she could see his face, contorted by anger and set determinedly. He shoved her against the bank so hard the air was knocked from her lungs, and grabbed at the hem of her dress.

They were perfectly visible from the other side of the river, but as Bea was fast learning, visible didn't equate to safe anymore. If someone saw them, would they realize she was in trouble? Or would she be just another slag giving a bloke a good time on a Friday night?

Like you always do, a voice in her head whispered. Karen's voice. *Haven't you learned your lesson after what happened? What's the difference between him and any of the other guys you've been with?*

It isn't like that, her own voice insisted back, the imaginary argument with her former best friend blocking out David's hand on her thigh, his other hand trying to grope for her nipple through her dress. *I know what I've said, I know the person I've pretended to be, but I'm not her. I'm scared and I'm broken.*

Had this been what it was like last time? Had she lain there, eyes squeezed closed, and just prayed for it to be over quickly? She could smell cigarette smoke and dirt and freshly cut grass, and she knew in that instant that if it happened to her again, she would never recover. This time she wouldn't come back.

It was frustrating, not being able to hear what they were saying, but from the way Bea was leaning closer to her date, her lips curving into a grin at whatever he was saying, it seemed to be off to a good start. I'd been more nervous than I imagined she was in the buildup to tonight. Up until now everything had been under my strict control, but not so anymore. Anything could happen, and the thought of leaving things to chance had made my skin itch. It was why I was there, the danger of being caught insignificant against my need to claw back some control over the evening. I told you I'm not evil, you see. I was there every minute, watching. Waiting.

I only just looked up in time to see Bea and her date heading towards the door of the bar. Not wanting to follow them too closely, I hung back, watched them cross the road and head towards the river. Before long they were almost completely out of sight, and I had to walk quickly to catch up.

They stopped, deep in conversation, and I wished I'd found some way to record their conversation. I didn't like not knowing what was being said without me in the middle to mediate. It seemed inevitable that they would discover the whole thing was a setup, but that was okay; that was part of the plan.

He had hold of her arm now, dragging her down towards the river where they couldn't be seen from the path. I looked around in despair, my heart thumping. No one had seen them—there was no one around to help her.

This was my chance. My opportunity to put everything right, to rescue Bea and be the hero. After all, wasn't that what I'd always wanted?

Only I wasn't going to get to her in time. It had been a stupid, risky plan; I'd become overconfident, spurred on by desperation and obsession, and now someone else was going to pay the price. Could I live with that?

I took a deep breath as I saw the couple approaching the embankment. Surely she would get help now? Ironic now that I was so concerned about that night, when what happened later was so much worse than anything I could have imagined.

- 64 -

BEA

It wasn't bravery that made her do it. Afterwards, when the images were running through her head constantly like a film on a loop, she couldn't explain that very second. She wanted to say that something snapped, but that wasn't it; it wasn't conscious. The only way she could remember it feeling was feral, primal. Fear merged with fury.

She screamed. His hand froze on the elastic waistband of the grotesquely inappropriate thong she had worn for their date.

"You don't want to do this," he snarled into her shoulder. She didn't stop screaming, kicking her legs, trying to free herself from his bulk weighing her down. Her heels found hard ground and she shoved upwards, arching her back the way she'd seen Toby do when he was younger, resisting his mother putting him into his car seat.

She didn't stop to think what would happen if no one was passing along the top of the bank, or if she had made him angry enough to simply knock her unconscious. He released her breast and shoved a hand to her mouth to stop her hysterics, but she bit down hard, causing him to cry out and sit back on his heels. "Bitch!"

Voices at the top of the bank got louder and relief coursed through her in waves as she saw two upside-down faces, a man and a woman, appear over the grass.

"You okay, love?" she heard the man shout down.

"Help me! Please, help me!"

David scrabbled backwards. "She's crazy. She's fucking crazy! We came down here for some privacy and she just . . ."

She didn't stop to hear what other lies he had to tell. With a new energy she threw herself to her knees and onto her feet, pulling at the grass to lift herself, then scrabbled up the bank, pushing past her rescuers onto the street.

You're not safe yet, her own voice told her. *He's still there. Run.*

It was like one of those dreams where you desperately need to escape from the bad guy, but your legs feel as though they're made of concrete. The world wasn't moving in slow motion; it just felt like she was. She didn't even know where she was running to, but she could hear the blood pounding in her ears, a haunting rhythm: *run, run, run.*

The taxi rank was deserted—the night was young, and no one wanted to go home yet.

"Taxi, please."

The man behind the glass looked up at her shaking voice, took in her disheveled appearance, the grass and mud caked on her new red dress, her hair sticking out like a crazed Medusa.

"You all right, love?"

She nodded, not trusting herself to speak without crying. He looked like he wanted to say more, but he didn't; just nodded. "Where to?"

Back in her flat with the door locked behind her, Bea finally felt safe. The taxi journey had been silent; she'd stared out of the window without actually noticing anything go by. Her chest was hollow and she could hear that her breath still hadn't returned to normal. All at once, the reality of what had happened, and what could have happened, hit her like a glass of water to the face. Tripping up the stairs she banged into the bathroom door and threw up violently until her throat was sore. Then she started to cry.

- 65 -

ELEANOR

Surrounded by presents, Toby ripped the paper from his brand-new iPad and grinned.

"Thanks, Mum, thanks, Dad, it's great! Can I set it up?"

Eleanor smiled, her heart aching at how genuinely thrilled her son was with the present.

"Not yet, sweetie, you've still got more presents to open yet. Oh, and the card from Auntie Karen! I left it upstairs."

She took the stairs two at a time, too excited to miss even a minute of Toby's happiest day in months. Ever since Noah had been born, he'd been sullen and moody, convinced he was being pushed aside in favor of the needy, screaming newborn. Today was all about him, and thankfully Noah had stayed quiet and content in his rocker so they could give their elder son all their attention. Adam had even got up early and made them a delicious breakfast. Everything about the morning had been perfect, thanks to their ability to still function as a family unit despite how exhausted and run-down they all were.

Retrieving the card from the top of her wardrobe, she held it up to the light, wondering what was inside. Knowing Karen, something ridiculously thoughtful that cost the earth and that Toby would be delighted with.

Eleanor's heart felt heavy when she thought of her friend. How could she bear to be with Michael knowing she was tearing a family apart? She had always thought of Karen as someone to look up to, the epitome of all that was good. Now that had been ruined by the lies she'd told them. Eleanor knew why she hadn't been truthful with them: there was no way she would have accepted her friend's relationship if she'd known that he had a wife and three kids at home, but at least she would have had a decision to make. This way, the last two years of their friendship she felt like Karen had been laughing at her and Bea's stupidity, at how gullible they were. No wonder Karen had never pushed the issue of having children; men didn't plan families with the other woman.

"Here," she said, handing Toby the envelope. She might be livid at her friend, but she shouldn't deny Toby his gift. He turned it over in his hands as if he could figure out what was inside by the weight of it. Then he put his thumb under the flap, tore it open, and pulled the card out. On the front was a mock-up of a newspaper with a picture of Toby in the middle and the headline TOBY WHITNEY SIGNS FOR MANCHESTER UNITED ON HIS NINTH BIRTHDAY!

"Cool card." He grinned, opening it up and looking confused. "There's nothing in it."

"That's strange," Eleanor replied, thinking of Karen's words when she'd handed her the card. *There's a little surprise in there for the birthday boy.*

"Just this letter." He frowned and started reading. When he hadn't spoken for a minute and the frown hadn't relaxed, Adam tried to peer around his arm, but the boy blocked him.

"What does it say, Tobes? Is it a riddle? Maybe you've got to solve it to guess your present."

Toby was still frowning, his mouth moving wordlessly as he read, struggling to make sense of what he was seeing.

"I don't know what it means, Dad. Is Auntie Karen tricking me?"

"Give it here, Toby," Eleanor said suddenly, her voice sharp. The mood in the room had changed dramatically in the last few minutes. Toby's face was screwed up and there was tension in his shoulders, and when she tried to take the card, he pulled it away. "I said give it to me."

Toby stood up, knocking the iPad off the arm of the chair and onto the floor. "Why is she saying these things?" he demanded, thrusting the card at Adam. "What does she mean? Is it supposed to be funny? I don't get it."

Eleanor watched as Adam scanned the words in the card, his jaw tightening with every line.

"Toby, take your new things up to your room. Your mum and I need to talk."

"No! I want to know why Karen wrote that letter—is it true?"

"Of course it's not true." Adam handed the card to Eleanor, his face gray with shock. "I don't know what kind of trick Auntie Karen is playing, but it's not a very funny one and we'll talk to her about it. Now please take your things upstairs and get ready to go. We're off to Frankie and Benny's for lunch."

"Oh yeah!" Toby ran upstairs and Eleanor sat down on the sofa, opened the card, and began to read what was written inside.

Dear Toby,

Happy birthday! I can't believe how old you are now, and how grown up you've become over the last few years. I'm certain you're old enough to understand what I have to tell you, which is why I've waited until now to say it.

Toby, your mum and dad love you very much, and what you're about to read doesn't change that fact. It doesn't change the fact that your mum held your hand while you were sick into a bucket for three days when you were just four, or that she stayed awake the entire night because you could only sleep with your head on her knee and she wanted to keep an eye on your temperature. It doesn't mean she is any less your mum than

*she's always been. A mother is so much more than the person
who gave birth to us—believe me, I should know.*

*But the truth is, Toby, Eleanor is not your biological
mother. She didn't give birth to you and she didn't meet your
dad until you were nearly two. Your real mother was not a nice
person, and Eleanor became like a mum to you, looking after
you and bringing you up as her own son. And I have loved you
as if you were my own nephew, but all these years I've told your
mum and dad that they should tell you the truth, that you have
a right to know. Ask them now—see if they keep lying to you
the way they have been all these years.*

*Please don't hate your parents. They did the wrong thing
but for the right reasons. They really do love you, it's just a
shame they couldn't see the grown-up young man I can see and
realize you deserve the truth.*

*Enjoy your birthday, Tobes. You are a man now and free to
make your own choices.*

Love always,
Auntie Karen

Silent tears rolled down Eleanor's cheeks as she read. How
could she? How dare she? She knew Karen had never approved of
them lying to Toby, but how could she feel it was her place to tell
him the truth?

"There has to be a mistake—Karen would not do this to us."

Adam rubbed his hands over his face as though trying to erase
what he had just seen.

"Wouldn't she? So that isn't her handwriting? So she hasn't
been going on at you to tell Toby the truth since he was three?"

"Well yes, but . . ." She didn't know what to say. How could she
defend Karen when what Adam was saying was true? Karen had
handed her the card herself; it had been in the top of the wardrobe

ever since. It was her handwriting—some of it was even things Karen had said to Eleanor herself. There wasn't really any doubt; the only question was why. She'd given Eleanor the card a week before the confrontation about Michael—and even if this had been about that, why involve Toby? It definitely wasn't like Karen to be so underhanded.

"I'm going to call her." She picked her mobile phone up off the sofa, but Adam took it out of her hand and placed it on the TV stand next to him.

"Not now you're not. We're going to get dressed, and then we're going to take our son shopping and out to lunch. And we're going to hope he doesn't believe a word that poisonous bitch said."

Eleanor was taken aback at his hostility, but how could she argue? What Karen had done to their family . . . it was unforgivable.

"And Toby? When are we going to tell him the truth, Adam? Don't you think this is the ideal time, now it's already out there?"

The living room door opened and Toby stood in the doorway. "She's right, Dad. You need to tell me the truth."

- 66 -

BEA

B ea, it's me."

Bea laughed. "Of course it's you, Fran. No one ever calls my house phone. It's either you or that woman who keeps ringing to ask if I've had an accident in the car I don't own and can't drive."

"Free calls to landlines. Anyway, I didn't ring to debate my choice of phone; I'm calling to tell you I'm doing dinner for Mum's birthday. Friday night at six—are you coming?"

"Chinese or Indian?"

"Chinese—I got some vouchers for House of Wok after Lewis found a Coke can ring pull in his rice last time we went."

"Jesus, Fran, probably best if you don't try to sell it to Mum like that. And yeah, I'll be there. Make sure you tell her I'm coming after the gym. Say that bit about the gym twice if she isn't paying attention."

"Great. Not sure I could put up with her excellent parenting tips without you there to make faces behind her. And Sam is bringing his new girlfriend. Gemma something. Sarah something? Oh God, what was the last one called?"

"Becky? Lydia? God knows. I wouldn't worry, there'll be a new name to remember next week. How're the kids?" Bea's mobile let out a long continuous buzz indicating the arrival of an email. She flicked her finger across the screen to unlock it and pressed the Outlook icon.

"Don't ask. Same as ever. We had parents' evening last night. Maisy talks too much, and the other day Lewis told his teacher to chuck it in the fuck-it bucket. Obviously I'm in hot water now because there's no way anyone in Rich's family would have taught our six-year-old son the F word."

The email was from an address Bea didn't recognize. Probably spam. She needed to tighten up her filters.

Subject: Recognize anyone?

She scrolled down, struggling to see the text on her tiny screen. There was a video attached to the message, and she tapped on the black box to play, wondering if Eleanor had been filming Noah allegedly laughing again. It didn't matter how many different angles she recorded it from, the kid had gas.

The circle on the video stopped turning, and the screen filled with the image of a dark room, a bed in one corner. Bea hoped she wasn't about to witness some dodgy porn movie. She couldn't afford a new phone if this one got some kind of virus. Clicking desperately on the screen, she attempted to cancel the video. Fran was still talking.

"Whoever it was, Lewis is protecting them. I asked him who he heard it from, and he said Mr. Tumble. I even told him I was going to complain to CBeebies and Mr. Tumble would be fired, but he's sticking to his story. I heard him telling Maisy this morning that she'd better find a new favorite program in case Mr. Tumble fell out of a tree and died."

The silence told Bea that her sister had finished her story, but she couldn't string together a sentence to reply. Despite her attempts to stop it, the video had started playing and the door to the room had opened. A woman had stumbled in, unsteady on her feet—obviously drunk—followed by a guy, who sat next to her on the bed. Within seconds they were kissing frantically, then he was pulling at her dress, lifting it higher until finally she broke away from the kiss to let him pull it over her head.

"Fran, I'll have to call you back." She hung up without waiting for her sister's response or tearing her eyes from the video.

The girl had only a tiny thong on now and was lying back on the bed as the man pulled at the buckle of his belt and pushed his trousers down around his thighs. Bea knew what was going to happen next. Of course, it was obvious. But it wasn't because she'd seen too many dodgy movies that she knew. She knew because the girl on the bed was her.

Why did you install spyware on your friend's computer?

I'm not going into this again. I told them, the police, that I didn't do that.

It wasn't to keep an eye on her? Keep her safe?

If it was me, then how did Jessica get hold of the video and email it to everyone Bea knew? What reason would I have to do that to my best friend? Haven't you been listening to a word I've said? If you don't believe me, there's not much point in us doing this at all, is there?

Oh, I see, the silence again.

Does silence bother you?

It does when I'm trying to have a conversation with someone.

Why did you get so upset just now?

You'd be upset too if everyone was treating you like a liar and a murderer. I'm a professional. I have a doctorate, for God's sake—a month ago I was sitting where you are now. Surely that counts for something?

Understandably, you're proud of what you've achieved, and of course it counts. I'm sorry to have upset you; it's important that I ask these questions to try and understand what life has been like for you and your friends these last few months. And I want to help you to come to terms with what's happened and to help you understand.

I already understand. I understand that they didn't believe me when I said they were in danger; just like you don't believe me now. I understand that none of this would have happened if I was just doing my job properly. I understand that this is my fault. I let this happen. I let it happen again.

Do you want to talk about Amy yet?

No.

- 68 -

ELEANOR

Eleanor fingered the soft hair on the right side of her head, where it still grew long and unmutilated. She avoided looking at the left side, where the patches made her look like she was suffering from some kind of disease. Tears pricked at her eyes but didn't spill down onto her cheeks—maybe they were drying up once and for all.

Adam had treated her as though she was made of glass ever since the horrific incident with her hair. At first she'd tried desperately to convince him it really was an accident, but he'd refused to listen, talking instead about doctor's appointments and asking Karen for recommendations. Karen. Whenever he mentioned her name these days, Eleanor found herself prickling and she had no idea why. She'd never noticed before how he spoke about her as if she was a higher class of person than them, as if she was a messiah rather than a psychiatrist. She'd found herself snapping at him, "She's not even a real doctor; it's not as if she's ever saved anyone's life." Adam had smiled, seeming not to notice the sting in her voice, and replied, "We don't know that."

She knew it was just a reaction to the news about Karen and Michael's relationship. It had made her paranoid about every time her best friend and her husband had been in a room together.

She thought back to the day of the hair incident. Karen had left their house before Bea to get back to the office—just as Adam was going to his meeting and she'd heard her tell Adam that if he needed to talk about anything he should call her. The way she'd said "anything," so loaded . . . Eleanor hadn't stopped thinking about it ever since.

"Did Toby leave his gym uniform in your car?" she shouted through to Adam, who was miraculously cooking dinner. Guilty conscience?

"Don't think so," he called back.

"I'm just going to check," she said, slightly quieter than before and hoping he wouldn't hear over the noise of the stove fan. He didn't object, so she lifted his keys off the hook and slipped out of the front door, closing it quietly rather than letting it slam.

The car was the junk heap she was expecting, crisp packets shoved in the door pockets and an empty McDonald's cup in the cup holder. She worked fast, opening the glove box and rifling through the contents. Nothing out of the ordinary: cables to charge a mobile phone, the GPS, a black leather wallet with the car's service history. She checked the boot—a pair of her old shoes, three of Toby's woolly hats, and a car-cleaning kit. She gave up, the chant of *crazy, crazy, crazy* reverberating in her ears as she went round to the driver's side to lock the door.

That was when she spotted it, just a tiny glint of gold on the passenger side, hooked over the side of the door pocket and nearly covered by rubbish. It was probably foil from a candy wrapper, she told herself as she opened the door and climbed over. A soda tab. A pen. She was still going through the list of things it was going to be as she picked up the delicate gold bracelet and lifted it to the light. It wasn't one of hers, but it was familiar. Her mind couldn't process where she'd seen it before; it was too busy reeling from the realization that Karen had been right. Her husband was having an affair.

- 69 -

BEA

The laptop seemed to take forever to boot up, and the minute it did, Bea clicked on her email app so many times, the screen froze.

Who the hell had sent her that video? Where had they even gotten it? Had he filmed it . . . Paul? He'd been one of her few attempts at a relationship in years, and if he had filmed it, he certainly hadn't . . . Her mind searched for the words as she slammed her fingers on "Ctrl" "Alt" "Delete" . . . He hadn't *obtained her consent*. The mobile phone tucked under her chin rang and rang, then switched over to voice mail once more.

"Eleanor. Ring me."

She didn't even want to think it, but she couldn't help herself. Had Karen sent her this? Karen had tried calling her a couple of times since her "date" with her fake work colleague, but Bea had had nothing to say to her so-called best friend. She would confront her, but in her own time and her own way. She'd had a lucky escape the other night, and every time she thought about it bile rose in her throat and hot, angry tears spiked her eyes. She needed to be calm and detached from the recent trauma before she faced her.

Obviously Karen was going to be mad that Bea had told Eleanor about Michael, but would she really do something like this to get back at her? Anyway, Bea's relationship with Paul had been way before that, so how would she even have this video?

The Outlook app launched and Bea felt bile rise in her throat when she saw the email sitting there with the subject line "Recognize anyone?" It sounded more like a threat the second time she read it—Karen's way of making sure she didn't tell anyone else about Michael's wife? It hurt Bea to think that her friend would have to stoop that low. Karen should know she'd never do anything to hurt her, even if she didn't agree with her decisions.

She double-clicked on the email, not wanting to see the images on a larger screen but hoping there would be something here she'd missed on the smaller screen of her phone.

There was.

The email had been sent to her personal inbox, where she was viewing it now. But that wasn't all.

Fear rose in Bea's chest, hammering at her rib cage as she scrolled down the list of names in the cc line. Some of them she recognized—Fran; her brother Sam; Eleanor; one, two, three girls from work; two of her friends from Slimming World . . . How had anyone even got hold of these addresses?

Panic rose in her chest. How many of these people had already seen the video? Her phone hadn't rung yet, so she suspected very few. She needed help to sort this out fast. Tomorrow was Monday, so there was a chance that some or all of them—especially her work colleagues—would see it then, perhaps while she was sitting in the office next to them. She imagined dozens of people around her all pressing "Play" at the same time, the office filled with the sounds of her and Paul moaning and grunting. This was no perfectly choreographed sex tape, all soft lighting and flattering angles recorded and leaked by a failing celebrity to revive a flagging career. This was sex in its true and highly unflattering glory, spare tires on display and legs akimbo.

Fran. The one person she could count on to keep a cool head and help her work this out. She grabbed her phone and dialed her sister's number, praying she wasn't bathing the children or reading bedtime stories.

Fran answered on the third ring.

"Bea, what the hell was all that about? Are you okay?"

"Not really, but I don't have much time to explain. Do you have your computer on?"

"Yeees," Fran replied slowly, obviously dying to ask more questions but too concerned by the desperation in Bea's voice. "Lewis is just finishing his homework."

"Right, can you kick him off for a minute? Get him out of the room, though, and log in to your email."

"Bea, what's this a—"

"Please, Fran?"

Fran paused. Bea knew she must be worrying no end, but she didn't have time to worry about that. She needed Fran to see exactly what they were dealing with. Of course she'd rather it wasn't necessary, but she needed help more than she needed her dignity right now. She heard Fran speaking to her son in low, urgent tones and Lewis protesting loudly.

"Okay, what do I do now?" Fran asked eventually.

"Are you alone?"

"Yes. Bea, what exactly am I going to be looking at?"

"Log in to your email."

Bea waited in silence while Fran did as she was told.

"I've got to say, this is all very cloak-and-dagger. I'm a bit . . . Okay, I'm in. What now?"

"Okay, find an email with the subject 'Recognize anyone?' Don't open it yet."

"I can't . . . Wait, there, got it."

"Right." Bea took a deep breath. "You need to open it. I'm sorry for what you're about to see, Fran, but you'll realize in a minute why I'm asking for your help. I don't need you to yell at me, or judge, I just need you to be a big sister and help me."

"Jesus, Bea, you're scaring me. Do I need to call a lawyer?"

"Just open the email."

She waited in silence, imagining her big sister double-clicking the email, pressing "Play" on the video and watching her baby sister doing things no one should ever have to imagine, let alone see. She closed her eyes, as if scrunching them up tightly could guard against the burning humiliation.

"What the fuck, Bea?" Fran's voice was hoarse. "I'm on my way round."

It took Fran just under fifteen minutes to make the twenty-five-minute journey, and when she arrived, she threw her arms around Bea and held her tightly. For the first time since she'd first seen the email—she could barely believe it had been less than forty minutes since her phone had buzzed with the message that had blown her nice normal evening apart—tears sprang to Bea's eyes.

"How much did you see?" she asked when Fran finally let her go.

"Enough to need a lot of alcohol to erase it from my memory," Fran replied. "Why couldn't you just have told me what it was?"

Bea threw herself down on the sofa, the laptop still in the middle of the floor. "I didn't want to spend half an hour listening to you tell me it couldn't be that bad and it probably wasn't even me and you probably couldn't see that much anyway. I wanted you to know how bad this was, exactly what all the other people on the list are going to see if they open that email."

Fran nodded. "And who was the guy?"

Bea closed her eyes in humiliation at the memory. "Did I ever tell you about Paul? He was friends with a girl at work. We went on a few dates and I decided to try taking it further. I had a few too many drinks beforehand, as you can see." She couldn't bring herself to tell Fran why she'd had to get so drunk before she had sex with Paul. Despite her bravado and the front she put on to her friends to make them think she was fine, she'd barely slept with anyone since university, and any relationship usually ended soon after she realized that the idea of sex made her skin crawl.

"Had he been over often?"

"No, we usually went out on dates. I don't think he'd been there before that night."

"So it couldn't have been him who filmed you."

Bea's eyes snapped open. "It must have been. Who else could it have been?"

"Come on, Bea, I know you've had a shock, but you have to be a bit smarter than that. That video started before the pair of you came into the room. Unless he had already been into your bedroom and set up a camera, there's no way it could have been him."

Bea let this sink in. She was right, of course she was. Paul hadn't been in the flat five minutes before she'd suggested going to the bedroom to get it over with, although she hadn't put it quite like that.

But if he hadn't filmed them, who had? The video had been close-up; the camera must have been on her desk, probably right next to her. . . .

She shot upright. "The laptop."

Fran looked confused. "What do you mean?"

Bea crossed the room and stepped around her laptop gingerly, as though it were a bomb waiting to explode. Standing behind it, she bent down and lifted it slowly, carried it in her outstretched hands into her bedroom, and left it on the bed, closing the door on it softly.

"The fucking laptop," she announced, marching back into the front room. "That's how it was filmed. On my own laptop. It must be bugged."

Fran's eyes widened. "Do you have any idea how mental you sound?"

"I know, Fran, but it's the only way! Like you said, that guy hadn't been anywhere near the bedroom before we went in together, and we were already being filmed. I sure as hell didn't set up a camera, and if there had been a tripod in front of my bed, I probably would have noticed."

"I don't know, the amount of alcohol you looked to have had, David Attenborough could have been sitting at the end of the bed narrating the session and you wouldn't have noticed."

"Thanks, Fran, that's exactly what I need right now, your goddam humor. I'm telling you, it could only be the laptop. "

Fran shook her head. "It just sounds so *Girl with the Dragon Tattoo*. Why would someone bug your computer? It's not like you're hiding government secrets. And who exactly? Who would have access to your laptop to do something like that?"

"I hate to even think this, let alone say it, but . . ." Bea closed her eyes as though just the thought caused her physical pain. "I think it might be Karen. She had access to my computer whenever she wanted. I think she's having some sort of breakdown. She's obsessed with this patient of hers . . . She sent me on a date the other night and . . ." She covered her face with her hands, feeling her cheeks heat up with the shame of what her best friend had said about her to this random stranger.

"Clearly there's a lot you're not telling me about what's going on with you and Karen, and as soon as we've sorted this, I want to know everything. But for now we need to deal with this. I was having a think on the way here, and there's one thing we can try."

"What, what can we do? Please tell me you can hack into people's accounts and delete the email."

"Not quite," Fran replied grimly. "But we don't need to delete it; we just need to make sure no one opens it. Do you have email on your phone?"

Bea nodded. "It's where I first saw that one."

"Okay, great. I need you to write an email to all the people who received that last one. Put in the subject line 'Virus warning: do not open emails from,' then type the address. Put it in capitals."

Bea did as her sister instructed. "Fran, you're a genius. Do you think it will work? Will people really not open it?"

"It's our best shot." Bea could have kissed her for using the word "our."

"Okay, now lay it on thick in the body of the email. Make it sound like if they open the email, their whole computer is at risk. Then you've just got to hope people open yours first."

Bea wrote what Fran had instructed and pressed "Send." She sighed. "I just can't believe this is even necessary. Why would anyone do something so cruel? I don't want to believe it's Karen; she's supposed to be my best friend. I mean, I can almost understand a threat, after what's happened, but this isn't a threat—she's actually tried to ruin my life. All because I found out about her and Michael."

"I think you have a lot to tell me," Fran said, sitting down next to her on the sofa. "Why don't you start at the beginning?"

- 70 -

ELEANOR

Eleanor backed gingerly out of the room, her shoulder hitting the door with a soft thud, making her cringe. Noah didn't stir and she silently let out the breath she'd been holding. She pulled the door closed behind her and hesitated for a second, waiting for the screams that didn't come. Maybe things were looking up. This was the third time this week Noah had slept in his crib during the day—yesterday she'd even managed a power nap without her Xanax.

She had to move fast if she wanted to make the most of her newfound energy. There were piles of washing in the kitchen, last night's dinner, and this morning's breakfast to wash up, and if he slept long enough, she might grab a cup of tea and watch some *Broadchurch*—she was falling behind with her TV viewing now that Noah was sleeping longer at night, and she had finally agreed to leave the house again after the incident with her hair. Bea had turned up one evening with an armful of beautiful hats she'd borrowed off a woman at work, and Eleanor had spent a good hour googling YouTube videos of side-parted hairstyles.

The house was strangely silent without the noise from either of the children. Not that it had been that much noisier the last few days, what with Toby barely speaking to them ever since his birthday and Adam out as much as ever. Her stomach hurt when she thought about the look on poor Toby's face as he'd walked in on her and Adam discussing whether to tell him about his real mother.

As it turned out, they didn't have much choice, and she'd called her mother to take Noah out for a few hours while they sat down and told Toby the truth. Or most of it, anyway.

He'd been silent throughout as they took turns to try to explain why they'd never told him before that Eleanor wasn't his real mum, but how did you explain a decision that was entirely based on selfish reasons? The fact was that if Eleanor hadn't been so desperate for her family to be perfect, so obsessed with making sure there were never any problems, never any obstacles to overcome, they would have told him the truth from the start, and he wouldn't be feeling so betrayed now.

It could have gone so much worse, she knew that, and however painful this was for Toby now, he would come to understand one day that all they had ever done was love him and try to protect him. At least now the secret wasn't hanging over their heads any longer, and the dread that had sat in Eleanor's chest ever since Toby's mother had walked out of his life had started to dissolve.

Kneeling on the kitchen floor, she shoved one of the piles of laundry into the washing machine, pushing it as far back in the drum as it would go to cram it all in. In spite of the fact that Toby hadn't run away from home—hadn't even shouted that he hated them—Eleanor still refused to be grateful to Karen for sending him the letter that had forced them into this position. She'd always known that Karen thought they were wrong to keep the truth from Toby—her and her *morals,* which were now basically a joke. But if all she had been trying to do was drive a bigger wedge into the gulf that was Eleanor and Adam's relationship—well, to use a child to do that was just sick.

She'd been trying not to think about it too much; she had no proof other than some late nights at work that Adam was having an affair with anyone. Was this Karen's way of breaking them up because her claim hadn't worked? Why would she do that? Because her own relationship was doomed to fail? What Karen had done with Michael didn't have to be the end of their friendship, despite how furious Eleanor had been when she'd first found out. Doing one bad thing didn't make someone a bad person, and maybe Karen didn't realize the damage she was inflicting; she had never been married, after all. If Eleanor was crossing things off her Reasons To Hate Karen list, that one was a question mark—she still didn't know if they could ever be as close unless Karen ended things with her married lover.

That just left the letter to Toby. Eleanor didn't want to lose someone she had been close to for her entire life over it, and maybe if Karen had replied to even one of her furious voice mail messages or missed phone calls, there might have been a chance that in time she would have accepted an apology from her friend. But there had been no apology, just one text message the evening before: *I didn't send that letter. I know who did and when I can prove it I'll come and explain xx*

Eleanor hadn't even bothered to reply. It was a pitiful attempt at shifting the blame, and not even a convincing one. Karen must know how devastated she would have been for Toby to find out about his real mother that way. It was almost as though she had made a conscious decision that Toby's birthday would be the end of their friendship, the letter the death knell at the funeral of their lives together. Maybe Karen was fed up with the drama that came with a close friendship like theirs, the petty disagreements, the self-justification that she wasn't even going to try and apologize, just a feeble denial so she didn't look like the bad guy. Maybe this was the end of them all—maybe it was for the best. Heaven knows they were at the age where friendships should be trinkets to be picked up and admired, then put back on the shelf until someone noticed they were getting dusty, not dishwashers constantly in need of refilling and emptying daily.

Eleanor grimaced at her choice of metaphor. Even thinking about her friends led her back to domestic tasks. She scanned the front room, unsure of where to start. Dusting could wait until Lesley came later in the week. She ran her finger over the top of a photo frame and shook the dust off onto the floor. That would have to do. Vacuuming she wouldn't risk until—

She stopped in her tracks, looking at the photograph she'd just run her finger over. It was a five-by-seven picture of Bea and Karen holding up a gigantic bedsheet with the words "Welcome Home" emblazoned across it in red, white, and blue sparkly letters. That one had been from when she'd spent two weeks in Italy on a work conference. She'd been in hysterics seeing them there, waving their banner as though she'd been on an expedition to the Amazon rain forest rather than at a two-week conference in a five-star hotel in Florence.

"We missed you!" Bea had declared when she'd asked them— tears running down her cheeks—what the bloody hell they thought they were playing at. "What's wrong with that?"

Now Eleanor looked at the smiling faces of her best friends, and tears stung her eyes again. What had it been about this picture that had given her reason to pause? Was it just the memory of a time when she'd thought there would be nothing on earth that could tear them apart? Karen had met Michael by then—she was already keeping the secret that had the potential to tear their friendship apart. How had she felt every time they had been out together, the five of them, to be playing a part? Had she experienced the same eternal dread that Eleanor herself had felt every time someone brought up the subject of giving birth in the days when she was a mother who had never experienced it?

Glancing again at the photograph, she felt that same pull that something wasn't quite right. There was something her mind was stretching to remember. She pictured Karen the last time she'd seen her. She'd left the café throwing one last disgusted look over her shoulder, clutching her handbag as though it were a force field against the awful revelation she'd just heard. Karen had been sitting there, her elbows resting on the table, her head in her hands, Bea blank-faced opposite her.

It still hurts, Eleanor told herself as she placed the picture back on the shelf. That was to be expected. Those kind of lies could cut a relationship to shreds.

An insistent beeping told her that the washing machine had finished its cycle, and she crossed the room to tackle the next load. Still, her mind kept pushing her thoughts back to Karen—her best friend and her husband, both liars. Did she even know either of them anym—

She cringed as her thoughts were interrupted by someone at the front door.

- 71 -

KAREN

Karen's mind was a whirlpool of dread and panic as she drove towards the river. What she'd done could never be undone and now someone was going to have to face the consequences. How had things gone so wrong? Everything she'd ever worked for had disappeared in a puff of smoke, all because of one woman. No one would ever trust her again. She'd probably never work again, and she and Michael would almost definitely not survive this. Her life was falling to pieces in front of her, and there was little or nothing she could do to glue it back together.

The river was angry today, angrier than she had seen it of late. It was almost as if it knew that Karen had failed to heed its warnings, the swirling dark mass of water chastising her, mocking her stupidity. *How could you? How could you?*

And what lay beneath it? Usually the idea of the life hidden under the water appealed to her, mirroring her own life, so much underneath the surface that people could not see. That people could not be allowed to see. The respected psychiatrist, the screwed-up mistress who used sex with nameless, faceless men to claw back some of the control she lost when she sent her boyfriend back to his wife and children every weekend. Who was she? Was she that woman who cheated and lied and used people? Or was she the loving, caring best friend who had dedicated her life to helping others through their problems, who held the hands—metaphorically, of course—of complete strangers who were at their lowest ebb? She knew she'd brought some of her patients back from the darkest places they'd ever visited. She'd saved lives. Was that the true Karen Browning? Which was real and which was the liar?

She'd spent what felt like hours sitting on the cold, wet grass that divided the icy water from the people of the town. Those banks kept them safe; when they failed, when they burst, homes and businesses were flooded with dirty, stinking river water, lives were ruined. She'd failed her friends as completely as those banks had failed their town time and time again. As soon as the rain got too much to bear, they gave in and let the place drown.

It was getting dark by the time she pulled into her street, the blue lights of the police car lighting up the sky intermittently. This was it, then. The water had filled her up and the banks had burst. She'd let them drown. She'd failed.

72

My hands were covered in warm, sticky blood and all I could do was stare at them stupidly. I hadn't even noticed that her head had been bleeding when I'd lifted it onto my lap, cradled it as her breathing changed from desperate, ragged spurts to light, strangled gasps. Had I known then that she was dying? The words didn't enter my head fully formed and with total clarity, but yes, I believe I knew it had gone further than I had ever planned or expected.

I didn't stay to see Eleanor die. I regret that now; I'd driven the train off the tracks, and I was too cowardly to stand and watch the crash. I now am aware that it will hurt her family to know she died alone and scared. But there are plenty of things in my life I regret—this is just the biggest. I'd lost control and I was ashamed—of everything, it was my control, that was the most important thing to me. I'd let her rile me with her callous words and her refusal to listen to the danger she was in—the true danger. And when she turned away from me, dismissing me as though I was no more than one of her children to be ignored or humored in equal measure, I grabbed her arm. I pulled her towards me and on her face I saw fear. She pulled back at the same time that I pushed her away. I don't think I hit her with anything. I'm certain she fell. I know I pushed her too hard, but she wouldn't stop saying those awful things. It wasn't my fault. Maybe now they'll all see.

PART 3

73

Tell me about when you were four.

You've asked about that already. I've told you, it's not relevant.

I think it is, and so do you. Is it hard for you to talk about?

Of course it is. I've never spoken about what happened with anyone.

Try.

I was three when Mum brought her home from the hospital. Amy. She was tiny, smaller even than the doll Dad had got me to prepare me for her arrival into the family. I loved that doll. I took her everywhere with me, I changed her nappy and fed her from my sippy cup. She was my best friend. And when Amy came home, I knew we would be best friends too.

Were you jealous of her?

Never. At least not that I can remember. She was so little, she needed our help with everything. She took up so much of Mum's time, and Mum was always exhausted, but I don't ever remember blaming Amy. If anything, I blamed Mum. I didn't understand how she could be so snappy and miserable when we had this wonderful little thing to take care of. When Amy cried, I would give her my teddy to make her happy, and she would look at me with those huge blue eyes, eyes too big for her little face, and sometimes I would pretend that I was her mummy and that our mum didn't even exist. Even at three I knew I wanted to take care of this baby for the rest of her life.

Go on.

My mum got worse. I didn't know what zombies were then, but

that's how I remember her now—like the walking dead. She would spend whole days where she never talked to either of us. Of course she kept us fed and watered, we were always clean and well dressed, but I didn't feel like I was even there. Sometimes I would pretend I was a ghost, and then it would be fun that she didn't talk to me because it meant my disguise was working. Some days the only interaction Amy got was from me until Dad came home.

Did your dad do anything about it?

That was the thing, when Dad got home it was like having a different Mum. She would sing while she cooked our favorite things for tea and she would play with us and read us stories before bed.

That must have been confusing for you.

I'm not sure it was. I mean, of course now I know it was, but at the time I got used to living like that. I used to call her "real Mum" and "day Mum."

How long was it like that for?

My whole life after Amy was born. But it didn't seem to matter. I had her to take care of, and to give all my love to, and she loved me back. Whenever I walked into the room, she would beam and put out her arms for me to lift her up, and at four years old I would carry her round like she was a doll.

What happened when Amy was eleven months old?

When she was born, I would sing to her as softly as I could and let her hold my hair while she fell asleep. I would put her dummy back in when she cried and I let her have my favorite bear—it was the same size as she was. When she was six months I taught her to crawl. I would put toys in front of her, just out of her reach, and demonstrate crawling across the floor to them. When she was eight months I would—

Do you blame yourself for what happened to your sister?

Of course I do. It was my fault. I wasn't taking good enough care of her. I know what you're going to say, but it doesn't make any difference how old I was. I should have been watching.

Tell me what happened, Karen.

My mummy is in her bedroom and I think she's been crying again. I've been as good as I really could be. I fed Amy her tea and played with her while Mum rested her eyes for a bit, and I haven't asked for anything today—Mummy hates it when I go on. Amy has been a bit loud, and even though I tried to shush her and sang to her loads, she wouldn't stop shouting and laughing at her pink singy bear.

I put my nose to Amy's padded bottom and sniff. It smells sweet and ripe and I start panicking. I'm going to have to go and disturb Mummy—there's a big orangey-brown stain on the onesie that Amy's been wearing all day and she won't hold still long enough for me to take it off. I wrestle with her a few minutes and manage to open a few of the snaps, but then she's gone, crawling across the floor towards the closed gate at the top of the stairs.

"Mummy?" I whisper, pushing open her bedroom door and hearing the slow creak. "Mum?"

She's lying on the bed—not in it—and her eyes are closed but I can't tell if she's asleep or not. She must be, though, because she doesn't answer me when I call her name. Her medicines are on the bedside table and I cross the room to put the lids on—if Amy sees them she'll think they're sweets, like I used to before Daddy explained they were grown-up medicines to help Mummy be happy. I understand that; my sweets make me happy so it makes sense to me that grown-up sweets can make Mummy happy too. It's just that they don't seem to work anymore.

"Mummy? Amy's pooed. It smells yucky."

Her eyes open slowly, and for a minute she looks like she doesn't know who I am. I wait for her to properly see me, and for a second I think she's going to smile, but she doesn't. Instead she says, "What's the matter now?"

"It's Amy," I say in my bestest indoor voice. I'm good at remembering the things that make her head hurt and how not to do them. "She's done a stinky poo and her nappy is leaking."

She sighs, but only a little one, and she doesn't shout or sound angry. She looks like all her parts are heavy as she gets off the bed and follows me to where Amy is still crawling around the landing, the stain on her onsie spreading down her leg now.

"Oh Jesus!" She's always talking to God and Jesus, as if everything that goes wrong in our house is their fault. I've never met Jesus, but Mummy doesn't seem to like him a lot—even though she's always asking him for things.

"Sorry, Mummy, I tried to help," I say. She doesn't answer me or even look at me, but at least she doesn't shout.

"Oh God." She has taken off Amy's onesie and the poo is everywhere. It stinks. One side of her nappy has come undone and her leg is covered in thick brown gloop. Mum puts her back down on the floor and pushes open the bathroom door, turns on the shower.

"Can I have a bath too?" I ask. I love the bath. We get to play and splash around and Amy always hugs on to me like I'm the mummy. "Please?"

"When I've got this mess off her," Mum promises, and she even smiles a bit at me remembering my manners. She strips Amy down and plonks her under the shower, the poo running off her into the plughole. Amy starts to scream straightaway and puts out her arms to me. I put my hand under the water.

"It's a bit chilly."

Mum doesn't look happy at my helping; she pulls her annoyed face and moves the hotter/colder switch.

"Can I get in now?" All the poo has gone down the plughole, and I'm desperate to get in to play with my sister. Mum sighs—I'm going on again—but she nods and I pull off my clothes, excited, and struggle to swing my leg over the side of the bath. I want to show her how much of a big girl I am getting in by myself, but she doesn't even notice. She picks me up and plonks me in the bath next to Amy. I put the plug in just like I always do and sit under the shower as the water fills up the sides.

"Watch her a second for me," Mum says, and gives me a frowny look. "Have you got her?"

I nod. Amy is sitting between my legs and I wrap my arms around her chest as Mum disappears from sight.

"Here we go, Amy." I show her the little blue boat with the squirrel captain, and she laughs when I duck it under the water and it bobs back up to the top.

The water on my head feels lovely and warm—I'm so grown-up now that I don't even mind anymore when a little bit gets on my face. Amy puts her hands out to the taps and grabs hold of one, tries to pull herself up. She's such a naughty little monkey—I always call her that—and she loves to stand up even though she can't walk yet. I'm trying to teach her but she always falls back on her bum after a few seconds. I laugh and pull her back down. "Oh, no you don't," I say to her like I've heard Daddy say. She laughs louder, like we're playing a game, and tries to crawl forward. The water isn't very high, and it's okay, it's not up to her face when she crawls yet.

I get a little shock when the water falling on my head goes cold. "Mum!" I shout. "It's gone chilly!"

Mum doesn't come, the water is freezing now and it's filling the bath. It's okay, though, I know how to turn it off, I can stop it freezing us before Mum comes to put it warm again. I'm so grown-up now, I think as I stand up to turn off the shower knob. I'm even going to school soon and my teachers will be really pleased with how grown-up I am. But I turn the knob the wrong way first time, silly billy me, and the water goes faster and faster. Quickly I turn it the other way, but my hands are wet now and the tap is wet and my fingers are just slipping round and round on the cold silver. "Mum?"

Phew, it's okay, the shower knob turns and the water goes off. "Thank goodness," I say to Amy with a grin. I've heard Daddy say that too, and I like the way it sounds. Goodness. Oh goodness.

I turn around to smile at my sister and laugh to see her messing around under the water.

"Oh, Amy! You silly monkey." I pull her back up to sit in between my legs, just like Mummy said, but she feels heavier now, and her eyes are closed. I didn't even know she was tired. "Amy, wake up, baba."

She's not waking up. And I know then that there's something very,

very wrong. I can feel myself starting to panic, the way I felt when I knocked my drink off the table and Mummy yelled and said why did I have to be so difficult? I give Amy a little shake—not too hard—but she is still sleeping.

"Mum!" I'm screaming really loud now, even though I've been told not to shout, not to give Mummy a headache, but I can't help it and I can't stop myself crying. "Mummy!"

Mum takes ages, but then she pushes open the door and suddenly she's screaming and crying and pulling Amy away from me, out of the water. This is bad, this is really bad, and I'm crying lots now, but Mummy doesn't even tell me to shut up or stop whining and I wish she would just yell at me or send me to bed and I wish Amy would cry or be a nightmare just like the other days. Then Mummy is on her phone and she tells me to get out of the way—only she uses one of those naughty words that Daddy doesn't like and is always telling me not to use—and I run away into my bedroom and climb into the bottom of my closet where I sit, naked and cold and being a crybaby until my daddy comes to find me and take me to Nanny's house for a little holiday. And Mummy and Amy aren't there anymore, and Amy never comes back again, and I know it's my fault.

- 74 -

BEA

Bea entered the bar area and scanned the room for Adam. She eventually found him huddled in the corner of one of the pub's private booths, staring at the table, his face a drawn gray.

"Oh, Adam." She slid into the booth and wrapped her arms around her best friend's husband, who sat rigidly while she squeezed him tightly.

"I shouldn't be here," he muttered. "I should be with the boys."

"Are they with your mum? How are they doing? If you need anything . . ." She trailed off, knowing how empty the platitude sounded. *If there's anything I can do . . . if you need any help . . .* She couldn't be a mum or a wife, and that was what they needed— the only thing they needed.

"They're doing awful. Toby hasn't spoken since I picked him up from school that day, and Noah hasn't stopped screaming. We're staying at Mum's because I can't bear to go back to the house, but we can't stay there forever. What are we going to do, Bea? What will we do without her?"

For the third time that day, hot, angry tears sprang to Bea's eyes, only this time she didn't sniff and wipe them away, just let them fall. She'd barely stopped crying herself in the two days since the call had come from Eleanor's mother, who had been barely coherent as she'd broken the news. Bea had tried to call Karen the minute she put down the phone, but there had been no answer; she'd taken a taxi to her house and there had been only darkness.

Karen hadn't been to work and they would tell her nothing—or they knew nothing. Bea was hurt, confused, and angry; it felt as though she'd lost two friends in the space of a week. She had no answer to Adam's question. She didn't know how they were going to cope; she didn't know if any of them would be okay ever again.

"Do they have any idea who was responsible?"

Adam laughed, a hollow sound with no humor. "I was prime suspect number one. Luckily I was in the office all day rather than traveling; there's no way I could have gone home. They don't think it was a robbery, as nothing was taken. The neighbors heard her arguing with someone. The police are questioning Karen—did you know?"

"Karen?" Bea was confused. "Why? Wouldn't she have been at work too?"

Adam looked at her, and for the first time she took in the red rims and the puffiness around his eyes. He looked completely broken. "She'd been suspended that week. I thought you'd know."

"We had a fight." Bea was ashamed to admit it; it all seemed so insignificant compared with their lives now. "About Michael. Surely . . ." She couldn't bring herself to say Eleanor's name. "Surely you knew that?"

"No." He shook his head. "Eleanor had been acting really strange, and not just new-baby strange. We barely spoke, and when she did speak to me, it was to snap at me about how little I did, or how little I understood."

Bea sighed. "We found out that Michael is married. Eleanor didn't take it well—you know how she felt about that kind of thing, the sacred family unit and all that. She hadn't spoken to Karen since she found out."

"Well, she must have started. That's why Karen was taken in for questioning: she was seen at our house the morning Eleanor . . . the morning it happened."

"I don't know anything about that. I haven't spoken to Karen in over a week. She won't answer my calls."

Bea thought back to the date her best friend had set up for her, the video emailed to her workmates. What the hell was going on with Karen? It wasn't like her; she'd always been so together, never one for nasty, malicious games. The conversation they'd had just a few weeks before flashed through her mind.

"I need to ask you a question." She looked down at the table, unable to meet Adam's eyes. "Before we fell out, Karen said she'd seen you with one of her patients. She thought you were having an affair."

If it was possible for Adam's face to lose even more color, Bea was sure it happened at her words.

"I wouldn't . . . I couldn't . . ."

She reached out a hand and touched his arm. "It doesn't matter now. Whatever happened, it's not important."

"Of course it is. I can't allow people to believe I could do that to Eleanor." He let out a sigh. "Let's face it, the last few months I was a shit husband. I worked late on purpose to avoid whatever I might have done or said wrong that day, when Els needed me there for her and the boys. I got out of the house at any opportunity; I went to the gym, for Christ's sake—I haven't been to the gym in years! I was so selfish, I just kept thinking about how I needed space and time to myself when I should have been spending every last minute with my family. Oh God, if I could just go back and be the husband she deserved . . ."

He was either telling the truth or a very good liar; Bea wasn't sure which. Her head was full of all the things that had happened to the three of them over the last couple of months, and she had no idea what the hell was going on. Karen wouldn't lie about seeing Adam with another woman. And this patient of hers, Bea was sure she was real too. So what was the truth? And with Eleanor gone and Karen missing, who could she trust now?

75

BEA

Bea, it's Michael. Can you let me in? We need to talk."
Bea pressed the "Talk" button on the intercom and injected as much venom into her voice as she could manage. "I'd rather shit in my hands and clap. Go away."

There was a silence, filled only by the static that indicated Michael still had his finger on the buzzer.

"Look," he said at last. "I know you think I'm to blame for what happened—"

"That's because it's your fault," Bea interrupted. "I know you aren't responsible for . . ." She couldn't say the words. *Eleanor's death.* "But you're to blame for what has happened to us. You're the reason none of us were speaking. Why are you even here? You should be with Karen, supporting her. Isn't she being questioned again?"

"I have no idea. We had a huge argument the night before . . . the night before Eleanor . . . about this patient of hers, and she told me to go back to . . . to go home. She won't talk to me, she won't let me in the house, and I don't want to let myself in—it's her home after all. I was hoping you could talk to her, make her see sense . . ."

"Piss off, Michael. Sounds like she's already seen sense. Go home to your family."

Bea released the button and wandered round the front room, picking up the remote and moving it from the sofa to the table, tidying the magazines from the table to the sofa. The buzzer didn't sound again. Was he still outside? She peered through the useless peephole; there was no one in the narrow hallway, no eye staring back at her. He couldn't be in the hall, not unless someone let him in through the front. She was just being stupid.

So Karen and Michael were no more. In that case, why hadn't she been answering Bea's calls? It had been nearly two weeks since they last spoke—had she been alone since Eleanor's death? Whatever their differences, Karen surely couldn't go through this alone.

From the front window of the flat she could see only a corner of the doorstep, but it looked empty. No cars waited in the street outside. She backed away from the window, letting the curtain fall limply back into place. Anger gave way to an uneasy feeling. Should she be scared of him?

Don't be ridiculous, she told herself. This is Michael. You've known him for two years. He sang karaoke at your birthday party and you've slept on his sofa. There's nothing dangerous about him.

Except there's a lot you don't know about him. You don't know his wife, or his children. You don't know where he sleeps on weekends, whether he reads his twin daughters bedtime stories or if he thinks of Karen while he's having sex with his wife. And there's someone else you thought you knew. Karen. But you didn't know she was a mistress. Or what had happened to her sister. Do you know she didn't kill your best friend?

She jumped at the sound of knocking at the front door. Someone had let him in—probably fucking Tara from upstairs, stupid cow. Now what was she going to do?

She picked up her mobile and keyed 999 without pressing "Dial." Edging closer to the door as quietly as she could manage with her heart beating a tattoo through her chest and her ragged breathing as an accompaniment, she pressed a hand against it. Would he go away if she didn't answer? Or would he try to kick it down?

"Bea?"

The voice didn't belong to Michael—not unless he'd had a sex change in the ten minutes since she'd told him to get lost. It was Tara, the dozy mare from upstairs and the least threatening person she knew. Bea had never been so happy to hear her voice.

"Thank God it's you." She threw open the door, half expecting at the last minute to see Michael with his arm around Tara's neck like a low-budget slasher-movie villain. But Tara was alone, a folded piece of paper in her hand and her usual vacant expression on her face.

"Some guy downstairs asked me to give you this." She handed Bea the note and waited expectantly for her to open it. Bea grasped the piece of paper and plastered on a bright smile.

"Thanks, hun!" She made a move to close the door, but Tara stayed rooted to the spot.

"Seemed pretty intense," she continued, either oblivious to Bea's desire to escape or pretending to be. "He your new boyfriend or something?"

"Or something," Bea replied. "I don't mean to be rude, but I was in the middle of cooking tea. Open flame and all that. Can't burn the building down!" And without waiting for Tara's reply, she closed the door in the waiting girl's face.

She practically threw the paper onto the coffee table while she went to pour herself a glass of wine. She was going to need to be sitting down and not completely sober to read whatever Michael had to say to her. Hearing him say Eleanor's name had been like stepping on a plug—a painful shock followed by a dull ache.

Glass in hand, she sank into the cream sofa and fingered the edge of the paper. She could so easily throw it away, burn it, flush it down the toilet, but she knew she wouldn't. People only did that in films. In real life it would take a heart of ice not to be curious, and hopeful. And petrified.

Breathing in through her nose, out through her mouth, Bea unfolded the paper.

She'd expected to see line after line of pleading and apologies. Instead she saw just two sentences.

I know who her patient was. Call me.

76

How did you feel when you saw the police waiting for you at your house?

I was scared, of course. I knew something bad must have happened. It was all part of her plan.

What do you think Jessica's plan for you was?

She was going to turn everyone against me. She wanted to take away everything I'd worked so hard for: my career, my relationship, my friends.

How had you worked hard for those things? Aren't friendships and relationships a normal part of life? How did you have to work harder than anyone else?

You know why.

Because you had to deceive people to get them? Michael's wife and family, your friends.

I suppose you could say that. I'm not going to pretend I haven't lied to people, but if you tell the truth, sometimes people get hurt. No one wants to know the truth anyway; they pretend to but they don't.

What do you mean by that?

Take Eleanor, for example. She always said that if she found out Adam was cheating on her she would get rid of him straightaway, and yet when it came to it, she didn't even ask him for the truth. She would rather not know and pretend there was nothing wrong than face the truth and have to make a difficult decision. And if you want to talk about Michael's wife—if there was ever anyone who didn't want to face the truth, it was her. Do you think she didn't suspect for a second that her husband might not be working away all week? He had a whole other life, for goodness' sake. If she'd wanted to find out the truth, she could have done it at any point. She only had to follow him once, or ask what the extra set of keys on his key ring was for. She didn't find out because she never wanted to.

So it's okay to lie if the truth would hurt people?

It's as good a reason as any.

Surely you could just stop doing the things that would hurt people.

I never said I was perfect. I've never said that.

- 77 -

BEA

Bea swilled back the dregs of her wine and reached out for the bottle to pour herself another glass. She knew she should keep a clear head if she was going to call Michael—and she *was* going to call him. She had so many questions. Her whole life had been blown apart by what had happened to Eleanor. Karen had been taken in for questioning, and Bea felt like she had no right to demand answers from anyone. The police had no obligation to tell her anything, and Eleanor's family were maintaining an icy silence. It hurt, the way she was being frozen out, as though she were a mere acquaintance, as if she hadn't known Eleanor almost her whole life, but she understood that they had the boys to think about now—and her pain was nothing compared to what they were going through.

It wasn't just Eleanor she had lost; it was as though her whole life had been rubbed out by a huge eraser and there was no rewriting it. It had always been Bea, Eleanor, and Karen. Without Eleanor she didn't even know who she was anymore. And she hadn't spoken to Karen since before it had happened—her phone was off most of the time, and when it wasn't, it just rang and rang. Her curtains were closed and she wasn't answering the door. It was as if they had never been more than passing acquaintances. Okay, so their friendship had come off the tracks, but surely something as enormous as this should bring them back together? If not this, then would anything?

The sound of her phone blaring out Sir Mix-A-Lot was unwelcome and distasteful at a time when smiling was unbearable. The tune only meant one person, though; the sole person she could tolerate talking to at the moment.

"Fran, hey."

"Hey. How're you feeling?"

"Like shit." Fran was the only one who asked that question and expected an honest answer rather than an "I'm fine." Bea didn't even have to ask how her sister was in return. Fran was a giver, not a taker.

"Of course you are. This whole thing is shit. I'm coming over in half an hour with *Fast and Furious* and toffee popcorn. Oh, and a vat of wine. I was just calling to see if you needed any shopping. I make a crappy lasagne, but I can fill your freezer with artery-squeezing ready meals."

At times like this, too many people asked if there was anything they could do, knowing that the person they were asking would say no out of politeness. Not Fran. If she wanted to help, she'd just do it. Knowing that her big sister had gone out and chosen a film and her favorite pick-me-ups made Bea want to hug her down the phone. She longed to tell Fran that that sounded perfect and spend the evening on the sofa in her comfy gray pajamas, but she knew she'd just end up wondering what the hell Michael thought he knew, and what he intended to do about it.

"There's honestly nothing I'd love more, Fran, but I have plans to be a complete moron tonight." She sighed and gave her sister an unedited account of her afternoon. "You may as well tell me I'm being an idiot and threaten to tattle on me to Mum now."

"I probably should . . ." Fran dropped her voice, presumably so Rich didn't hear her being irresponsible, "but I wouldn't be able to resist finding out either. You don't think Michael had anything to do with what happened to Els, do you? Hasn't his wife given him an alibi? The police obviously don't think he was involved; they've got their heads firmly up their asses trying to prove it was Karen."

"You're not telling me *you* think she didn't do it? I thought you'd be the first with the torch and pitchfork."

"What, the doc? Come on, Bea, seriously? You've known her for years—admittedly not as well as you thought you did, but still, you were all so close."

"I don't know her at all, Fran." Bea sighed, sadness and exhaustion threatening to take her over completely. "Her boyfriend is a married man! I don't know either of them. She set me up with that creep and she probably emailed all my workmates a sex tape I didn't even make! And I told you what happened to her sister, right? How do we know she didn't do that on purpose?"

She heard Fran take a deep breath. "Don't be a bitch, Bea. You told me she wasn't to blame for that. She was a kid!"

Bea sighed again. "You're right, that was horrible. I'm just so confused at the moment. Why hasn't she been in touch? Although, you've changed your tune. You never got on with Karen. Why the sudden bleeding heart?"

Fran let out a laugh. "I never really disliked her. It was her relationship with you I didn't like. She was like a big sister to you. I didn't particularly relish the competition from someone who had never glued your Barbies' heads together."

"I knew that was you," Bea muttered, tears pricking at her eyelids. "You never had any competition, Fran."

"I know that really. Now go and prove your best friend isn't a nutcase and I'll bring Vin Diesel over tomorrow."

"Love you, Fran."

"Love you too, Bea."

- 78 -

BEA

Who is this girl, then? And what makes you suddenly so sure you know her identity?"

Bea had called Michael as soon as Fran had left and told him to pick her up immediately, on the condition he didn't talk about Karen or Eleanor. He'd agreed, and Bea was relieved he'd stuck to his word.

"I would have known all along if Karen had been allowed to tell me her name," Michael replied. "When I went back to the house to pick up some stuff, she wasn't there and I had to let myself in. There was a file on the table. It didn't take a genius to work out whose; Karen had been verging on obsessed with this girl for weeks. When I saw the name, I recognized it straightaway."

"Old girlfriend with a grudge?"

Michael snorted. "I almost wish it was. Jessica Hamilton was a friend of my daughter's at college."

"Your daughter?" Bea whistled. "Jesus, Michael, were you in college yourself when you had her?"

Michael sighed and rubbed a hand across his face. "I'm forty-five, Bea. Anne is twenty-two now. We adopted her when she was nearly seven. Anne was—*is*—Emily's niece. Her sister had a drug problem. We didn't even realize until social services contacted us to say that Anne would be taken away and placed with a new family if we didn't take her in. Emily was distraught that she hadn't seen any signs—her sister lived miles away—but we agreed to take Anne on.

She'd been through a lot, seen more than a seven-year-old should see. She was difficult, but not in the normal seven-year-old way. She could be quite sly; she'd lie to me and Emily, play us off against each other. There were incidents, things that put a lot of pressure on our relationship. I wasn't there enough."

Bea could read between the lines as though the words were written across his forehead. Karen wasn't the first—he'd been cheating on his wife for years.

"And this girl, Jessica, where does she fit in?"

He shook his head in reply. "I honestly don't know. Like I said, she was a friend of Anne's at college. Anne didn't mention her friends much, so when she started talking about Jessica, we were pleased she'd met someone she got on with so well. Then she met someone else, a girl called Ruth Carrington. According to Anne, Jessica didn't like her having someone else she was close to. She was a jealous girl, possessive. I got the impression she didn't have many friends herself."

"You never met her?"

"Like I said, I wasn't around much." Michael switched lanes. He was silent for a moment while he chose the correct exit at the roundabout, then began to speak again. "Anne said Jessica's family was well-off, but she was a bit of a loner. I assumed that was the reason they'd connected."

Bea could well imagine the awkward young girl, shoved from pillar to post, embarrassed about her past and confused that her new family wasn't the catalog picture she'd hoped for.

"When Anne and Ruth started spending more time together, Jessica became hostile towards the other girl. Started sending her nasty text messages warning her to stay away from Anne. When she told us this, I told her to steer clear of Jessica, even suggested I go and see the head of the college, but Anne said there was no need. Jessica was harmless. Then one evening Anne came home in a state. I wasn't there, but Emily told me about it afterwards. Anne said that Jessica had attacked Ruth. She took it badly, as though it was her fault. Emily tried to calm her down, but she locked herself in her room, stayed in there all weekend. Em thought she seemed scared of her so-called friend. I said I'd go to the college that Monday, but something came up, and when I got back, Anne was fine. She said she'd been to college and everything was being dealt with. Ruth switched colleges and Anne never talked about her or Jessica again."

"It sounds as though this Jessica has some problems."

"That's not what I'm worried about," Michael replied grimly. "I'm concerned that Emily and I only got one side of the story. I called Jessica Hamilton before I spoke to you. The way she tells it, it was Anne who attacked Ruth because she started seeing someone and Anne couldn't handle the rejection. Jessica Hamilton has been at university the past four years and has never moved back. My daughter, however"—he grimaced as though it caused him physical pain to say the words—"has been living here all along. And from what Jessica told me, if she found out about Karen and me, God knows how she would react."

Bea let his words sink in. *God knows how she would react.*

"When you said you knew her patient's identity, I assumed we were going to see her. If Jessica doesn't live here anymore, then why are we going to her house?"

"We're not," Michael replied. "We're going to find my daughter."

- 79 -

KAREN

Released pending further investigation. It was hard not to laugh at that. Everything in her life seemed to be pending further investigation. Her job, her relationship, now her freedom.

She'd called Michael from the station, unwilling to believe that their argument days ago would stop him from being there for her upon her release. She needed him. She needed him to explain, to tell her that "released without charge" meant that the police believed she'd had nothing to do with Eleanor's death—or, better still, that this was all part of Jessica Hamilton's sick plan and Eleanor wasn't really dead at all. Above all she just needed him to be there for her as though for that moment there was no wife, no other family, just her.

The phone had rung and rung, and just when she thought he'd picked up, she heard the familiar voice of the automated voice-mail message. With a sinking feeling in her stomach she had stepped out of the station and onto the main road, on her own. It was obviously how she was going to have to face this now. No Michael, no Bea. No Eleanor.

The thought of Eleanor brought a black curtain down in front of her eyes, and she stumbled, grabbed hold of the chipped blue railing outside the police station and retched into the greenery at its border. To anyone passing she must have looked like another reveler who had spent the night on one of the wooden slats with a sheet that passed for a bed, sleeping off a good time.

When her throat was sore and her stomach empty she paused
for a second, trying desperately to catch her breath and wipe stinging water from her eyes. The town was a twenty-minute walk she
knew she wouldn't be able to make, but not wanting to call a taxi
to pick her up from a police station, she forced her shaky legs to
take her to the nearest bench.

The taxi took as long as the walk would have. While she waited,
her mind probed cautiously, looking for a reaction that she could
analyze. When she thought of Eleanor, a screaming pain threatened
to escalate into a full-blown migraine, something she couldn't deal
with here and now, but despite her efforts to think of something
else, *anything else,* all she could picture was her best friend's little
boys, now motherless children. Noah had been found in his crib
upstairs, completely unharmed but in considerable distress. The
call had come from one of the neighbors who had seen a woman
perfectly fitting her description walking up the path towards the
house shortly before the screaming and banging started.

"Bea, it's Karen. Listen, I don't know what you've heard about
anything . . ." She hesitated. The last thing she wanted to do was
talk to Bea about what had happened to Eleanor in a voice mail.
"Look, call me please, it's urgent. I'm sorry."

She didn't bother going inside her house, instead getting straight
into her car. There wasn't anything there for her, and the emptiness
would be too much to bear. She didn't care about how she looked
or smelled after seventeen hours in a police station. She'd told them
about Jessica Hamilton but they hadn't seemed particularly interested, concentrating more on her.

There was only one way to find out. She had known as soon
as she'd taken it from the office that it was going to end this way.
She'd told herself when she'd written it down that to go there would

be career suicide. But now it seemed she had no career, so she had nothing left to lose.

She took the slip of paper out of her bag and laid it on the steering wheel in front of her.

Jessica Hamilton's home address.

Karen turned the radio up so she didn't have to think about the dozens of police officers who were working on the evidence that would lead them to Eleanor's killer. It was only a matter of time before she was dragged back in for questioning again, and this time she might not be coming out. Not unless she could prove that Jessica Hamilton at least existed. Then maybe she wouldn't be the sole focus of their investigation. Jessica might be twisted, she might be smart, but Karen doubted she was an evil genius. It happened all the time on TV, killers being so clever that they took care of all the evidence, led the police round in circles until the very end, but the truth was that in real life it was unlikely that she'd erased all the fingerprints she'd made in Eleanor's life. All the police needed was someone to match them to, and while Jessica remained a ghost, Karen's was the only direction they were looking in. Hers and perhaps Adam's.

Her phone buzzed inside her handbag and she fumbled for it, trying to keep control of the wheel with one hand and rooting around inside with the other. When she had no luck, she upended the bag, tipping the entire contents onto the passenger seat, and grabbed the phone, which promptly stopped ringing. Shit! Number unknown. She waited to see if a voice-mail message appeared, but nothing. To be honest, it was for the best. If it had been Michael or Bea, she would have had to tell them where she was going, and they would only try to stop her. She'd made up her mind and had no intention of being swayed by reason or logic. She felt like she'd been possessed by an impulsive, reckless spirit and she was going to embrace the feeling for as long as it took her to get there, like a drunk determined to dance until she was sober. She'd never acted without consulting her senses before; everything she did in her life was carefully measured and considered. Even the casual sex had had none of the reckless abandon of a normal one-night stand, each episode planned methodically and executed for the exact purpose of convincing herself she was in control of the situation with Michael. He went home to his wife; she went and screwed a nameless stranger. Tit for tat to prove to herself that she couldn't be in too deep—not if she could cheat on him so easily and without the slightest bit of guilt. Well, until the last time.

The houses on Jessica's street were of the detached, three-story, bay-windowed variety. They all had names rather than numbers, "Tontine" and "Valley House." The one she was looking for was "Underwood," and she found it at the end of the street, facing out onto the others as though it were at the head of the table. She didn't feel nervous despite the fact that she believed she was about to come face-to-face with the person who was responsible for her best friend's death. She supposed that part of her expected Jessica wouldn't be there, that she would have gathered her belongings and fled the country like the ghost she had come to be. So she was surprised to see lights on, a car in the drive.

Ringing the doorbell, she felt a lump form in her throat that threatened to choke her. She wasn't sure she'd be able to speak if the door even opened. But it did open, and instead of mousy Jessica Hamilton, she was confronted by a face she knew very well.

She stood dumbly, the ability to voice her intentions lost. The woman in the doorway smiled nervously. Everything about her was miniature; she was thin enough to knock sideways with a deep breath, and so pale. She gripped the frame with her tiny hands as though to steady herself, and Karen wondered if she'd had a drink.

"Can I help?"

"I'm . . . I'm looking for Jessica Hamilton."

A flicker of recognition crossed the woman's face with a frown, as though she knew the name but couldn't quite place it. Instead of turning Karen away, however, she studied her intently, as though her face was the one she was trying to identify. And then a hand shot to her mouth.

"You're her, aren't you?" She stepped back as though to close the door on her, but Karen lurched forward in desperation.

"Please, wait! I need to find Jessica. It's very important for all of us. You recognize the name, I know you do. Can you help me?"

The woman took several deep, slow breaths, the kind a therapist would teach you to take when your feelings were overwhelming you.

"I've been waiting for this, you know. I suppose you'd better come in."

And with that, Michael's wife stepped to one side and Karen entered the house.

- 8 0 -

KAREN

I've waited for this for ten years," Emily repeated, leading Karen from the hallway into a front room the size of her entire house.

"Ten years?" Karen replied without thinking. "But Michael and I have only been together two."

Emily recoiled at the sound of his name coming from Karen's lips, and instantly she regretted her lack of tact. She was so used to Michael being fully hers when they were together that it was hard to make herself believe that he was actually married to someone else.

"You, one of the others, I was always expecting someone to turn up. You do know you're not the first, I presume?" The way she said it made Karen sound like a commodity, a replaceable part in an everlasting machine. "But no one ever has. I assume you didn't come today to tell me tales of the affair?"

She'd always known what Emily Lenton looked like, from the Facebook photos she tortured herself with so often. In real life she was more delicate, breakable even, and her hands shook slightly when they weren't clasped together in front of her. Karen could tell she had been beautiful once, but the strain of her situation had taken its toll. Her hair was salon-finished but it was thinning in places, and her makeup looked like a mask against the accusations that she'd lost her husband because she'd let herself go. She made a small motion for Karen to sit down and perched herself on the edge of the large plum-colored sofa.

"This isn't Michael's house." Karen looked around the room at the solid oak furniture, the marble fire surround. Why was Michael's wife here?

"This is our daughter's home. She rents it from a family friend. We have three children, three girls. The youngest are twins." The words were designed to sting, and they did.

His children. Another inconvenience Karen had managed to block out, pretend didn't exist. Twin girls of about thirteen years old. She'd seen the pictures: Bethany and Rose. Beautiful children who didn't deserve an absent father. She realized that she was furious at Michael for what he'd done, for what he'd allowed her to do. She'd known before now, probably for a long time, that their relationship couldn't go on, but now she was certain and she felt nothing but a slight regret. Regret that they hadn't met under different circumstances, regret that they had let themselves believe that what they were doing didn't matter as long as his wife didn't find out. It did matter, and this woman sitting before her was the victim of their actions. Karen had never even known about another daughter.

"So why are you here? To find this Jessica Hamilton?"

"Yes, she's a patient of mine and I'm very worried about her."

"I don't understand how you ended up here if you didn't know Anne lived here."

"Because this is the address Jessica gave the practice when she signed up."

"Not possible. I haven't heard her name in five years, and she's never lived here."

"But you do know her?"

"I know of her. She was a friend of Anne's at college. I've not really seen her since."

"Is Anne here? Can I speak to her?"

"She's gone out, thank goodness. She doesn't need to see you here. How do you think I know who you are? I found a picture of you and Michael at some event tucked into a book that Anne lent me last year. She doesn't need to be confronted by her father's mistress, thank you. It's bad enough she knows you exist. I never wanted her to find out what her father was really like." She stood up.

"I'm sorry I can't help you find your patient. I have no idea where Jessica Hamilton lives. We haven't heard from her in years. Good-bye."

The confrontation Karen had imagined more than once had been nothing like the fiery affair she'd expected. The wife and the mistress bidding each other a civilized farewell.

Emily spoke again as Karen was walking through the front door, hesitantly, as though she didn't want to speak at all but would regret it if she didn't. "You and Michael . . ."

"It's over," Karen replied, knowing it was true. There was no pretending Michael's other life didn't exist after stepping into it, even for just a minute. Emily let out a breath, something almost like relief, and then the mask was back in place.

Karen's hand was on the door handle of her car when she heard her name being called.

She glanced up. Emily was pointing to where a car had pulled into the cul-de-sac and was coming towards them.

"Looks like you're about to get your wish after all," she said. "That's Anne's car."

Anne slammed on her brakes at the sight of Karen outside her house, put the car into reverse, and began to spin her wheels backwards up the street. Karen swung open her door, slammed it behind her and started the engine, shoving the car into first. Emily screamed something after her, but she had no time to stop and explain. She was chasing Anne Lenton's car, but the person behind the wheel was Jessica Hamilton.

What happened the day you met Jessica Hamilton?

Nothing. I thought she was just a regular patient until I saw her with Adam. That's when I knew she was a danger to my friends.

Not to Bea, surely? How was Jessica sleeping with Adam a threat to Bea?

Jessica hated Eleanor, she told me. She wanted to hurt anyone Eleanor loved. Me, Bea, Noah.

Did she say those words? Did she say their names?

Of course she didn't. She didn't need to.

How do you feel about your friends, Karen?

What kind of question is that? We're like sisters. I love them.

Eleanor and Bea's bond was particularly close, was it not?

We were all close. All three of us.

And you never felt jealous of the bond shared between the others? It must have been difficult, them being so alike and you keeping the secret of what happened to your sister. Never being able to tell them what life was like at home for you.

We were best friends. I've told you, all of us. I wasn't the odd one out. I wasn't different. I was one of them. I *loved* them.

- 82 -
BEA

What the hell has Anne done?" Michael was still shaking his head and muttering to himself as they drove towards where his daughter lived. It was clear now that Anne was involved in all of this, possibly even the instigator, and Bea thought he might be having a breakdown with all the information he was trying to process. She attempted to summon up the smallest bit of sympathy for him, but she couldn't force herself to feel anything other than disgust. Her friend was dead, her other friend was under suspicion of murder, and at the moment she was laying all the blame firmly at his door. If Karen had never met him, if he'd not been a liar and a cheat . . . if, if, if. Unable to think of anything constructive to say, she bit her bottom lip and stared out of the window.

They had tried calling Anne's mobile several times, and eventually it had cut straight to voice mail. Now the mobile sitting in the cup holder buzzed to life, the words "Emily mob" flashing across it.

"My wife," Michael said, reaching down to take the phone. Bea could almost taste the disgust in her mouth.

"Emily, what is it?" He flicked the speakerphone on so he didn't have to pull over.

"It's Anne, Michael, she's just turned up at the house."

Michael looked at Bea. "Is she okay?"

"I don't know, she didn't come in. She took one look at your mistress and drove off."

Bea let out a gasp. Michael looked as though he was going to deny all knowledge of Karen but obviously realized it was too late for that.

"Is Karen there now?" he asked. "Put her on please, Emily."

"She took off after Anne. What's going on, Michael? That woman was looking for one of Anne's old college friends. Is Anne in trouble?"

"Yes. You need to call the police. Tell them the make and model of Anne's car and that she might hurt herself or someone else. Can you do that?" There was a mumbling at the end of the phone. "Please, Emily, can you do that?"

"I said yes, Michael, I'm not totally useless! But I want you to know that if anything happens to her, I'll never forgive you for bringing that woman into our lives."

"If anything happens to either of them I'll never forgive myself. I'll call you as soon as I know anything." He rang off.

Bea was staring out of the window stone-faced.

"Where to now?" she asked. "Where are they?"

"I have no idea." Michael shook his head. "The only place I can think to go is home. Our home. Or I suppose I should say Karen's home."

- 83 -

KAREN

Anne's silver Fiat was parked across two of the spaces in the riverside parking lot when she reached it, the motor still running, door flung open, and the driver's seat empty. Karen pulled into a space and cut her engine, her eyes scanning the empty banks. She should walk away and call the police—stop trying to fix everyone and everything. If there was one thing she should have learned from all of this, it was not to try and save the world. She slammed the car door behind her and, not bothering to lock it, ran towards the riverbank. Maybe she hadn't learned anything at all.

She found her standing on the concrete underneath the bridge, staring into the dark water as though in a trance. As Karen approached, she didn't even look up. Karen stopped walking and studied her.

Anne Lenton, the woman Karen had known as Jessica Hamilton for the last five weeks, the woman responsible for her entire world imploding, was just a child. She could see now the nervous girl from that very first encounter, her face pink and devoid of makeup, her hair thick and frizzy. How had things gone so far from that first day? Should she have realized sooner how much of a threat Anne was? Had she failed again?

Anne looked up, saw Karen watching, and took a shaky step backwards. Gone was the cool, calm Jessica Hamilton, in control and holding all the cards. This girl—Michael's daughter, for God's sake!—looked petrified. It was difficult for Karen to reconcile her with the murderous psychopath she had felt so sure she was just a few hours ago.

"Stay away from me," Anne said as Karen moved closer. She had one hand held out in a traffic-stopping pose, as though she could stop her with some unseen force. "Stay the fuck away from me!"

Karen stopped and held up her own hands. "I'm not coming closer unless you want me to. I just want to talk to you."

"I don't want to talk to you."

"Jess— Anne, you've nothing to fear from me." She inched closer, trying to utilize her years of training. She'd never been in a situation like this before—they didn't teach you at university what to do if your married lover's daughter turned out to be a dangerous psychopath. "Jessica paid for five sessions, remember? Well, she's only had four. Let's do your last session right here."

Karen held her breath while Anne stood rigid, a look of confusion on her face. "What do you want me to talk about?"

"Well, now that I know the real reason you came to see me, I think we need to take another look at the aims of your sessions. What do you hope to achieve?"

Karen felt calmer now. Although she wasn't in her familiar office setting, just the rhythm and intonation of the psychiatrist's role readjusted the control in the situation, brought them back on an even footing. Anne dropped her chin and studied the concrete.

"Dad spent more time with you than the others. He was gone all week, expecting mum to believe he was *working*. So I followed him, saw him practically living at your house. I found out everything I could about you. At first I just watched the pair of you coming and going, then—I don't know what made me do it—but I booked an appointment with your practice. I suppose I just wanted to see what you were like up close. I don't really know what I expected. Then when you didn't recognize me—you didn't have a clue who I was, and I knew all about you—I started to think that maybe I could make you realize the damage you were doing. That's why I invented the story about seeing a married man. I . . . I never even . . . I didn't expect it to turn out like this."

She looked out over the river and Karen took the chance to move forward half a step, a movement so imperceptible that the other woman didn't even notice when she turned back to face her.

"Why not just tell me who you were?"

"I thought you knew that your boyfriend had children. I saw you once, sitting in your car outside mum and dad's house. It wasn't like you didn't know he was married. If you already knew, what would be the point of telling you?"

Karen felt the shame wash over her as she took in the damage she and Michael had caused. She had always insisted to Michael that she didn't want to know about his family, that it would make it impossible to continue if she knew what it was she was keeping him from, but the truth was she hadn't been able to stay away. She hadn't known about Anne, though. Emily's Facebook page was full of pictures of the twins, but there wasn't one picture of Anne on there.

"You're right," she said. "We were selfish and it was wrong of us. But why involve my friends?"

For a second Anne looked as though she was about to deny it; then she said, "I sent them the emails because I wanted them to see what you were really like. I've been watching you, the things you do when you think no one knows. I wanted them to see."

"How long have you been watching me?"

"For a while. Long enough. Long enough to know I'm not the one who needs a psychiatrist."

"You could have just told them."

"You'd say I was crazy. You'd lie your way out of it. You're a good liar, Karen, I'll give you that."

"And the story about your sister?"

"I just wanted to get some kind of a reaction from you. I hated seeing you so calm and composed every week while I knew what was really happening under the surface. I just wanted to see you rattled."

"Is that why you broke into my house? Stole my things?"

"I didn't break in; Dad has a key. He didn't even suspect that I knew about you, so there was no reason for him to hide it. Who's going to ask which doors his keys are for? Mum was turning a blind eye as always."

"So the woman you were talking about when you said you blamed her, you hated her for being weak and allowing her husband to be stolen . . ."

"She never even tried to stop him, you know." Anne's voice was filled with bitterness now, and for the first time Karen thought she could see the angry girl she recognized from their sessions. "I love her, of course; she's my mother and she saved me from going into foster care when I was seven years old. I owe her everything. But all I ever wanted was a stable family. She could have given me that, but instead she chose to let him screw you. You've met her; she's weak. I bet you walked up to my house and she just let you in. She probably offered you a cup of tea."

Strangely, Karen wanted to defend her boyfriend's wife, but she couldn't. Emily hadn't asked her to stop seeing her husband. Karen had always wondered about the type of woman who turned a blind eye, but when it came to it, that was exactly what Eleanor had done. How did Karen know she wouldn't do the same?

"You shouldn't blame your mother. You don't know what it's like."

"To feel like someone you love is giving up on you?" Anne snorted. "No, I've got no idea of that." She kicked at the clumps of dried soil on the concrete. "So what do we do now?"

"I don't know," Karen replied. Her shoulders sagged at the weight of all that had happened, all the pain she had caused. "I guess we should go to the police."

Confusion passed momentarily over Anne's face. "You don't want to do that."

"They'll find you anyway, Anne. It's better to hand yourself in. They already know all about what you've been doing to my friends and me. You left fingerprints at my house. They're looking for you now, it's only a matter of time before they arrest you for Eleanor's murder."

It was a risky lie and Karen had no way of knowing if Anne would believe her. Anne's eyes widened in fear, and Karen could see no trace of the confident young woman who had sat across from her in her office, mocking her with her questions of morality and taunting her with her knowledge of Karen and her friends.

"Me?" Realization dawned on her. "No. NO. You know I'm not responsible for those things, you know her death wasn't my fault. You can't do this to me!" She sank slowly to her haunches, doubled over as though hit by a sudden stomach cramp. "It wasn't supposed to be like this." She began muttering something, but Karen couldn't hear what she was saying. She didn't feel like a threat anymore. Karen moved to kneel down beside her, but she didn't even seem to notice, and instead carried on mumbling the same sentence over and over.

"Look, Anne, I'm sure they will take everything into account. It was an accident, that much is obvious. If you admit it, they will go easy on you."

The girl looked up, a mixture of fear and defiance in her murky blue eyes, and in that second Karen knew she'd underestimated her for a second time. She'd been wrong about what fear could make a person do.

"You won't get away with this," Anne hissed, and grabbing hold of Karen's shirt collar, she dragged her towards the still brown water.

- 84 -

BEA

This doesn't feel right," Bea announced, following Michael up the stairs of Karen's home. "I feel like an intruder."

"We're trying to help. Besides, I live here."

Bea scowled. "Don't get me started on that again. I just don't see how this is going to help Karen with your lunatic daughter. No offense. We should be driving around screaming her name out of the car window, not creeping around her bedroom."

"I hoped she'd have given up chasing Anne and come back here, but as she hasn't, there's something I wanted to show you." He emerged from the master bedroom with a cardboard box in his arms and passed it to Bea, who took it cautiously, as though she was expecting it to burn her. She sat down on the top step of the stairs and opened the lid, Michael pacing behind her.

"What am I looking at?"

"I found this once, hidden under some of Karen's things. I opened it up and it had your name in it, and Eleanor's, so I put it back, thinking it was personal."

Bea pulled a notebook from the top.

"There's all sorts in here. It's like a dossier of everyone she's ever met. I'm in here, and Eleanor," Bea murmured, pain shooting through her chest at the picture of her friend. "What we like, what we dislike, what we're scared of, practically everything about us. It's like one of those journals you make as a kid."

"Maybe that's what it is. Maybe she's just kept it for the memories."

"Then how come you're in here?" Bea held up the notebook, open at a page that contained a picture of Michael, along with every detail of his life: where he lived, the names of his wife and children, even their pictures.

"Not Anne, though, she's not in here at all," said Bea, scanning through. "It's like Karen never knew about her."

"She might not have. Like I told you, Anne's adopted. We were never allowed to put photographs of her on Facebook, because of the legal protections in place, and she moved out before I met Karen. Jesus," he breathed. "I always thought she didn't want to know about them. She never asked."

"She never really needed to, did she? I mean, she has it all written down here. What is this even for?"

"Maybe it's just a really detailed way of not forgetting things about the people she loves. Like some people keep lists of birthdays and special occasions; maybe this is just an extreme version of that."

"Fran's in here. Adam too. There's half a page on Gary from work. That's hardly memories."

Bea turned page after page, details of her own life jumping out at her. It was like how *This Is Your Life* would be if the host was actually a deranged stalker.

"See this?" She pointed to a yellowing newspaper article glued to one of the pages. "I knew this guy." A hand clenched at her chest to see the picture of him staring out from Karen's album. "At university."

Michael studied the article. "Says he had an accident. Why has Karen kept that?"

"No idea," Bea murmured. Or rather, she didn't want to have an idea.

"There's a train ticket here for Shrewsbury to Liverpool; it's dated two days before the article."

Bea shook her head. "I don't understand. Why wouldn't she have told me she was in the same city when this happened?"

"There's a lot she hasn't been telling either of us, by the looks of it."

Bea held up some photos that had been left loose in the box. "Look at these."

Michael looked at the scenic shots, each one showing the place Karen went when she needed to think.

"I think I know where they've gone."

We were holding on to one another so tightly that it didn't matter anymore who was dragging who down. All that mattered was the freezing, dirty water that waited to suck us under should we lose our footing.

She was stronger than me, surprisingly so for someone so slight. Or maybe she was just more scared. There is a certain strength that comes from fear, and from the knowledge that you no longer have anything to lose. She knew what I had done, what I was capable of, and she didn't want to meet the same fate as Eleanor. Maybe she'd thought she wouldn't care anymore, but everyone fights back in the end, when they feel the life slipping from them; however much they have craved death, moved towards it like an old friend in the last moments of their life, everyone fights for one more breath.

I'd heard the splash a second before I felt the breath sucked from my lungs by the freezing water. She released me then, the shock of the impact rendering her temporarily immobile. She's not going to fight, I realized, even as my legs were propelling me towards the surface. She's just going to give in.

But the survival instinct had been stronger than her despair, and she'd broken the surface of the water seconds after me. The river that had looked so calm on the surface was a churning tide underneath that threatened to drag us both down to our death. Maybe that was the way it should have been. We were both guilty in this; we'd both had our part to play. Mine had been the hands that had taken Eleanor's life, but she had been to blame as surely as if she'd been there with me. We were partners in a crime neither of us ever intended to commit. And now we were going to pay our penance.

How would you feel if I told you that Adam wasn't sleeping with Anne Lenton?

He was. I saw them together.

You saw what you wanted to see.

What is that supposed to mean? Why would I want to see my best friend's marriage fail? Why would I want her to be in danger? Myself in danger?

So you could be the one to fix it when it all fell apart. Like you always did.

Say what you want—I know what I saw.

Take a look at this, please, Karen.

Who is it?

It's the manager of the Pandora shop. See her hair? It's similar to Anne's, don't you think? She recognizes Adam; he checked the store's electrics a couple of months ago. And here, here's a still of the store's CCTV. See how he's touching her arm as she leaves? She was going on her lunch break; it's why you couldn't see her uniform.

Why are you doing this?

Adam wasn't having an affair.

Yes he was.

No. He remembers working at the shop. He's never seen Anne Lenton.

He's a liar. What he's saying can't be true.

Why not, Karen? Would it be so terrible if you were wrong? If your friends had never been in danger?

They were. I know they were. It wasn't for nothing. I was just trying to protect them. Like I always did.

Is that why you took Noah? As a warning?

I just wanted to make her see. She wasn't taking me seriously.

And the other things? The hair cream? Bea's date with the man from the Internet site?

Nothing I did made them see the danger they were in. What she was capable of.

What Jessica was capable of?

Yes! That they were in danger.

And yet Anne Lenton never went near your friends, did she? She lied about having an affair with a married man to make you ashamed of what you were doing with her father, but she never did a single thing to hurt anyone. The only danger to your friends was you.

Liar. Liar. Liar LIAR LIAR.

- 87 -

BEA

They found both cars pulled up at the spot in the third photo they had found, but neither woman was in sight on the banks. Bea jumped out before Michael had even cut the engine; she was at the edge of the river before she heard his door slam.

"Can you see them?" he shouted, jogging up to meet her. Bea's eyes scanned the river.

"Oh God." She reached out to grab his arm, but he'd already seen the two women surface fifty yards away and had broken into a run, shrugging off his jacket as he went.

"Call 999!" he shouted back to her.

Bea was rigid with fear. Her fingers fumbled as she pulled the phone from her pocket and swiped in, punched 999. Afterwards she couldn't even remember giving the operator the details; all she could recall of that moment was the question running through her mind about the horrific choice Michael had to make.

His daughter or his lover. Which one would he save?

88

What happened then? Before Bea and Michael pulled you out of the river?

You know what happened. I told the officers already. She grabbed me. She dragged me in. She tried to kill me.

Your boyfriend—

He's not my boyfriend.

Your ex-boyfriend saw you both come up for air and then he said you pushed her back down.

He's mistaken. How can anyone have known what was really happening? What was going on under the surface? It was an accident.

Are we still talking about what happened in the river?

What happened in the river, what happened to Eleanor, what happened to Amy—does it matter? I couldn't save any of them in the end, could I? She was right about that—they all were. You can't save everyone. Some people are beyond saving. I tried.

Your sister's death was an accident.

It was still my fault. I could have saved her. She would still be alive if I had done my job.

You weren't old enough to be put in charge of your sister in that situation. She was your mother's responsibility.

Do you think I don't know that? I've dedicated my entire life to helping people who had childhoods like mine. You can tell yourself over and over that you weren't to blame, you can reason and plead with yourself, but in the end there is always that voice whispering that if you'd only paid more attention, been more responsible, no one's life would have been ruined. A baby wouldn't be dead. You wouldn't be evil.

Is that what you think? That you're evil?

Most people go their whole lives not killing anyone at all. I've killed my sister and my best friend. Do you think I'm evil?

I think you need help.

You can't help me. No one can. You can take me back to my cell now.

89

The first time I killed someone I was just four years old. For so many years I tried to tell myself it was an accident—I wasn't responsible for the death of my sister. But I didn't save her either. I have spent my whole life trying to protect the people I love, to try to make up for the baby girl I couldn't save. Sometimes I'll admit that I went too far, but all I ever wanted to do was protect them. I blamed myself for what happened to Bea at university; I should never have been so far away from her. It's why I installed the camera in her laptop—to look out for her when we couldn't be together.

As we grew up, me on the outside of our triumvirate looking in on the friendship Bea and Eleanor shared, I made sure they always needed me. I suppose, looking back, I felt like I couldn't be phased out if I was indispensable. When it looked as though things were ticking along too neatly for them, all it ever took was a little help from me to make sure their lives were shaken up enough for me to save the day. At school it was a rumor, or a boyfriend caught cheating; as we grew up it was easier to show my worth without having to intervene in the first place. Thoughtful gifts when they were having a bad day, dates I remembered that they barely remembered themselves. I prided myself on making these women the center of my universe without them even knowing. And in return they gave me a taste of normality, a peek into an ordinary life with family feuds that came from stealing each other's clothes rather than from the aching loss of a baby girl.

I honestly thought as we entered adulthood that they were mine and I was theirs. I had integrated myself into their lives so completely that I was part of the machine rather than the third wheel.

Until that day.

I'd gone into town on my lunch break to post some letters when I saw them together. Without me. It will sound meaningless to you; in thirty years of friendship of course we'd met without all three being present before, but not often, and usually only because the other couldn't make it. We'd dropped into one another's houses without sending out group invites, but if you asked me why this time was different, I'd say I just knew. In that moment all my fears were confirmed—theirs was the true friendship and this would be the beginning of my descent into loneliness. You see, I had no one else. I had put all my eggs in their basket, so to speak; even Michael wasn't really mine. There had always been something stopping me from giving myself fully to relationships, and this was the consequence. How many clandestine meetings had there been? How many furtive glances—*don't let Karen know, let's make it just the two of us.*

And once I'd seen them, and I'd known, it was all I could think about. Our every interaction was tainted with their imagined betrayal; my time in their reflected sunlight was coming to a close.

Jessica Hamilton walked into our lives at just the right—or the most horrifically wrong—moment. As soon as I met her I knew there was something not quite right about her, that she was wearing a mask not too different to my own, but it wasn't until I saw her with Adam that I knew how dangerous she would be, to me and my friends. I didn't know what she wanted or why, but I knew that I had to protect them from her. This was my chance to show them how much they needed me. My psychiatrist, Sheila, tells me that I can't have seen what I thought I saw; that Adam was there innocently, but I don't believe that. If all this was for nothing, then what does that make me?

But they couldn't—or wouldn't—see the danger that was right in front of them. I had to make them realize! The things I did—moving Eleanor's car, setting Bea up on a date doomed to remind her of the past—I was never putting them in real danger. I was always right there, ready to swoop in and remind them I was the only person they could rely on. Not Adam or Fran. Not even each other. And when they realized how much of a threat Jessica Hamilton was to them, it would be me they turned to, to tell me I was right all along. To ask me to help them.

The police say that Jessica, or Anne Lenton as we now know her to be, was never interested in my friends; that it was me she wanted to cause trouble for, but I know that can't be true. I was protecting them. And when I went to Eleanor's house that afternoon, I just wanted to make her see. I'd been careless; she'd recognized the bracelet I'd hidden in Adam's car from an old photograph—so stupid to use an old one of my own, but I hadn't worn it in so long, I never thought she'd remember it—and she started accusing me of all sorts of things. She thought I was the one having an affair with her husband. Me! She didn't even believe Jessica existed. It was far from the vision I'd had of promising her I would fix everything for her and her falling gratefully into my arms. I can't pretend it wasn't frustrating, or that when she lashed out at me I didn't push back, just a little harder than I'd intended. When I saw the blood, I realized what I'd done.

And there it was. The second person I'd loved was dead because I couldn't save them. First from my mother, and then from Jessica Hamilton. Because she was responsible—I wasn't in any doubt about that. She might not have been in the room, but it was her fault. All I ever wanted to do was love them, protect them from everything. They needed me. I just wanted to save them all.

You can't fix me. Those were some of the first words she said to me, and I remember thinking she was wrong. I fixed people all the time, it was my job. It turned out that she never wanted to be fixed.

She was there to fix me, she was my inspector, my Marley's Ghost. But I don't feel fixed. And I don't think I ever will be.

Final report—Karen Browning
Psychiatrist: Dr. Sheila Ford.
Length of treatment: 1 year and two months.

Karen suffered severe trauma as a result of bereavement in childhood, resulting in her blaming herself for the death of her sister. Although she recognizes that the responsibility for her sister lay solely with her mother, she still bears the emotional scars caused by guilt and as such has spent her life trying to atone for the accident by protecting those around her. The almost symbiotic relationship she has cultivated with her close group of friends has reinforced her belief that she needs to "save" these women, and when there was no immediate threat, her mind manufactured one in the form of her patient Jessica Hamilton.

There is still much work to be done with Karen. The God complex that she has cultivated since the death of her sister in childhood has given her the inflated belief that the harm she caused was all collateral damage in the grand scheme of keeping her friends safe from the outside threat, and I understand from police reports that it is believed she has been manufacturing ways in which she can protect her friends for quite some time—although the events of twelve months ago mark an accelerated decline in her mental state. Confronting what really happened will be the last emotional barrier to breach, after which I fear we may see a complete breakdown. Once Karen loses the image she has of herself as protector and admits that she was the sole threat to her friends, there will be considerable fallout.

Having worked with Karen Browning for over a year now it is my opinion that she remains a high-risk patient, with the severest risk she poses being that to herself. It is my recommendation to the courts that Karen Browning should remain in custody for the maximum sentence available.

ACKNOWLEDGMENTS

My first thanks go, and I hope will always go to my wonderful agent, Laetitia Rutherford. A wiser woman than me once called you the "author whisperer," and that couldn't be truer. You always have enthusiasm for whatever I'm babbling on about, and you continue to have more faith in my ability than I ever have. Thanks also to Megan and the rest of the team at Watson Little, and Camilla and everyone at the Marsh Agency.

Thanks of course to my wonderful editor Emily Bestler at Emily Bestler Books; to know my work is reaching a wider audience is just amazing and I am forever grateful. Also to Lara Jones, who always answers my questions without making me feel like a complete newbie, and the entire team in the United States, you have made a dream come true for me.

I'm petrified at this stage of forgetting someone, so please rest assured that if you have ever congratulated me, asked how the book is going, or emailed, tweeted, or Facebooked me to say you enjoyed my first or referred to me as a "real author," then this thank-you is aimed at you. Every message from a reader is like a big hug.

It's not easy working two jobs and bringing up two hyperactive children, so a special thanks to Maxine, my day-job boss for much of the writing of this book. Without your support and shoulder to vent on, I don't think I'd have ever finished it.

In the year since *How I Lost You* was published I have been fortunate to meet some wonderful bloggers, readers, and book lovers, far too many to name here. I have to mention, however, the amazing Liz Barnsley and Tracy Fenton; for giving me their time and honesty on my final draft of this book, I will always be grateful. Also to the wonderful Anne Cater and her team of Book Connectors. To each and every member of THE Book Club; to try to name you all would be impossible but I have never met a group more supportive of authors—you all rock. I do have to say a special thanks to Teresa Nikolic, who has possibly championed my work more than my own mother (and that is saying something).

The crime scene is a wonderful community to be part of, and I feel so lucky to have been welcomed in. Thank you to every single one of you for your help and support—you have genuinely kept me going over the last twelve months. Special thanks to Susi Holliday for guiding me into the fold.

Now for the gushy bit. I'm lucky enough to have amazing friends and family by my side always. Thank you never seems enough to say to Mum and Dad for their immense love, support, and babysitting skills—I love you both. Thank you to my mother-in-law for always being there to help out even though the last year has been the toughest one of our lives; the kids couldn't ask for better grandparents and will never forget Granddad Ken.

To my gorgeous ginger twosome, Connor and Finlay—without you this book would have been written in half the time, but I wouldn't swap you for the world. You make it worth being in.

And finally, always my last thank-you but always the most important. To the man who has to live with me while the words aren't coming, who has to do all the housework when they are, and who knows exactly when edits are due just by the tone of my voice. To Ash for still being my everything.

ABOUT THE AUTHOR

Jenny Blackhurst was raised in Shropshire, where she still lives with her husband and children. Growing up, she spent hours reading and talking about crime novels—writing her own seemed like a natural progression. *Before I Let You In* is her second novel.